A FLIGHTY FAKE BOYFRIEND

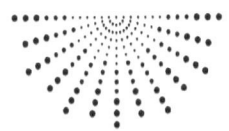

Z.A. MAXFIELD

Authenticity is the daily practice of letting go of who we think we're supposed to be and embracing who we are.
Brené Brown

CHAPTER ONE

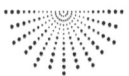

Today, the server's name badge read *Muse*. I'd been to Bistro a total of four times this trip, and he'd been Bob, Jeremy, and Jackson.

That wasn't the only reason he interested me, although I love a mystery. The kid was college aged, bright, and funny. Plus, he had a winning, affable personality.

He always remembered the last thing I'd eaten and asked how I'd enjoyed it. He was also remarkably bossy. Like on the first morning the hostess had seated me at one of his tables, he decided I needed avocado on my omelet due to the fact I looked...well, like me.

Driving to Luis's wedding in Santa Barbara had seemed like a pretty good way to unwind, but I hadn't been taking care of myself. The route was long with lots of lonely stretches.

I didn't expect the thing that drove me—the restlessness that made me burn the candle at both ends at work—to sit on my shoulder the whole time.

I seriously needed this vacation. Too much work and stress resulted in a badly misused body—namely, mine.

Muse, Bob, Jeremy, whatever his name was, noticed things like that. He treated every customer to his particular brand of mother-henning. He made suggestions and even overrode the unhealthy choices of those he knew best in a gently teasing way that probably doubled, even tripled his tips. I'd been unusually generous, and I had a reputation for tipping well.

I couldn't take my eyes off him when he was in the room.

As I scrolled through the many urgent messages on my phone, "Muse" brought water.

"Good morning. Did you want coffee today?"

Oh, I did. I wanted coffee so badly my eyes would probably bleed. But with the hangover I had after partying with Dan and Cam at Nacho's Bar the night before, coffee might be a bad idea. Going easy today might save me.

"Herbal tea if you have it."

"Certainly. Have you decided on breakfast yet, or do you need another minute?"

I didn't bother looking at the menu a second time. "Oatmeal, please. And dry toast."

His eyebrow rose. "Would you like the usual accompaniments?"

"I'm sorry?"

"We serve steel cut oatmeal with brown sugar, dried fruit mix, and half-and-half."

"That's fine."

He narrowed his eyes. "Are you sure?"

"Is there something wrong with that?"

"Not a thing. I just wondered—because of the oatmeal and dry toast—if you'd rather have soy milk."

"Half-and-half is fine."

"Okay. Sure. That was really weird, wasn't it? I'm sorry." He took the menu from me and walked away, shoulders tight.

I went back to the messages on my phone until he slid a pot of water onto the table before me and said, "Teabag?"

I opened my mouth to offer an off-color reply, then closed it. "Sure."

"We have several herbal teas." He opened a chest and let

me look at the variety within. I picked one at random. Usually, I had no choice. I didn't know what the difference between the teas he offered could be.

"Thank you." I removed the teabag from its packaging and placed it in the hot water pot.

Oatmeal and toast arrived shortly after that. My server stood next to the table until I looked up again.

"Is there anything else?" he asked.

"No, thank you."

He didn't leave. "Are you sure?"

"I'm sure." I glanced around. No one else seemed to think he was acting weird. Weirder. More weird than normal.

"Okay. Thank you." He walked away again, his shoulders as tense as before.

I tried a bit of my oatmeal. It seemed okay—at least my stomach didn't rebel. I added some dried fruit and half-and-half and had another few spoonfuls.

Nausea fluttered, making me swallow several times. Herbal tea usually helped with the sensation, so I took a long swallow. This was the hangover talking, right? There was no reason to invent a connection between the wedding and any digestive issues I might be having.

I felt eyes on me. To my left, my server peeked over the half wall that hid the point-of-sale machine. When he saw me, he ducked. I briefly wondered if I'd missed a news report about spree killers who matched my description.

The tea was good. I ate my breakfast slowly. At home, the entire purpose of food was fuel, and I managed as much as I could before pushing the bowl away. Beads of sweat itched at my hairline.

When the waiter came back, he dropped the check and whispered something in my ear.

"Excuse me?"

"Meet me out back." He jerked his head. "By the dumpster."

My need for a cigarette caused me to linger in the parking lot, so I thought why not?

"Muse" slipped out the back door, glanced both ways, and called out, "Hey. *Pssst*. C'mere."

Intrigued enough to solve The Mystery of the Very Weird Waiter, I strolled his way.

He pulled something from behind his back. My heart gave a jolt. Leaped? Stuttered? Nausea crept into my throat, and I nearly lost what little I'd eaten on the pavement. I backed away, hands up.

Turned out he wasn't holding a gun or a knife but a creamy orange drink.

My reaction probably seemed absurd—at least to anyone who hadn't recently traveled to a part of the world the US State Department considered too dangerous for Americans.

"Jesus," I reached out and fell against the wall. "What is wrong with you?"

"Me?" He held a to-go cup in one shaking hand. "I just wanted to give you this. For later, you know. If you want."

I still couldn't believe this was happening. "What is it?"

"Mango lassi." He bit his lip. "With whey protein. It's, um…it's easy to digest, and—"

"You made me a mango lassi?"

"It's on the menu." He said this like, *Duh*. "I recommend it because you seem so"—he glanced away—"not okay today."

While my heart rate went back to normal, I studied him. Thick dark hair, pale skin, and piercing blue eyes. The rest of him was hidden beneath a typical Parisian waiter's uniform: white shirt, white apron, black vest, and trousers.

I fidgeted when he frowned at me. He made me want to straighten things like his tie and my spine.

"I'm not very hungry this morning."

He let out a breath. "Look, it's none of my business, but my grandmother swears by these for hangovers. You looked like you could use one."

4

I rubbed my forehead with the heel of my hand. Then I heard my hair sizzle.

"Whoa, pyro." He took the cigarette from my hand. "You singed your hair."

"Aw shit. I hate the smell of burning hair. It stays with you forever."

"I...did not know that." He didn't give the cigarette back "I'm keeping this. You're not allowed to play with fire right now."

"Do you always get so involved in your customers' lives?" I felt like a pitcher who'd gone three and oh with a batter he'd never faced. I meant to brush him back. Change things up. "Or am I special?"

"I meddle all the time. Ask anyone." As if I needed to. "And also, I think you might be special. You're staying around here, right? I've seen you around."

"Yeah?" I made the word a question.

He toed the ground shyly. "I hope we bump into each other again."

"Maybe we will." I took the drink he offered. "Thanks for this."

There was no reason I shouldn't try the drink. It could be drugged. Poisoned, for all I knew. Maybe Bob, Jeremy, Muse was a serial poisoner, and no one would ever know because he only poisoned people who were passing through.

I pulled out of the Bistro parking lot and headed back to the highway. A tentative sip of the drink told me it was delicious. Mango and yogurt. What was not to like about that combination? Plus, instead of roiling around after it went down, it quenched the nausea building inside me.

Even if the waiter was a serial poisoner, his drink did the trick in the meantime. I'd take it. If I keeled over later, it was almost worth the price.

THE MAIN REASON I'd stopped in St. Nacho's at all was to visit my friends Daniel and Cam Livingston. We'd known each other for ten years—ever since Daniel had become interested in supporting StolenLives in the fight against human trafficking. He'd reached out to my boss, Lila Newcastle to learn more, starting out as a benefactor and becoming a very good friend. Since then, he'd divorced, come out as gay, and married Cameron Rooney. I'd broken up with Luis. Things had changed for both of us, but we'd remained close.

Their house sat just outside Santo Ignacio. As soon as I pulled into the driveway, I was greeted by three dogs and a goat. Their miniature horse stared at me from inside its little paddock.

Daniel had taken well to life in his adopted home. He and his firefighter husband were so in love you could write epic poetry about it. Understandable, because Cam was as gorgeous as he was sweet and caring. I couldn't be happier for them.

I'd arranged to stay with them for a few days before driving the rest of the way to Santa Barbara to meet my plus-one. Dan worked from home, so I normally found other things to do while he was busy.

I stepped inside and noticed again how homey Dan and Cam's place looked. The house he'd shared with his ex-wife had been sleek and modern and—I privately thought—ice cold.

This new Ralph Lauren adjacent country elegance suited the Daniel Livingston I knew much better.

"Have a seat. I was just about to get some coffee." Dan wore jeans and a button-down. He still looked as elegant as he had when his suits were bespoke. He had dark hair and serious brown eyes in a handsome face. Since I'd known him when he was married to his ex, BreeAnna, I never saw him as anything but a friend, but I often wished I had someone like him. Intelligent and kind. Dedicated.

I cleared my throat. "No thanks."

"I feel like hell this morning," said Dan. "Note to self: Ryan Winslow's idea of a bar crawl is madness."

"I'm hungover as fuck," I admitted. "I drink too much. It's habit. I drink coffee to stay awake and liquor to wind down."

"You think you have a problem?"

"I think I will if I don't do a little more to protect my health. Our favorite server at Bistro accosted me with this today." I held up the drink. "You're not the first to tell me I look like hell."

"I think it's going to be a theme if there are people who know you at Luis's wedding."

I shrugged.

"What's got you so messed up?" he asked. "The wedding or work?"

"I'm always messed up about work, but yeah. This wedding's fraught with anxiety. Luis and I are playing chicken. I doubt the invitation was sincere, but I couldn't refuse because I don't want him to think his marriage bothers me."

"Does it?"

I hesitated. "I'm glad he found what he's looking for."

"But…?" Dan knew me so well.

"But his fiancé is a barrister specializing in international law and human rights. He's dedicated, invested in his work, but has somehow made time for a personal life. It's as if Luis is saying, 'This could have been you if you weren't defective.'"

"Don't compare. People handle stress differently."

"It's becoming clear I don't handle stress at all. According to you and the waiter of mystery, I store it on my body like *The Picture of Dorian Gray*." I sank farther into the comfort of a buttery soft couch and pretended not to notice that one corner of the skirting had been chewed down to the foam padding.

"Maybe you should talk to a therapist?" Daniel always got to the heart of things.

"Probably."

"I'm putting that on my checklist of things to badger you about when you get home. You can't keep going like this."

He was right, of course. "No. I can't."

"I'm glad you've at least taken these days to visit. I've enjoyed spending time with you."

"Me too. I love it here." I snapped my fingers for Blue the Queensland heeler. Between her, a border collie with one blue eye and one brown named Malarky, and Molly, a younger border collie, I'd rediscovered my love of dogs. I wished I could adopt a dog, but I lived in an apartment and spent long hours working. "How come you have so many animals? When you were with BreeAnna, you never had any that I knew of."

"Cam grew up on a ranch. He adores them. I love watching him with them. There's nothing in the world like a hot man romping with dogs at sunrise."

"I work too much, or I'd get a dog."

"We have plenty to share. Our place is turning into a petting zoo. Stop by any time."

I smiled, wishing it was that easy.

"About your plus-one." He grinned knowingly. "You never did say who you're taking. Is he hot?"

I gasped in mock outrage. "Do I appear shallow to you?"

"Yes. Now spill."

"I'm taking Lawrence Dunbar." I tried not to sound smug.

He gasped. "The guy from the Marvel movies?"

"That's the one. He's meeting me in Santa Barbara on Friday night."

"I am in awe of your choice." He sat back. "Gorgeous, out and proud, A-list actors aren't thick on the ground."

"He's a friend and benefactor. Lila brought up his name when we were working on our media campaign two years ago. He's a great guy. He agreed to be in our public service ads, and while we were shooting them, he and I hit it off."

"Go you." Daniel widened his eyes. "He's pretty hot. What's it like, dating such a big name?"

"He and I don't date." I finished the last of my drink and set the cup on the coffee table. "We're just friends."

"Too bad."

"He offered to act as if we're more than that for the wedding."

Dan snorted. "He's a very good actor. Take him up on it."

"I'm no good at that kind of subterfuge." I stretched. "How can I be so exhausted right after breakfast?"

"Why don't you take a nap. We'll be lazy today."

"That sounds wonderful." I stood.

The food in my belly was comforting on both a physical and emotional level, and hanging out at Daniel's place was a balm to my spirit.

I never slept like I did in St. Nacho's. I put it down to the clean sea air. The taste of salt on my tongue. Being with friends I didn't have to impress. But it was more. When I strolled along the boardwalk, everything around me seemed more vivid. Colors brightened. The air filled with music. Everywhere I looked, someone was smiling, laughing, performing some small act of kindness—like my mystery server and his grand-mother's hangover cure.

Blue followed me into the room and hopped up on the bed after I got in.

Despite the emotional pain of Luis's wedding—despite the pressure building as work went undone—as soon as I laid my head on the pillow in Daniel's inviting guest room, I drifted into a dreamless sleep.

CHAPTER TWO

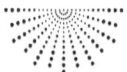

T he sun had set before I woke up. Groggily, I made my way to the kitchen where I found Daniel feeding the dogs.

"Hey, I'm so sorry," I said. "I can't believe I slept that long."

"You must have needed it."

"I probably won't sleep tonight, though."

He brushed his hands off on his jeans. "We can get dinner and walk along the boardwalk. Let's stop by the firehouse and say hi to my man."

"I'm up for dinner and a drink or two. Nothing like last night."

"You got that right. Let me get changed then. Back in a bit."

"Me too." My clothes were rumpled and a little damp from sleeping in them. "I'll be out in a few."

Still on the fuzzy side of waking, I rummaged in my suit-case for something appropriate. The temperature had dropped. I opted for a white T-shirt, jeans, and a thin sweater. When I saw Daniel, I asked if he thought I'd need a jacket.

"Probably, if we're going to walk on the beach. The wind can really cut through knits."

"Okay," I went back to the guest room and got a light-weight blazer. "You mind driving?"

"Not at all. Let me just make sure the dogs are set." I heard running water before he came back, ready to go.

As we walked to his car, I glanced back at his house. With the porch light on, it welcomed visitors with ruthless charm. This was nothing like what I expected, but it suited this happier, less-driven Daniel well. I envied him.

"You have a pretty awesome life here, don't you?"

He smiled fondly. "Oh, yeah."

We got into his car and buckled up. "You ever see BreeAnna?"

"Yes, she remarried, and they have a kid. I wouldn't be surprised if by now she had another on the way. She's a great mom."

"So you're still friends?"

"Improbably, yes." He pulled onto the road. "I think we're better friends now than ever."

"That's good."

"It will get easier between you and Luis too, you know. Let him have his moment without resentment."

"I don't resent him for finding someone else. I resent him for…I don't know. Inviting me? Making me feel bad about my choices? Couldn't he have just left well enough alone? It's as if he's taunting me."

"I'm sure that's not the case."

"I should have refused to go. Instead, I arranged for this date with Laurie, and —"

"You call Lawrence Dunbar *Laurie*?"

"Everyone does. It's the name he came with."

"Ah."

"He's a really great guy. I would probably date him, but he's already with someone who isn't out."

"I see." Daniel made a turn onto the stretch of Main Street where bars and restaurants clustered. "I'm going to look for a place to park, then we'll walk to the restaurant."

"We're going past the firehouse, I presume."

"Of course."

He parked behind a veterinary clinic that looked closed for the evening, and we got out. I drew my jacket closer. "That wind is a little brisk, isn't it?"

"Yeah, it's gusty tonight." He locked the doors and we headed for the firehouse. "Pity we didn't come during the day. Cam's usually out here polishing the vehicles like a porn star."

I laughed at that because I could picture it. "Cam's not a shy boy, is he?"

"He hasn't got a modest bone in his body. Well, except when he's being all humble about his work. 'Aw, shucks. Just doing my job, ma'am.'"

We went inside the station to look for him, and the first thing I noticed was the absolutely irresistible aroma of garlic in oil. Even if my testy stomach didn't approve just then, I loved that smell.

"You guys decent?" Daniel called out to the men in the lounge area. Of course they were decent, more's the pity.

"Hey, babe." Cam came from the kitchen with a towel slung over his shoulder. They kissed like high school sweethearts. "Mm."

"Mm, yourself. You taste yummy." Cam turned and wrapped his arms around me. "Ryan, you're just in time. Eat something. You drank enough for three people last night."

I winced. "Et tu, Cam?"

"Guys, you remember Daniel's friend Ryan?" He reintroduced me to his colleagues, some of whom I remembered getting drunk with the night before. The ones who were watching the news on the big screen waved tiredly at me. A few said hello.

"I'm making pasta arrabbiata." Cam motioned for us to follow. "This way. I have to keep an eye on the garlic."

We followed him into a huge kitchen where one man was draining cans of San Marzano tomatoes, another was chopping basil, and a third was grating parmesan cheese with a microplane. Cam had a huge amount of garlic cloves frying in olive oil. My mouth watered.

"Expecting a vampire invasion?" I asked.

"Preparedness is key." Cam handed me a hunk of sourdough bread after lashing it with soft butter. *Oh, my god, yum.*

Daniel kissed his cheek. "We were just stopping by on our way to Nacho's for dinner."

"Have a good meal." Cam said this smugly as if he knew that nothing we ate could compare to what he was making.

"You guys having a salad with that?" Daniel teased. "Man cannot live on pasta and cheese alone."

Cam seemed to consider this. "There are tomatoes involved."

"Eat. A. Salad." Daniel intoned.

"You too, my love." Cam leaned in for one last kiss. We left with waves all around and promises from Daniel to catch up at poker night.

Outside, the crisp mineral tang of sea air hit like a wall after the warm sensory overload of the firehouse.

"Still obscenely happy, I see."

"We have our ups and downs. More ups than downs, though. God, I love that man."

"You're still glad you moved here?"

"I honestly couldn't live anywhere else anymore. St. Nacho's is home even if we technically live outside the city limits."

"I could love it here." I glanced in the direction we'd come from. "Things are pretty chill."

"Absolutely." Dan put his arm around me. "Considering a move?"

"No, I couldn't. Vancouver puts me close to work."

"But how often do you even need to be at headquarters? Isn't most of your work online? You work remotely when you travel."

"Last year I traveled a fair bit. Things have settled down lately." We both knew that for the lie it was. Human trafficking was as old as time, and nothing could stop it. It was a wildfire that never ran out of fuel.

Dan gave me a slight hug, then let me go. "I don't have to tell you that you can't keep going like this."

"I'll be fine."

"I don't think so, Ryan. Not if you don't take regular breaks."

"I'm taking a vacation right now," I pointed out the obvious.

"Some vacation. Your ex's wedding has you tied up in knots."

"Well, parts of this trip will be very fun, and there's good news too. Apparently, I won a humanitarian award, and it comes with a sizable check for StolenLives. I'll be heading to LA for a banquet to collect it next month."

"That's wonderful news." Dan patted my back. "Well deserved. Nobody I know works harder for less money and accolades than you do."

"I make plenty. I don't even spend my salary because of the corporate apartment. Travel expenses are covered. What do I really need beyond that?"

"What you mean is, you don't spend much on yourself."

"I live pretty simply," I admitted. "Which is a good thing because this wedding weekend is going to empty all my savings. The nightly rate at the hotel is appalling."

"You deserve some luxury now and again."

"That's what I figured. Might as well enjoy my vacation in style."

"That's the spirit. Good man." Dan gave me another hearty, approving pat on the back.

Salsa music announced the cantina before we got there. A cluster of club-kid types stood outside the doors. I saw my server from the restaurant among them and waved.

"Hey, hello." He detached from the group and came toward us. "Hi, Daniel. How's Cam?"

Daniel smiled indulgently. "Cam's doing great. Thanks for asking. You out here partying?"

He nodded. "I worked this morning so I have tonight off."

"Thanks for the drink you gave me earlier," I said. "I felt a hundred percent better after drinking it."

"I told you." He winked. "Mango lassi's my grandmother's cure for everything. But maybe don't get hungover again."

"I'll try not to." I glanced over at his friends; three men and two women. They stared and whispered amongst themselves. They were probably still in college and they were obviously checking me out. Awkward. "Thanks again."

"We dine." Daniel drew me toward the restaurant's door. I waved a limp goodbye and went with him.

"You know him?" I asked.

Daniel glanced back at the knot of kids. "Epic? Everyone knows him."

"So, his name isn't Bob?" I asked dryly. "Or Jeremy or Muse?"

Daniel laughed. "Was he wearing the Muse name tag at Bistro this morning? You can't go by that. He just picks up whatever badge he feels like from some box. His name is actually Epic. Nice kid."

"Epic." I'd met a ton of kids with street names over the years. Epic fit him brilliantly.

Daniel opened the door and let me precede him. "I met his parents once at some charity thing. Very straightlaced but nice."

"With a kid like Epic?" I barely knew him, and I couldn't

picture him in a straightlaced family. He was flamboyant. Or no, maybe just buoyant. He seemed lighter than air. And that smile of his…"That can't be."

"Guess rebellion is still a thing." Daniel walked to the hostess station and asked for a table by the window.

A woman about halfway between Epic's age and ours smiled brightly as soon as she saw Daniel. "Sure thing, Mr. Livingston. Follow me."

"Hi, Espie." Daniel talked to the hostess as we walked. "How're Brandon and June?"

"Doing great. They always love the start of summer vacation, but they'll be bored soon, and I don't know how we'll make it through until fall."

"They can come and see the animals anytime." Dan offered. "Just call ahead."

"Oh, thank you. That's great. I'll save it for a last resort though. In case of emergency, visit the Livingstons." She waved us to a table in front of floor-to-ceiling windows. During the day the view must be spectacular, but there was little moonlight, and beyond the boardwalk the ocean was a vast void, faint light barely shimmering over inky blackness.

There was plenty to see on the boardwalk though. People biked, jogged, walked with strollers and dogs on leashes. Moths hovered around the old-fashioned electric streetlamps. Between the salsa music playing in the bar and the bustle outside, it was hard to reconcile this place with the quiet I'd sensed earlier.

Since I'd been there, we'd mostly eaten at Bistro and done our drinking at Nacho's Bar. Falling into the lovely lassitude of life in St. Nacho's had proved ridiculously easy.

"St. Nacho's nightlife, such as it is," Daniel murmured, eyes sparkling. "The cantina is the beating heart of downtown Santo Ignacio."

"Downtown," I said doubtfully.

"Yep. This is where the magic happens."

"Okay." Beyond the beach area, St. Nacho's felt more like Mayberry. "Do you even have to lock your cars?"

"Sure. Lots of transients pass through here." Daniel picked up his menu. "We have all the usual crime."

Sad. Even in a town where everyone seemed to know Daniel by name, there was crime.

"What are you having tonight?"

"Carnitas. They're a specialty. It's good for people who drink too much."

"I'll have that then. Just to be proactive," I teased. "I'll start with tortilla soup."

"That's spicy."

"I like spicy." Whether he believed it or not, I would not be drinking as much as I had the night before. A soup with a chicken base, even a spicy one, sounded delicious.

"If you're sure you're not going to throw it back up." Daniel put his menu aside.

"Last night was an anomaly." I'd gotten maudlin, dwelling on all the mistakes I'd made with Luis. That wouldn't happen again. "Tell me about you. How's business?"

He shrugged. "It's good. The Feds lowered the interest rate again, which is always good for the housing market. What about you? Working on anything in particular?"

Just the thought of work made me itch to check my phone. I wasn't going to. Talk about diving into a bottomless cesspool.

Not tonight.

Not unless there was something really important. Maybe there was? I took out my phone.

"Let me just—"

"Don't. You said you were on vacation." His hands closed over mine, covering the screen. "Work messages will only upset you."

"Right." I slipped the phone into my jacket pocket. "You're right."

"You're supposed to be relaxing, remember?"

"It's hard." If there was a whine in my voice, he didn't call me on it. "I can't kid myself that everything won't be waiting for me when I get back."

"I understand."

"It piles up."

"I know." Daniel's eyes were kind, his voice gentle. "But take it from a fellow workaholic. It will *still* be there. You can't do your job if you burn out."

I knew that. I was just a piece on the board, and while I was gone, other people—capable, dynamic, intelligent people—were doing their best. Only I found it impossible to let go when lives might hang in the balance.

"It's hard to ease off the throttle." I fussed with my silverware.

"Oh, don't I know it." Dan trapped my hand against the table. "But you can't help anyone if you don't take care of yourself."

Throat tight, I nodded.

I'd hidden the truth from myself for so long that I'd begun to believe my lies. The reality—my reality—was that I was an emotional and physical mess. I'd been barely hanging on for so long that letting go seemed insurmountable.

If you let go now, the lie whispered, *you'll never get a grip again. Keep going. Keep going. Don't stop until you can't go any more.*

At some point, soup appeared before me, along with home-made corn and flour tortillas. I tasted nothing. I ventured a beer, and then over the course of dinner, I had two more.

"Last one." I felt pleasantly buzzed but not drunk.

"That's good." Daniel eyed me sympathetically.

I tried not to take it personally. "I don't usually drink like this. But this fucking wedding..."

"Come on. You've been over Luis for years."

"I know."

"You can't be that nervous."

"I'm not nervous, precisely. I'm ordinarily paralyzed somewhere between outrage and fear. If you add in Luis's fantasy five-star wedding? I feel catatonic. Might as well drink and enjoy the oblivion."

"Hold on." Daniel sat back in his chair, his brown eyes filled with anxiety and pain. "I'm really starting to worry about you. Will you promise me something?"

"I'm fine, Daniel."

He ignored that. "Promise me you'll talk to a therapist the minute you get home."

"Oh, I plan to, even though I already know what they'll say. Quit drinking. Quit smoking. Eat healthy. Reduce the work hours. Meditate. Try yoga."

"So why don't you do those things?"

"I will." The promise didn't feel like a lie. I was pretty sure it was, though. "Plus, I'll go to the doctor as soon as this goddamn fiasco is over. Will that make you happy?"

Dan cuffed my arm. "I'm already happy. It's you I'm worried about."

"And?"

He reached across the table to cover my hand. "It's a start."

CHAPTER THREE

W hile Daniel caught up with some friends in the bar, I went outside for a smoke. The look of protest he shot me would have stopped a better man. I promised to change after the wedding, and I would. I just couldn't bring myself to think about quitting then.

My buzz gave me a pleasantly swimmy head and a full belly.

I lit up a smoke.

I knew my lifestyle wouldn't help me with my problems, but lately I'd lost my way. When that happened, I never turned around to go back the way I'd come, or asked for directions, or did anything rational like look at a map. I always kept going forward at full speed, certain I'd find where I was going sooner or later. Nobody but me had to know how lost I felt.

Of course I compounded my misery by checking my phone for messages.

I had close to a hundred emails from different people and news organizations. Our negotiations with regard to getting vital shipping manifests were breaking down in one region of the world while it looked like local authorities weren't making any headway in securing the release of nine trafficked schoolgirls in another. On top of that, drone footage of a particularly troubling series of encampments that could only be forced labor camps had suddenly stopped transmitting.

I was only a conduit, really. I received and collated data from people who risked their lives to document the work of traffickers and the suffering of their victims. Yet I felt the responsibility keenly. It made me sick to envision failure.

I held my cigarette with shaking fingers and shoved the pack into the pocket of my jacket.

"I thought I saw you out here." Epic, my mysterious server, climbed onto the wall separating the boardwalk from the sand and slid beside me. "Are you going to light your hair on fire again?"

"God, I hope not." I received another email but didn't open it.

"You want to tell me why you look like your dog just died?"

"My dog just died."

He reacted with an exaggerated expression—part shock, part horror. "Oh God. I'm so sorry."

"I'm kidding. Just wanted to see what you'd do if you were right."

"That's not okay!" He punched my arm lightly. "Letting me think a dog died."

I blew smoke away from him. "No dogs were harmed in the making of this moment."

"You're funny." He didn't sound like he meant that.

"I'm sorry. Bad news from work."

"Really?"

I nodded. "It's all bad news, actually. I don't know why I'm still surprised."

"What do you do?"

"Dog catcher." I smirked at him. "Too soon?"

He glared at me. "Just say it's private if you don't want to tell me."

"It's fine. I work for an international nongovernmental organization called StolenLives."

"A nonprofit?"

"Exactly."

"What's your area?"

"Prevention of human trafficking."

"Wow." His brows furrowed as he took my cigarette, hit it, and gave it back. "Tough stuff."

"Yeah. Now, can I ask you something?"

He glanced at his feet. "I might not answer."

"How old are you?"

"Oh," he smiled. "That's an easy one. Twenty-three. You?"

"Thirty-six."

"Silver fox."

I coughed out smoke and surprise. "More like aging roadkill."

"No. I dig older men."

I hardly knew what to say to that. "Are you hitting on me?"

"Duh. You're new around here. And you're a friend of Daniel's. He's like...the ultimate business Daddy. Plus, you look like you need me."

"I what?" My phone vibrated again. I couldn't stop myself from reading the message that time, and my heart sank. "Motherfucker."

Laurie: Don't hate me. Please don't hate me. I have to cancel.

"Something wrong?" asked Epic.

"Wait. Gimme a second." Instead of replying to Laurie's text, I walked a few steps away and called him back. He answered on the first ring.

"I'm so sorry. Don't hate me."

Despair made me sag. "What happened?"

"You know the actor Kelsey D'Angelo?"

"The dude that got arrested for statutory rape?"

"That's him. He had a small part in the film I just finished, so now we either need to cut his scenes or reshoot them. The director made the decision to hire another actor, so I'm due back in Vancouver tomorrow. I am so sorry, Ryan. You know I'd do anything for you, but—"

"It's not your fault, Laurie." I stared at the sky and swallowed my initial reaction, which was to scream. "Don't worry about it."

"Will you be able to find someone else? Should I ask around?"

"No. God no. I don't want to go with a stranger. I'm comfortable with you, so I just thought..." I don't know what I thought. He was handsome enough to be arm candy and kind enough to make the wedding bearable. He was someone I could have a good time with. "It's all right."

"You could hire someone to go with you."

"An escort? I bet if you think about my life's work for a second, you'll see why that might be problematic for me."

"Bro, I was talking about hiring an actor."

"Oh."

"Yeah, *oh*. I know a dozen actors who'd be happy to do it."

"But how would we get them up to speed at this stage in the game? At least you know me. If we were forced to make small talk—"

"Listen to you. Actors can improvise. That's part of our training, you know."

"No improvised relationship talk would fool Luis into thinking any actor I hired was a real date. He's way too shrewd for that."

"I'm really, really sorry, Ry. If there was any way I could postpone this, I would, but as it is, this is costing the production a boatload of money, and—"

"It's all right, Laurie. I know there's nothing you can do even if you wanted to. I understand. I'm just whining."

"I'll make it up to you somehow. We'll go out to the lake

house and spend some time fishing or something. Just you and me."

"Sounds great." I couldn't stand fishing, but he wouldn't really make me do it. Besides, neither of our schedules would allow time off. "You tried, and I love you for it. I've got to go. Someone's waiting for me."

"Okay, bye. See you."

"Soon. It's a plan." I disconnected the call and just stood there, staring at the barest sliver of moon in the sky. We had something in common, the moon and me. I'd planned to bask in the sunlight of Laurie's glory at Luis's wedding, and even though I was sort of a reduced, barely there bit of myself, I could have reflected his light. But now, without Laurie...I was an eclipse.

"Are you okay?" I turned and found Epic staring at me. "Bad news?"

"Nothing I can't handle." I took a deep breath. The cigarette I'd been holding was nothing but ash. I stubbed it out on the wall.

"Look, it's none of my business—"

"Since when has that stopped you?" Even as I spoke the words, they felt cruel.

"Sorry." His mouth snapped shut.

"No. I'm the one who ought to apologize. I shouldn't have reacted like that. I'm sorry. My plans changed, and I'm disappointed."

"Somebody cancel a date?" Why was he so fucking curious?

"Sort of," I admitted. "Now I have to decide whether I'm going to go ahead with my plans alone or slink home with a white flag flying."

"Oh." He sat on the retaining wall. I flopped onto it. It's worth noting that it hurt, since I had very little padding at that point.

With the sea behind him and the wind blowing his thick,

dark hair, Epic looked like a young Kennedy. His bone structure was fine and strong, and his pale blue eyes glimmered brightly. He wore a soft blue V-neck sweater over a white T-shirt and skinny jeans.

I was flattered by his attention without a doubt. But wary.

"Is Epic really your name? Or—"

"That's what most people call me."

"You were Bob when I first met you."

"Because you came to Bistro on a 'Bob' day." He leaned back and kicked his legs. He wore red Vans without socks. Even his feet looked confident. If I'd had his kind of poise at his age? Well, I only wished I had it now.

"Why do you wear name tags that aren't yours?"

He looked sheepish. "I lost my name tag, like...three times in the first week. Now my boss won't make me a new one, so I just take one out of the box he keeps after waitstaff leaves. It started out of necessity, but now it's kind of my trademark."

"You realize having a trademark that changes every day defeats the purpose?"

"For some people. But I assure you it works for me. Everyone knows me. Uncle Brian says the food competes with me to bring people in."

"Your uncle owns Bistro?"

He nodded. "We're not really related. He's an old friend of my dad's. I've always called him uncle." He straightened as if something important had just occurred to him. "Brian and my dad used to surf competitively. That's where they met, but if you knew my dad now you wouldn't believe it. Dad teaches *economics*."

His expression said what he thought of that fact.

"What's wrong with that?"

"It's so boring."

"I don't know—"

"No, it is. My dad was like this super chill guy, and my mom met him on the beach in Costa Rica when she was in some women's cult or something, and the next thing you know, they're both teaching economics, and it's like whatever made them spontaneous disappeared."

"Is that so?" I hid my smile. Epic overshared. I liked that because I didn't have to talk, but it still felt like having a conversation.

He grimaced. "They have these pictures of themselves smoking dope and lying around with half-naked people in yurts. Honestly, it makes me believe in alien abduction."

"Does it?" In spite of my problems—or maybe because of them—I kept the kid talking. His voice was low and velvety. As soothing as the susurration of the waves behind us.

"Well, not really. But it's amazing how people change. Some people become concentrated if you know what I mean. As they get older, they become more of what they started out as. Others do a total one-eighty and go the opposite direction."

That...was very true. "I agree. It's as if some people believe in a magical maturity line. Once they pass it, they're supposed to leave behind the things they were passionate about when they were younger."

"Exactly!"

"But that's total horse shit." I was speaking from experience. My "causes" could never take a back seat to relationship building and starting a family. Luis's wedding to another man was proof of that. "Maybe some people only lose interest in old things because new things take their place."

"Yeah, but why economics? *Blech.*"

"Didn't they also build a stable home and raise a family?"

He shrugged. "You don't have to turn your back on everything you once believed in to do that. Imagine going from a commune to teaching at a private university."

"Okay. I can see how that seems like a bit of a backslide."

He nodded vigorously. "To the dark side. Oh, that's good. That's going to be the title of my first memoir—*Backslide to the Darkside.*"

"You plan on writing more than one?"

"Sure." His grin was wide and white and impossibly sweet. "I want a record of where I've been in case I get lost or do one of those about-faces like my parents."

"You mean if you should wake up teaching economics?"

"Imagine me teaching." He shuddered. "My luck I'd end up at some Christian college."

"Do your parents teach at a religious school?"

"Not unless you count obscene wealth as a religion."

I laughed. "Some people do. Don't knock it, though. Without big money where would we find philanthropists?"

"Oh, right." He leaned against my shoulder. "You work for a nonprofit. Well, money has its uses."

"It does indeed." I barely had time to accept the contact of his body before he moved again, but while he'd been pressed against me, a sensation like an electrical shock had torn through me. The contact had been fleeting, but the jolt made me feel strange and vulnerable and exposed—as if I were a hermit crab and someone had torn my shell away.

At a guess, I'd have said Epic was educated and intelligent. He was certainly articulate. The way he used words created comfortable clouds around uncomfortable subjects.

I knew a lot about his family from what he'd said but more from what he hadn't—that maybe he'd been lonely growing up. He didn't feel understood by his mother and father nor did he understand them even though he wanted to connect on the level he admired and understood.

He hoped he wouldn't turn out like them, hoped he wouldn't simply stop being the man he wanted to be for some goals that weren't his.

Maybe I was reading way too much into the encounter.

Probably, I was.

Maybe I superimposed my experience on him because he seemed a lot like the kid I'd once been. Not naive by any stretch, but still optimistic. He hadn't been broken by disappointment after disappointment. It almost hurt to look at him because I knew how the fairy tale would end.

And yet...

And yet I was drawn to him. I was iron shavings, and he was magnetic north.

"Are you free this weekend?" I asked.

"What?" He blinked as if he'd just noticed I was there. "This weekend?"

I nodded, certain I was doing the right thing. "How'd you like to go to a wedding?"

"YOU ASKED Epic to Luis's wedding?" Daniel's incredulous expression worried me a little as we walked to the lot where we'd left his car. "The waiter, Epic?"

"Yeah. He liked the idea." I didn't think it was that big a deal. "Apparently he has his own black tie, so I won't even have to rent him a suit."

"Epic the waiter has a tuxedo," Dan repeated.

"He said he had a vintage tux. I hope it's not powder blue."

"I could totally see him showing up in a powder-blue tux."

If he did, so be it. "It's fine. We'll be fine."

"I can't believe you're so calm about this." The street was empty. The sounds from the bar faded the farther we walked.

"I don't know why you're so shocked. He's a nice enough kid."

"I think he's wonderful, but he's so young."

I agreed, but Epic had held his own in our conversation. "When Laurie cancelled and I was feeling awful, Epic and I just started talking. He's funny and very bright. I think he'll be great."

"Does he know you asked him because you want to poke your ex in the eye?"

"I'll fill him in on the drive down. We've got a couple days before the ceremony to get to know each other."

Daniel shoved his hands into his pockets. "You were so worried about this event you were going to bring an A-list actor as your date. Now you're going to abandon that idea and take a kid you just met?"

"Laurie suggested I hire an actor. How is this any different?"

"Because with an actor, presumably you get to write the script. With Epic…anything can come out of his mouth. You know that, right? He really is the neighborhood eccentric—and that's saying something in St. Nacho's."

"You say that like it's a bad thing. Maybe since I can't have my envy producing A-list actor, I simply want to go with someone pleasant."

"Pleasant?"

"Yes. I want a pleasant fake boyfriend. Why is that so hard to understand?"

"It's not." Daniel reached the car and opened the driver's side door. "I admire your ability to adapt, but I'll warn you. Epic is well liked around here, and you will get your ass kicked if you mess with his head. Make sure he knows it's a *fake* date, okay?"

"I explained the situation when I asked him. He's going to take the weekend off to stay in a posh hotel and attend an aristocrat's wedding. There's no downside—his words, not mine."

"And here I thought you couldn't surprise me."

I opened my door and got into the car.

In truth, I'd surprised myself. This wedding had been a log jam in my peace of mind for almost six months. Everything that came before and after stood in stark contrast to the time I had to take off to attend, the worry finding the right date caused me, and the anxiety I felt about going.

Making the decision to throw my plans to the wind and

invite someone entirely by chance broke that log jam. My life felt "in flow" again.

When we got to Daniel's place, we talked for a bit more before heading to bed. I slipped between the sheets in the guest room without setting an alarm for the morning and had the most peaceful night I'd had in a long time.

CHAPTER FOUR

T hursday morning began like a lot of coastal mornings—with the sound of a foghorn in the distance and mist so thick it was nearly impossible to see. The worst of it burned off before Daniel, Cam, and I finished breakfast.

Dan and I drank more coffee on the porch while we watched Cam play with the animals under the guise of "getting a little exercise."

It seemed a little sacred, the way Cam became a boy around his dogs. Despite his size, despite his thickly muscled body and beard shadow, Cam's eyes lit with happiness every time he tossed a Frisbee and one of the dogs caught it. I could only imagine how lovely he would be with his children if he and Daniel decided to have any.

"You're a lucky man, Daniel Livingston. Ever thought about having kids?"

"Actually, that's the plan." Daniel smiled softly. "We've been looking for a surrogate."

"That's wonderful." I almost teared up. "You'll be great dads."

"Knock wood." He tapped his knuckles lightly on the porch railing.

I picked up my bag to take it to the car. "I've got to get on the road. I promised Epic I'd pick him up at nine."

"Come here, you." Cam ran over and threw his arms around me. It wasn't enough he could crush me with a hug, but he lifted me into the air and swung me around. Despite the indignity, I liked that a lot more than I should have.

"Hey!" I made a weak protest.

"Don't take so long to come visit next time," Cam said sternly. "We've missed you."

"I won't."

"And eat something. My God, that was like lifting a middle schooler."

"I'm not that light."

"You need to get some meat back on your bones." Cam's smile dazzled me a little.

"Take care of yourself," Dan said, patting my shoulder.

"I hear you both. I promise." I couldn't look Dan in the eye. "I'll do better."

He hugged me hard. "Please do. We love you. You know that."

"I do. Love you too."

I opened the door of my car. "Bye!"

Cam threw the Frisbee so the dogs had to run in the opposite direction, then he gave me a big smooch on the cheek.

"Bye, Ry. Take a break before you go back to saving the world."

"Will do." I ducked into the car and started the engine. I waved a final time before I drove off. As their pleasant cottage got smaller in the rearview, I was subsumed by envy, which was so unusual for me I almost didn't recognize it at first.

I attributed my emotions to missing their company and the peaceful home they'd built together, but at the core of my feelings was a sense of unbearable loss and a quagmire of whys — why did I pursue my professional goals to the detriment of my personal life? Why would a personal life have been so bad? Why couldn't I have what they have?

The answer, as always, was because I wasn't strong enough, or smart enough, or organized enough, or brave enough to have it all. If I had to choose, then what I did professionally was so much more important than anything I could do privately. It wasn't even a contest for me.

Instead of bemoaning what I couldn't have, I should have rejoiced in what I could. And sometimes, I was able to do just that. Sometimes a win on the international front—if we were to find the missing schoolgirls or cut the head off an operation that dealt in slave labor, then I could celebrate my choices.

It was only when I was at loose ends, like I was then, trying to gather together the tattered scraps of what little personal life I had, that I was aware of how unbalanced my priorities were.

Dan and Cam were right. I should have eaten more. Drank less. Smoked less. I should have found a way to handle stress that didn't take years off my life.

Note to self: Install meditation app on phone and learn to use it. Mentally, I added, *after the wedding* because I just knew I'd be using old familiar coping mechanisms on this trip.

And Epic.

Because surely I would use my colorful fake boyfriend as one of many crutches to lean on so I could limp through this event without losing my mind.

I pulled up in front of Epic's apartment building to find him waiting on the sidewalk surrounded by what looked like a garage sale's worth of inexplicable junk.

He waved. I parked and got out of the car to ask over the roof, "What's all this?"

He picked up a suit bag and said, "Tuxedo."

"Okay." I went around the vehicle and took it from him. I hung it inside the car next to mine. "And?"

He pointed to each thing, "Snacks, drinks, clothing, pool toys—"

"Pool toys?" Did he seriously expect to bring a giant inflatable unicorn? "Is all that necessary?"

"I can deflate it." He pulled some plug and the poor thing just sizzled and got smaller while I watched. "I wasn't sure what kind of car you had."

"Epic—"

"Don't worry, it's not as hard to blow up as you'd think."

"I—"

"It's fine. I promise. Pop the trunk. I'll have everything packed up in a sec. We'll need the snacks inside on the floor of the back seat where we can reach."

"What if I don't allow eating in my car?"

"How do you do road trips without eating in the car?" His apparent shock shouldn't have made me want to laugh.

"I rarely drive long distances."

"Oh. So maybe you don't know how this works, then?" he asked, all bug-eyed and innocent. "Healthy snacks are an absolute must, along with things that are just tasty—like Frito's and bean dip."

"You plan to eat *bean dip* in my leased Lexus?"

"Well, I can't make you stop every time I want a snack, can I?"

I opened my mouth. Closed it.

"Don't worry," he reassured. "This is all part of the fake boyfriend service plan."

"But it's only a two-hour drive."

"And by the time we're back in St. Nacho's, I'll have you inducted into the road trip hall of fame."

I wasn't sure that was a good thing, but swept along by Epic's enthusiasm, I let him shove all his stuff into my car.

When at last the sidewalk was empty and my car looked like the Griswolds would be driving it to Wally World, Epic beamed at me over the roof.

"I'm really honored you asked me to come with you, Ryan.

It means a lot to me that you think I can be a good fake boyfriend for such an important event."

"And I'm honored to have you, Epic. Honored and...pleased."

He got in, and I joined him. "Ready?"

"Of course." I keyed the engine.

"Wait." His mouth formed a surprised *O*. "I need to sync my phone to your Bluetooth. Can I do that? Or do we need a USB? I made a road trip playlist."

"You can sync it. Here." USB indeed. Did he think I lived in the Dark Ages? As soon as I took his phone and linked it with the audio, a cello introduced me to a familiar but elusive overture. "What is that?"

"*The Pirates of the Caribbean* soundtrack. Perfect start, don't you think? *Bring me the Horizon!*" he said, quoting the film.

"Oh my God." I muttered, not unhappily. "You're going to be the weirdest fake boyfriend ever."

"There's nothing wrong with weird," he said primly. "Grape soda?"

I almost gagged. "No. Absolutely not."

"Okay. But you don't know what you're missing."

"Yes, I do. I have grown-up tastebuds."

With a knowing smile, he handed me a grapefruit LaCroix. "Okay, then, mister. You'll probably like this."

I probably would. Goddamn it. How had he known that?

I put the car in gear and took off as the music swelled around us.

"It really isn't that long a drive."

"Then we must begin right away. Eat up, my good man." He pulled a couple of Kind bars out of his bag, stuffed them into the console, and then turned back to rustle around until he came up with chips. It looked as if Epic planned to feed me like a goose on the way to the foie gras follies. If only Cam and Daniel could see me now.

It was still early. We reached the nearly empty highway, and I felt as expansive as the road in front of us. Was this happiness? I wasn't sure I had the skill set to know happiness when I saw it. Did I feel lighter than usual? Yes. Did I feel optimistic? I did.

But I also felt strained in a way I wouldn't have had Laurie been in the car beside me. Laurie was the known, and Epic was very much part of an unfinished map with the words: *That be danger past these waters* on it.

What was it about Epic?

I'd already asked myself this question several times. Epic seemed to act on impulse, and in my ordered life, I had only made room for things or people I could predict.

"Can we stop at the miniature golf place?"

I slid a glance his way. "Now?"

"Yes, now. There's a place ahead that features a fairy-tale theme. You can see the castle from the highway."

"I played mini-golf once. I hated it." I'd gotten to the ninth hole, realized there were eighteen, and nearly opened a vein right then and there.

"Of course you did," he said sarcastically. "What happened? Didn't you win?"

"I don't have to win all the time."

"But?"

"But mini-golf is so frivolous. I mean, golf is frivolous—"

His eyes widened. "Apologize right now. My ancestors invented golf."

"I despise golf. My experience is that it's the last bastion of 'old boy' handshake deals and classism."

"You've never used that to your advantage? The networking possibilities seem to dovetail with fundraising. I'd think you'd golf if only for that."

I had to give Epic the point. He was absolutely right. "The networking possibilities would outweigh my personal disdain for the sport if there weren't others better suited. I have colleagues who play. They work within social circles I don't have entry to anyway."

Epic sent a calculating look my way. "You're more a boots-on-the-ground man, then?"

"I'm not as comfortable on the fundraising side. Since I'm unattached and willing to travel, I'm more useful in analysis and negotiation."

"I see."

"We have the whole day to get to the hotel." I dug into the bag of chips he held and used one to scoop a dollop of bean dip from the can he'd also produced from his snack food cache. "Do you really want to mini-golf?"

"I love mini-golf," he said wistfully.

"Then mini-golf you shall, Epic," I said. "I have some work to do. I'll wait for you in the bar, or wherever passes for a watering hole, while you play."

"That's adorable," he mused while we crunched our chips. "It's almost like you think you have a choice."

My mouth went dry. "I don't mini-golf, Epic. Honestly. Don't set yourself up for disappointment."

"Oh, I won't." He hummed.

I may have had a picnic's worth of snacks and sodas in my car and a deflated pool toy in the trunk, but I had to draw the line somewhere. Epic wasn't going to get his way *every* time. This was *my* horrible wedding weekend, not his. I was going to decide which horrible things I'd do, not him.

"Mini-golf really isn't for me," I said firmly. "There will be no negotiation. Mini-golf is off the table as far as I am concerned. You are, of course, free to enjoy yourself."

"And I will. I assure you."

I didn't trust his sweet, smug smile when he said those words.

I was right not to.

CHAPTER FIVE

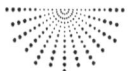

Three tiny hobbit houses sat at the base of a fiberglass tree with a kindly Green Man face. Two of them sent my mini-golf ball into an underground chamber, causing it to shoot out from somewhere behind me and hit the heel of my shoe painfully. Of course it took me three tries to find the one that didn't. Fortunately, we weren't keeping score. After me, Epic got it on the first try, but he'd played this course before and knew all the ins and outs.

A crisp breeze blew in from the ocean, cooling my skin. It bore the sticky fragrance of frying corn dogs and funnel cakes and cotton candy. Screaming children and pink adults ran amok everywhere. They obviously didn't have someone like Epic around to slather them with sunscreen until they shone like the domes of a Russian Orthodox church.

The sun blazed down, and the light bounced off everything. I'd remembered my Oakleys at the last minute, glad they were reflective so people couldn't see how miserable I felt.

I'd had plenty of practice keeping the impassive face of a benign diplomat, no matter what situation I found myself in. I was certain that to anyone watching, I looked like I was enjoying myself.

We moved on to another hole. This one had a giant loop-de-loop that required exactly the right speed and velocity to carry the ball through to the green without turning it into an antipersonnel device. I admit my timid approach didn't cut the mustard for the first, oh, three tries.

"You're going to have to hit that a lot harder," said my fake boyfriend.

"That's what he said." I tried again, and this time my ball shot off a topiary hippo, landed on the cement pathway, and rolled away.

"Alas, your poor meatball. It's under that bush."

"Sorry, I'm not hooked into mini-golf lore."

"Wait here. I'll get it."

As I waited, a woman walking a boy of about five in the direction of the entrance smiled at me. "Having a father-son outing?"

"That's my husband, ma'am." I don't know why I lied. I might have gone with the father and son gag if I thought I could trust Epic not to do something outlandish like...kiss me or something. He really was taking the fake boyfriend thing very seriously.

The woman gave me a frozen smile and nodded. "Sorry."

"Happens all the time since he was still in high school when we hooked up." Her eyes widened. "I'm just kidding. Epic's my friend. He likes mini-golf."

She obviously didn't know what to believe, so she grabbed her son's hand and hauled ass.

Epic came back. I gave him an abbreviated version of events.

He grinned widely. "You're kind of a troublemaker, aren't you?"

"Not at all," I protested. "I just reacted in a haze of fury to her calling you my son."

He studied me calmly. "You still doing okay?"

"If I say no, can I quit?"

He shook his head as if I'd truly disappointed him. "You have to get the loop-de-loop. Each stage of mini-golf is important. You learn vital life lessons that will last a lifetime."

"Does your family run some kind of mini-golf mafia?"

"Hit the ball, Dad."

"Oh, for fuck's sake." I hit the ball, and this time I used exactly the right force to propel it onto the green. It took me two putts to sink it, but that was one more hole down. Only eight more to go.

As we arrived at our next hole, Epic squatted to look at a complicated system of swirly runnel-like features, one of which would lead my ball to yet another Astroturfed green.

"Now, I want you to really look at what we have here," Epic golf-whispered. "It's a lot like life isn't it? There's a choice to be made, and each path leads in a different direction. Some you can follow, and some are occluded because they go under the cartoon school bus. They require blind faith."

I eyed the fiberglass school bus full of woodland creatures with scholarly aspirations. There were five channels into which I could putt. One spilled a ball out right next to the cup, another returned the ball from a hole behind me. Who knew where the other balls went? Please God, let there be one that led to an alternate universe where I could sit in an air-conditioned bar with a smoking section.

Epic stood, patted my shoulder, and said, "Choose wisely."

At that point, I simply didn't care. I tapped my ball, and it fell into a pink glistening channel that if I thought about it at all, seemed a little too obvious.

"Going with Freud on this one?" He glanced up at me. "When was the last time you got laid?"

I followed my ball, which—it turned out—had landed only three feet away from the cup. I knocked the ball in with one putt and felt rather proud of myself.

"I see how it is," Epic teased. "The student becomes the master."

"Hardly." I might have smirked a little as we walked up to the next hole, which was just more of the same. This mini golf thing wasn't unbearable, I thought. I could do this. Then the last hole gave me such fits we had to let two families and a children's birthday party play through.

"C'mon," Epic coached. "In every game of mini-golf, you'll find the dreaded windmill. You have to learn to time your shot. Get the rhythm of it. Think of yourself as an inmate in a Turkish prison, timing the guard rounds. Freedom is life, baby. You've got this."

"That's oddly specific." He had no idea how close I'd once come to such a fate, though it had been a Syrian interrogation site.

In this case, the windmill guarded the fairy-tale castle we'd seen from the highway. It was made up of four drawbridges that spun on a wheel. You had to get your timing perfect in order for your ball to go between them.

I started to swing. Epic shouted, "Quiet on the green, please." And I missed my shot.

He laughed like a troll then spoke through his cupped hand, "While the game is not on the line here, Ryan Winslow is still looking for a personal best on this hole."

"Oh, shut up."

"Look at the concentration on his face. That's the look of a champion right there. He's seen what he needs to do. He lines up his shot..."

I did it. It only took me about twelve tries. My ball swirled around the green and landed about three inches away from the cup. I tapped it in.

"It's over, right?" I asked. "Please tell me it's over."

"It's over when I say it's over," Epic held his putter like a rifle. "You don't stand a chance, puny human. *Pew, pew, pew, pew, pew, pew.*"

Every goddamn eye in the place was on us as he laughed maniacally.

"The castle is mine!"

Like a man freed from that prison he mentioned, I stared at the sky. A few little mare's tail clouds drifted in from the ocean. I smelled plumeria on the breeze along with the bright verdant scent of ornamental grasses and chlorine from the park's water features.

Epic might have had a point. *Mini-golf is full of life lessons.*

There was a place to drop off our putters and balls.

"Food." Epic turned toward the snack shack, but I maneuvered him out of the park with the promise of a nice lunch at a restaurant with a bar. At the car, I rested my back against the sun-hot metal of the driver's side door and took out my smokes.

Epic eyed me. "You really need to do that?"

"For now? Yes."

"Why? Are you that nervous about this wedding?"

"I'm not real comfortable with the invite, but that's not why I smoke."

He mirrored me, leaning against the car and looking up, watching each exhaled smoke cloud waft away. "So I'm assuming you're not in the wedding."

"What makes you say that?"

"Well, you wouldn't be in a wedding you were uptight about, would you? Unless your sister was marrying someone you hate. Or your mom. Who's getting married?"

"My ex."

"Ooooh." He winced. "It's totally reasonable to get uptight over that."

"I'm not uptight. I said I'm uncomfortable."

"Okay, let's break that down. Who broke up with whom?"

I bit back the reply that it was none of his business. "It was a mutual decision."

"Actually mutual? Or like, *you can't fire me because I quit.*"

"Okay, it was mostly mutual." I took another drag. "I work a lot."

"So?"

"So, I was dating the billionaire scion of a Spanish noble family, and he liked everything to revolve around him."

Epic widened his eyes. "Meow."

"Yeah, well. I'm probably a tiny bit bitter."

"Isn't it weird he invited you to his wedding?"

I took another drag on the cigarette. "Yes."

"So you think, what, he just wants to rub your nose in the fact he's marrying someone else?"

"I don't know what there is to rub my nose in. He's a catch. The guy probably loves him."

"And you're going to prove you aren't drowning in despair over the loss, right?"

"I never drowned. It's been years since we were together."

"How many?"

"Six"

"That's a lot of years."

"Enough to find his one true love, I guess." For me the time had gone by so quickly I'd barely had time to get used to the idea he wasn't around.

"You have to walk that bitterness back, Ryan, or he's going to smell it all over you."

"I know." I stubbed out my cigarette and opened the car door. "Mount up. We're not far from the hotel."

"Isn't it still a little early?"

"The room should be ready. It will be by the time we've eaten lunch."

"Okay." When we were both inside the car and buckled up, he said, "You know, I don't mind if we have to share a bed."

I glanced at him. "You don't?"

"No. I thought about it a lot, and I figure if you were supposed to come here with a date, you probably don't have a room with two beds."

"I see." I started the engine and left the lot, making my way south toward the hotel.

"Yeah, so I wanted you to know it's fine. As long as it's a king-size because I need my space."

"We have two beds."

"Oh." He sighed. "Okay."

Was that disappointment? "The date I was going to bring is a friend. We don't hook up."

"Really?" That was definitely disappointment. "It seems a shame for you to go to all this trouble for a wedding you don't want to attend with a guy you don't even boink."

"Yeah, that's my style. I snatch defeat from the jaws of victory at every opportunity."

"So...this guy who had to cancel at the last second. Just a friend? Really?"

"Yeah. We planned to get some sailing in. He's got a boat."

"Nice." Epic rolled his window down to let his hand fly on the breeze. "What's he do?"

"Actor."

"An actor...He do anything I might have heard of?"

I hesitated before answering. "I doubt it."

"I thought about being an actor." Epic turned to me with a wry expression. "My parents couldn't stand the idea."

"It's not really up to your parents, is it?"

"Well, no. But they'll ride my ass until I decide what I want to do, and whatever it is will probably freak them out just as badly. They have a career in mind for me, and I hate it."

"You finish college yet?"

"Yup. I got my BS at Santa Cruz and an MFE at Berkley Haas, but there's no way I'm going into finance."

Epic had a graduate degree? "Seriously?"

"What?"

"You have a master's degree in *financial engineering*?" I couldn't help my surprise.

He frowned at me. "Why is my education so shocking to you?"

"You...You're twenty-three, aren't you?"

"Yeah, but"—he began ticking things off on his fingers—"I took every advanced placement class I could in high school; I graduated early, so I went to college at seventeen; and the MFE only takes a year."

"Still. That's an amazing accomplishment."

"What's on your CV?"

"Undergrad at Georgetown's Walsh School of Foreign Service in culture and politics. Master's in foreign service."

"Spy school." He hissed the words.

"They originally tapped me for intelligence work, but there are two reasons I can't do that."

"What are they?"

"Illegal drug use in my past is one. I'd have never passed the polygraphs."

"Oops. And?"

"I hate politics," I said. "I'd have had a nervous breakdown in the first week."

"I get you. Totally." I felt his eyes on me. "But what does someone with your skill set do at an NGO that prevents human trafficking?"

"Now *that* is a very good question."

He let a few seconds pass before asking, "You plan on answering it?"

"Later, maybe. If you're very good. It's complicated."

He glanced out the window. "Everything worthwhile is..."

CHAPTER SIX

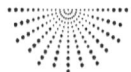

The traffic concentrated dramatically around Santa Barbara. We crawled for some time before I could pull into the entrance of the resort complex. I parked beneath a porte cochere with massive, vine-covered arches. I got out, slipped on my jacket, and gave my keys to the valet while Epic exited the car and explored everything with a child's delight.

"Holy cow," he shot me a happy smile. "This is amazing."

"Right? This resort is the quintessence of old California glamor." I tipped the valet, who opened the trunk for the bellman to get our luggage.

"Follow me, sir," he said. His name badge read Arsenio, but thanks to Epic, I was now suspicious of badge wearers.

I've stayed in some pretty nice places, but the Four Seasons represented a different level of luxury. There was history here. Grandeur from a bygone era.

A lot of the wedding guests, if they were staying in town, would no doubt choose a less luxurious option. But I hadn't taken a real vacation in close to six years. As soon as I saw the resort, I wanted to stay for the week after the wedding too. I had to have Laurie book the room for me because I didn't have the clout to get a reservation in my name.

At reception, there was some confusion, and for a dreadful moment I saw my beautiful getaway disappear before my eyes. That was before I said the magic words.

"Lawrence Dunbar made the reservations, so they might be in his name."

The receptionist didn't blink, but Epic gave one of those *owooga* double takes you only see in cartoons. "What did you just say?"

"Oh, of course." The receptionist, whose badge read Gale, smiled. "You're Mr. Dunbar's guests."

"*Lawrence Dunbar?*" Epic clutched his heart.

"I'm not sure what you mean by guests," I told Gale. "Mr. Dunbar meant to meet me here, but he had to cancel at the last minute."

I took out my credit card, but she waved it away. "Mr. Dunbar phoned yesterday and had you upgraded to the Santa Cruz suite."

"Wait. I wasn't meant to have a suite."

"The—Oh my God," Epic gasped. "Your plus-one was Lawrence Dunbar?"

"Mr. Dunbar took care of everything. He left a note, I believe. It says: Enjoy anything that strikes your fancy, and you are absolutely not"—she squinted at her computer screen —"to wallow. You're a prince among men. Indulge like one."

"Oh my God. Is this my fifteen minutes?" Epic patted his hair. "I'm not even dressed cute!"

"Oh, hush." I took the keys along with a gift bag I assumed contained water and snacks. "Thank you so much, Gale."

"My pleasure." She gave us a map of the grounds and marked it with arrows. "Arsenio will see you to your suite. Enjoy your stay, Mr. Winslow." She nodded to me and turned to Epic. "You too, Mr.—"

"Epic. Just Epic. Thank you so much." He whirled around, head turned up to study the dizzying array of multicolored tiles on the ceiling. I steadied him when he nearly fell.

Z.A. MAXFIELD

"Just *wow*."

Arsenio gave a little bow and asked us to follow. My heels clicked over what seemed like acres of pristine marble flooring, then down a thickly carpeted hallway.

"When Luis and I were thinking of making things permanent, this place was on our shortlist of wedding venues."

"Wait. Is the wedding going to be here?"

"Yes."

"Doesn't that mean you could bump into your ex and his fiancé any time?"

"I doubt it. This is a huge property."

"But they're staying here?"

"Yes, the wedding party will probably stay in suites like ours. I'm pretty certain Luis booked one of the bungalows."

"And that doesn't bother you?"

"No." *Yes, liar.* "Luis was a long time ago, okay? It didn't work out. I'm happy for him, and I am getting a much-needed vacation. Win-win."

"But you're not going with a *movie star.*" His face fell. "They upgraded your suite, but I'm kind of bargain basement compared to Lawrence Dunbar."

"I don't think so. You're fun. We get along."

"But my tux is vintage and everything." He splayed his hands over his mouth. "Oh God. I've ruined your revenge."

"I'm not here to get revenge. I wanted to bring someone who makes me laugh. I'm glad I met you. I think we'll have a blast, don't you?"

"Really?"

"Of course."

He took a deep breath. "I'm going to be the best, most complimentary, starry-eyed fake boyfriend ever. I promise. I'll have everyone eating out of my hand."

"No doubt."

Arsenio led us past an arch covered in flaming red

48

bougainvillea. "Oh, I already have so much to tell my room-mate, Bea. She would love this place."

"You can text her from the room."

Arsenio unlocked a door with a plaque that read Santa Cruz and ushered us inside. The suite had a breath-stealing fireplace with a white mantle and a painted yellow plaster chimney. A high red writing desk and a red and gold couch delineated the living room, and there was a dining table with four chairs.

Epic seemed more interested in the large picnic hamper with its gift bow and fancy tag.

"What do you suppose this is?"

I shrugged. "Open it and find out."

"Yay." He undid the large red silk ribbon. "Oh, wine and treats. I want to live here forever."

"Suitcases in the closet, sir?" Arsenio asked.

"Yes, please."

"May I bring you anything else?"

"Ice would be great. Thank you."

After Arsenio left, we checked out the rest of the suite. In the bedroom, we found a king-size bed.

"Oh, shit." Of course there was only one bed. "Lawrence thought I was coming by myself. I'm sorry, Epic."

"No worries. It'll be fine to share."

"Probably the couch folds out."

"This room is amazing." He peeked into the bathroom. "Come look at this. It's huge."

I looked. "The tile was all handmade, I think."

Epic turned to me. "Did you ever see the movie *Zorro*?"

"You mean the one with Antonio Banderas? Or Tyrone Power?" I narrowed my eyes. "Choose wisely because only one answer is correct."

"Tyrone Power FTW." He pumped his fist and quoted, "'This is California, where a man can only marry, raise fat children, and watch his vinyards grow.'"

"Oh, thank goodness. I was afraid I'd have to find a place to hide your body."

He shoved his windblown hair off his face. "I love old Hollywood."

"Me too."

In the living room, I opened the cabernet sauvignon, poured two glasses and took a long, healthy sip.

This. I needed exactly this. The artfully manicured—yet made to look wild—gardens. Sand between my toes. The chance to sit still and consider what was next for me. Because it had been a long, long time since I'd slowed down enough to take stock.

Arsenio came back with ice. I thanked him in the customary way since I could afford to be a big tipper if Lawrence was footing the hotel bill. "Thank you. Have a nice afternoon, Arsenio."

"Thank you, sir." He smiled and left us.

Once we were alone, silence fell like a blanket of fog.

Epic, who rarely shut up, simply took the wine I offered him.

"To your health," I said.

"And yours." We clinked our glasses together.

He fussed with the contents of the hamper for a few minutes. Three cheeses, a couple of different types of charcuterie, some fruit, honey, and nuts. He even dug out caviar and crème fraîche and some packaged blini to go with them.

"This is quite a spread," I said. "Guess if you like this stuff, we could snack on the patio."

He nodded.

"Hey, did I do something?" I asked. "If it's about the bed, you can take it. I've slept on a ton of pullouts in my day."

"No. It's not that." He picked up the hamper and headed for the patio. "It's just that this is so much more amazing than I thought it would be. I'm totally unprepared for this level of... good fortune."

"Are you saying you're not normally lucky?" I followed him outside, where we sat at a wrought iron table for two with a glass top.

"No. I am." He frowned down at the cheese board he was crafting. "But when we started this adventure, I thought we were just two guys off on a lark."

I lifted his chin. "And now?"

"Now, I don't know how to act. Not around a guy who pals around with A-listers and stays in places where they give you caviar and wine."

"I'm pretty sure the gift basket is from Laurie."

"OMG. You call him Laurie?" He made a little heart throbbing gesture. "That is so adorable."

I helped spread out our little picnic. "You know I work for an NGO, right? Laurie and I became friends because, not only does he support the work we do, he believes in it. I know a lot of so-called A-listers who give us money but would step over a half-dead Uber driver to get another ride. Laurie's not that guy. He's decent. I don't know what he was thinking, doing all this for me of all people."

Epic's steady blue eyes met mine. "You mean because this level of luxury becomes complicated if you think about the armies of unseen hands who make it happen."

"*Yes.*" I breathed the word. For a single, wonderful moment, it seemed as if someone truly saw me. "Thank you."

Epic, the boy with the absurd name, had hidden depths.

He picked up a cracker and a little spade-shaped cheese knife. "I spent the summer before college working with a group that makes no-cost home repairs for low-income households in Appalachia. After that, my grandma wanted to meet me near Raleigh to celebrate. We stayed at the Umpstead, I think? We had a suite on the spa level. It was nothing like this, but I still got whiplash."

"You spent a summer doing free building repairs, *and* you have an MFE?"

He smirked. "See? Not just a pretty face."

"But it is." I'd had too much wine to keep that in. "Pretty, I mean."

"Thank you." He flushed. "How do you make it all work inside your brain? Doing what you do and taking advantage of this kind of luxury at the same time?"

"I try to patronize businesses that value their staff. I get nosy sometimes. I look up anything I can find in the media. Dig into the finances of a business if I think it has shady employment practices."

"What about this one?" He gestured past the patio to the masterfully detailed gardens beyond.

"I didn't want to know this time." I hadn't really looked beyond making the reservation and getting a date. "Don't get me wrong, I would have looked into it if I'd been the one using it as a wedding venue. Too many beautiful things hold ugliness inside."

Not Epic, though. Despite only knowing him for a day, I'd have bet on Epic being lovely all the way through. I took another swallow of my wine. We chatted while we ate our charcuterie picnic and finished off the wine. The warmth of the sun and the meal made me so sleepy, I gave Epic his key and told him he was free to explore.

"You look beat." He started packing up what was left of the food. "I'll just clean up here, then take a look around."

"Maybe make a dinner reservation? There are several restaurants on site."

"What time do you think you want to eat?"

I checked my watch. It was only two. "Seven, maybe? We'll get the sunset."

"I'll see what they have available." I could tell by the coltish way Epic moved that he was tipsy.

"Don't do anything I wouldn't do."

"I'll be fine. Just need some fresh air."

"Have fun."

He turned back at the door. "I thought you said I shouldn't do anything you wouldn't do?"

Very funny. Just because I didn't love mini-golf... "Get out."

He smiled, winked, and left me with the impression I was in way over my head. I had asked a goofy waiter with a silly name to be my plus-one for this event. I'd seen him as arm candy. A bit of fluff. A diversion.

The warm, sweet man I'd come to know in just a few hours had a great sense of humor. I liked being around him. He had depth and values that aligned with things I'd rarely spoken about to anyone.

Danger lurked here.

If I got attached to a guy like Epic, I might not be able to walk away.

Epic could turn my quiet, purposeful world upside down.

CHAPTER SEVEN

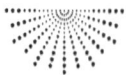

I showered when I woke from my nap. As far as I knew, Epic hadn't returned to our suite, but he probably would shortly, and I wanted to get shaved and dressed before he came back.

The bath was nothing short of miraculous. It featured an extra-long tub, a separate shower, and two pedestal sinks. Lovely tilework evoked both the resort's Spanish colonial heritage and the gardens outside.

I'd just finished shaving when the door opened.

"I'm back."

"I'll be out in—"

"This place is…" Epic had walked in with his usual bonhomie, but he stopped short when he saw me in only a towel. His cheeks reddened. "Sorry."

"No worries. I'm through with the bath if you want to grab a shower before dinner."

"Sounds good. What are we wearing?"

"I thought I'd wear slacks and a button-down with a jacket."

"Okay." He went to the closet and took out the duffel he'd brought. "I guess I should've hung things up, huh?"

"There's an iron." I indicated the cubby over the closet. "I could press anything you need while you shower."

"Oh God. No. It'll be fine tonight. The penguin suit's all I'm worried about. I'm a great packer. I just hate living out of a suitcase."

I'd already hung my shirts and slacks and put the rest into dresser drawers, so while I dressed, Epic unzipped his duffel and took his clothes out to hang them. He was right about packing. He'd employed some strategy that saved space but kept his clothes from getting rumpled.

"How much did you bring?" I asked.

"Enough," he said coolly. "Is that a problem?"

"No. I admire how you Tetrised your things. You'll have to teach me." He'd run out of hangers and he was only half done. "I'll call housekeeping for more hangers."

"Okay. Thank you."

Only a few minutes passed before a woman — name-tagged Linda — brought a nice stack of hangers.

"Thank you." I tipped and took them from her. "Appreciate it."

"Have a good afternoon, sir."

I helped Epic hang up the rest of his things. "I feel like I've been knighted with as many times people have called me sir today."

"I know, right?"

"I'll go out to the patio while you get ready. I'll take my laptop and check on work."

"Should you do that if you're on vacation?" he asked.

"Probably not, but it's a compulsion."

He turned back to the closet. "Maybe we can break you of that while we're here."

"Bigger men than you have tried."

"I'm surprised at you"—he shot me a calculating look —"thinking size matters."

I left him standing in the bedroom with a spark in his gaze.

On the patio, I thought about Laurie. I missed our chance to get together, but Epic might actually be a much better plus-one. Like it or not, Laurie drew unwanted attention wherever we went. Epic and I could leave the room, walk on the beach, swim, and sail. We could dine without curious onlookers and strobing flashes interrupting us every five seconds.

But I began to sense that Epic attracted attention in his own way.

He was a handful. A lovely, teasing, mischievous handful.

If nothing else, this weekend would be interesting.

"HOLY COW," Epic said when we were seated at a table in the glass-enclosed space overlooking the sunset on Butterfly Beach. Still half-visible on the horizon, the sun bled purple and pink and fiery orange ripples onto the water. "This is spectacular."

The hostess responded with a pleased smile. "Enjoy your evening, sirs."

"Thank you."

The menu at Tyde was brief and pricey. It featured things like oysters mignonette and beef tartare.

I found it charming that the ordinarily opinionated Epic stayed quiet as we looked the menu over together. I assured him he could get anything he wanted, but he kept asking me what I planned on having.

"I'm torn between the pasta and the sea scallops."

He bit his lip. "Those sound good. I love scallops."

"Then why don't you order those, and I'll order pasta, and we can share. Would you like that?"

"Okay." He lowered his gaze. "Is your friend paying for this too? I don't want to take advantage."

"If it matters, I'll find a way to pay Laurie back. Not for the suite because honestly, that's on him for upgrading me like that. But the incidentals shouldn't be at his expense."

Epic leaned over to whisper, "But this is ridiculous. We serve the same things at Bistro, and they're nowhere near this expensive."

"We're paying for the view, the experience, and the chef's reputation. It's all right. I haven't had a vacation in six years. I assure you, I can afford it. Let's enjoy ourselves, shall we?"

I handed him the wine list. "Find us a nice wine, unless you'd prefer a cocktail?"

"Wine with dinner, I think. Cocktails later?"

"Sounds like a plan."

He bit his lip. "Maybe we should request the sommelier?"

"Oh, indubitably." I put on a snooty accent. "Let's do."

I ended up getting Brussels sprouts for the table along with spring pea and prosciutto tagliatelle while Epic settled on the sea scallops. We got a bottle of crisp, dry white wine the waiter recommended to enjoy with dinner. After the meal, we ordered an artisanal cheese platter and twenty-five-year-old port.

"I can't believe I'm drinking port that's older than I am while eating after-dinner cheese."

"If this meal doesn't give me a heart attack, we can do it again tomorrow."

"Don't even joke."

I leaned back and studied Epic's profile. He had patrician features, which I found odd because his actions were pure squirrelly California boy. Outgoing and approachable—maybe even a little frivolous—wasn't Epic's entire story. There was something distinctly noble about him in spite of his antics.

And I knew nobility. There was likely to be a lot of it around this weekend.

Luis carried himself in a way that made people respond with automatic deference. He drew the eye. He commanded attention. People naturally made way for him in social gatherings based on a subtle undercurrent of expectation that was probably several centuries in the making.

There was no comparing the two, and yet they were opposite sides of the same coin. They both felt things deeply. They were both willing to work for the things they believed in.

Apparently I gravitated toward a certain type of man.

I wondered what would happen if Epic was older.

Or if we were dating for real.

Could he ever be interested in someone like me, or was I simply an adventure to him?

He lifted his drink and sat back in his chair. "I really like port."

"Me too." In the glow of candlelight, we shared a quiet companionship that warmed my heart. Who knew? Epic understood when to fill a silence and when to let one linger for a bit.

When the waiter arrived, I signed the meal to the room.

I didn't ask if there was somewhere I could smoke. Better to apologize and all that. Instead, Epic and I made our leisurely way along the convoluted pathways toward the beach. The landscape featured ground lights and up-lit trees and palms wound around with thousands of fairy lights. A slightly chilly breeze blew Epic's thick dark hair all over, but it mostly fell back into place. Mine, of course, curled—especially in humid weather. There would be no controlling my slightly too-long mop this trip.

As we walked, I noticed Epic had wrapped his arms around himself.

"Cold?" I slipped out of my jacket. "Here. Take this."

"I don't want to take it from you."

"You know I live in Canada, right?"

"Do you?" He stared at me blankly. "I guess I didn't know that. How'd you end up there?"

"Oh, that's right. I was going to tell you more about all that." I shrugged. "Well, I had the languages and skill set to work in National Security, but it was 2008, and everyone was still paranoid about the Middle East specifically and Muslims in general. I didn't like the direction the country had taken back then. I couldn't see myself breaking codes or analyzing bits of information for the US's war on terrorism."

"I understand. Why work for HUD when you can build houses?"

"Right, well, HUD has its place, but I was very young and had wild ideas. Not all of them were good ones. I traveled in Southeast Asia for a while after grad school, and that's where I first became aware of sex tourism."

Epic winced. "Oh, man."

"Sex tourism made me see a different way I could use my education. The University of British Columbia offers a doctorate in Gender, Race, Sexuality, and Social Justice, so I applied."

"Did you get in?"

"No." I laughed. "I was pissed off about that. Then I talked to the department chair and told her what I wanted to do. She referred me to StolenLives, an NGO whose purpose aligned with mine—that is, to stop human trafficking for sex or labor."

"So you felt like you had a calling?"

"I guess I did." At the seawall, we turned and followed the walkway to the very farthest edge of the property. Hopefully no one would throw me out if I was super discreet.

I lit a cigarette as we slipped into the shadows, where trampled ice plant gave up its familiar, sharp fragrance. A brisk wind whisked the smoke from my mouth almost before I had a chance to expel it. Epic hoisted himself onto the low wall.

"I wish I had a calling." He pulled my jacket tighter around him.

"You'll find one." I had the urge to wrap my arms around him too. I had never talked with anyone like I'd talked with him. Never shared even half of what I'd let him see. But things were already complicated enough between us.

"Maybe my calling is waiting tables."

"Maybe it is. Would that be so bad?"

"My parents would go nuclear if that was the case. They expect better things from me."

"But it sounds like your grandmother sort of champions you."

He nodded. "We're very close. When I was a kid, she seemed almost magical to me. Things were always better when she was around. In the long run, she's the one I want to make proud. I don't know if my parents even have that setting."

"I'm sorry."

"No, it's all right. I'm just being stupid. Chloe—that's my mother—says I've been hiding in St. Nacho's in order to avoid responsibility."

"Do you make enough to pay your way?"

"With a roommate and the food I get from Bistro, sure."

"Are you happy there?"

"Oh yes. I love it in St. Nacho's." His face softened.

I sent another stream of smoke into the air. "My friend Daniel says the same thing."

"Livingston? Of course he does. He's got Cam Rooney to go home to."

"Yes, there's Cam, but I think originally he was there for business and because his brother lives there. He stayed because he loves it."

"I understand that. When I first saw the place, it was as if a big weight fell off my shoulders."

"How'd you end up there?" I leaned my elbows on the wall beside him and shifted my weight ever so slightly. Our arms pressed together.

"I was supposed to go to LA with an actor friend. He planned to get headshots and start making the rounds. It was pilot season. He was going to try to get an agent."

"Oldest story in the world."

"Right?" Epic chuckled. "I didn't really even want to go.

LA isn't my idea of a nice place to live. Anyway, we got as far as the valley, and he started talking about porn. I was outta there so fast I burned the streets up. On the way back, I stopped in St. Nacho's and never left."

"You're happy there."

"I am." He turned to meet my gaze. "You would be too, I think. St. Nacho's would be good for you."

"Think so?" I carefully crushed out my cigarette and tossed the butt into a nearby trash bin. "Kind of a tough commute to Vancouver."

"You should open a satellite office. With the border, the ports, and the I-5 corridor, California is a major artery for human trafficking from both Mexico and China."

"I am aware," I pointed out.

"And are you aware you have a ton of stress-related habits that seem to be taking a toll on your health?"

"Who are you, my mother?"

Epic giggled at that. He fucking giggled, and the sound was so endearing I found myself wishing this was a real date.

"C'mon," I said. "I could use a good night's sleep."

We turned to walk, but a shape moved out of the shadows and a flame limned a horribly familiar face. The man stepped forward.

"Hello, Ryan."

Of all the lousy seawalls in the world, why'd he have to show up at mine?

"Hey, he smokes the same weird brand you do," observed Epic.

"Hello, Luis." It wasn't the wind that chilled me to the bone. "Congratulations on your upcoming nuptials."

CHAPTER EIGHT

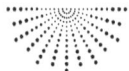

L uis nodded his head regally while I took stock of his appearance. He now wore his dark, curly hair long, but his smoldering black eyes and hawkish nose were the same and still achingly handsome.

"Thank you, amorcito. It means a lot to me that you are here to witness my happiness." He spoke the words with a memorable Castilian *θ*, and I had to swallow past the tightness in my throat.

"Wait. Is this—"

"Allow me to introduce you. Luis Acebo y Ibarra, meet Epic."

"Epic?" Luis's brows rose. "Short for Epictetus, I presume? Father of stoic philosophy?"

His expression was that of a cat toying with a mouse, and I burned with anger on Epic's behalf.

"Got it in one," Epic answered. "Robert Epictetus Alsop. Pleasure to meet you."

Luis nodded. "The pleasure is mine."

I stared at Epic in shock. "Epictetus *Alsop?* Really?"

Epic shrugged.

"How are you enjoying your stay so far, Ryan?" Luis

asked. "As I recall, you always wanted to spend time at this resort."

"It's lovely," I said tightly.

Luis blew his smoke away and turned back with a sheepish grin. "William is making me quit after the honeymoon, so I must make the best of these last few opportunities to smoke."

Epic slipped his arm through mine. "I've been waging a similar campaign with Ryan."

I stared at him. "Good luck with that."

"Ryan's habits are very ingrained, you see," Luis murmured. "There is his work, whatever it takes to support his work, and little else."

"Oh, I don't know." Epic rested his head against my arm. "I didn't have to take his phone away while we were playing mini-golf today."

Luis eyed me. "You don't enjoy golf of any kind."

"I don't," I offered. "But Epic wanted to go."

I still didn't know how he'd talked me into it.

"I see. Well, don't let me keep you on such a lovely night."

I hesitated, uncertain, but Epic drew me away. "It was a pleasure to meet you, Luis. My best to William."

"Good night." Luis saluted with his cigarette. The tip of which glowed faintly as he pulled back into the shadows.

When we were far enough away, Epic whispered, "That wasn't awkward at all."

"Was it?" I'd nearly died on the spot, but I didn't understand why it might have been awkward for Epic.

"Of course it was. Oh my God, I've never been so blatantly dick measured in my life."

"What's this about your name? You're really Epictetus? I thought everyone called you Epic because you're--kind of —extra."

"I'm *extra?*"

"Bubbly. Effervescent. You know what I mean."

"Extra," he muttered. "So he really is a Spanish aristocrat?"

"Titled and everything."

"He's pretty good-looking." Epic pursed his lips. "If you like the Antonio Banderas type."

"I thought we established I'm on team Tyrone Power."

"We did, didn't we?" His lips curled into a shy smile.

In a way, Epic reminded me of an old Hollywood heart-throb. He had that look—dark hair, impossibly blue eyes. He was tall but still coltish. Elegant in jeans, a button-down, and my jacket.

Epic had the ability to blend in, whether he was waiting tables, eating cheese and drinking twenty-five-year-old port, or bantering with my intimidating ex. He had a poise so unexpected that if I'd blinked, I'd have missed the transitions.

I'd been drawn to him from the first, and he hadn't let go of my arm. Suddenly, I was aware of his body and the fact there was only a king bed in our suite. Pullouts were notoriously uncomfortable, plus, they required taking out at night and putting back in the morning. Even if the maids did all the work, it still meant moving furniture and ruining the aesthetic of the room.

Of course, the last time I'd considered the *aesthetic* of a room...was never.

"You're awfully quiet. Did it hurt seeing him?" Epic asked.

"Maybe a little."

"I take it your work came between you? What does he do?"

"He manages his family's philanthropic trust, and he's on the board of trustees for a children's hospital. He also has a number of social obligations each year, and he's a brand ambassador for Piaget."

"Of course he is," Epic muttered.

"So you can see why it didn't work. He needed a husband who would support the work he's doing."

"But so did you."

"Bullshit." I couldn't imagine that. "The last thing I'd want in a husband is staff."

"You think William's going to be his staff?"

"William has a career of his own. I can't imagine how they're making things work." I checked the signs to make certain we were headed in the right direction. "This way."

He stopped and looked around as if to memorize the path. "This place is confusing, isn't it?"

"What Luis wanted was someone willing to make being his husband into a career."

"And you would hate that."

"I spend too much time pressing the flesh frivolously as it is. Imagine me at a banquet for a hospital board or a photo shoot on a yacht."

"So where are you happiest?"

"What do you mean?"

"You travel for work, right?" I nodded. "Do you like to travel?"

"Not really. I'm most comfortable in my office at home. I have alerts set for certain types of news, and my team and I follow whatever trails we can to uncover where dirty money starts and where it ends. Missing persons, mail-order brides, drug mules, sweat shops, employment scams. Trafficking anything is a multibillion-dollar industry, and someone has to clean all that cash. That's where you start to see the big picture."

"Hey." Surprise stole over his features. "You're an intelligence analyst after all."

I gave a nod. "It helps to have those skills."

"What do you do when you find something?"

"We notify the proper authorities so they can look into the information we've gathered, and that means we create a dossier of everything we've discovered and why we think it's problematic. Or we might undertake negotiations on behalf of people involved. Arrange legal fees for those needing help, either with immigration or charges related to crimes they might have been coerced into committing."

"This got awfully serious all of a sudden."

"I'm so sorry. I can go on and on. Stop me when that happens."

"I like that you talk to me. I guess I didn't expect it to be such a serious answer."

"So I should have said, I'm happiest in my office on my computer."

He bumped my shoulder with his. "Right."

"I'm sorry." I'd gotten us lost in a jungle of tropical plants. "Is this the way we came?"

"I don't know." He pointed out a sign. "Looks like the pool is that way."

"Then we're the other direction. I think I've got it now."

"I don't mind walking some more." Epic sighed. "I drank too much at dinner."

"I ate too much," I admitted. "I don't usually eat like that."

He poked me. "No kidding."

"Ah, here we are." I recognized our building. At the door, I swiped the key, but before we went inside, I stopped him. "Look. You're right. We're both super tired, and the bed is huge. If you want to share it, I promise things won't get weird. I'll be asleep before my head hits the pillow."

"Thanks." He bit his lip over a cheeky grin. "I really didn't want to sleep on the pullout."

"C'mon." I opened the door.

Inside the bedroom we discovered the maids had performed a turndown service. They'd left little boxes of chocolate on the pillows.

Epic kicked off his shoes and leaped on, rolling around a little. "I could totally get used to this. Wonder if I could get my roommate to do it."

I slipped my tie off and started unbuttoning my shirt.

"Need to use the bathroom?" Epic asked. "I'd like a quick shower before bed."

I went and took care of business. When I came out, Epic

was down to his boxer briefs, but he'd hung his clothes—and my jacket—neatly away.

"Back in a bit." He slipped into the bathroom but turned at the doorway where he hesitated a few seconds, holding his dopp kit. I'd stripped to my boxers and put on a T-shirt. There was no doubt he was watching me. His eyes warmed with appreciation. "I'll just…"

"I might be asleep by the time you get out."

"I'll try not to wake you if you try not to snore." The door closed behind him, and I let out the breath I'd been holding.

God, he was sweet—in both temperament and looks. His body was beautiful, he had nice shoulders, a slim waist, and long lean legs. His skin was luminescent, lightly dusted with hair the same dark color of the hair on his head. His buttocks was firm and pleasingly bubbly.

He was perfect.

And he was sleeping in my bed.

And I hadn't brought Ambien.

Shit, shit, shit.

I'd said I was sleepy—that was very true—but I was also a red-blooded man who hadn't gotten laid in the better part of a year. In no way could I break my word and come on to him now, so I lay down and counted on the wine we'd had at dinner to do the trick.

It had been a long day. I'd gotten too much sun, and between my nerves and mini-golf, I was barely awake when Epic came in and made himself comfortable. Thank God between the white noise of water from the shower and the waves I could hear from the shore, I fell into a pleasant, languorous sleep.

Of course, I didn't stay that way. At three in the morning I woke again, feeling refreshed and wide awake. That gave me the opportunity to study Epic at leisure.

As I'd thought, he had an old Hollywood face. A square-jawed, East Coast, old money look that made him appear masculine and at the same time a little dreamy.

I could totally picture him on the big screen with Jimmy Stewart and Henry Fonda. He was still young, but he'd season into one hell of a handsome man. In the light coming through the window, I saw he'd put on a Chain Smokers T-shirt. He lay on his back, exposing his profile, and I almost laughed when I recalled Luis sizing him up.

He didn't snore, but I did. I wondered if he'd noticed. If things were different, if he wasn't my fake boyfriend, would snoring be a deal breaker?

It had bothered Luis.

A lot had bothered Luis—from my job, to my snoring, to the fact that I didn't like ostentatious gifts and didn't care who designed my clothes. He didn't like that I wouldn't take time off work for an impromptu trip to Greece on someone's yacht.

I sighed and tried to get out of bed without waking Epic. I picked up a robe and padded into the living room part of the suite where I took out my laptop to check messages and get a look at the nightly news.

I was streaming a feel-good story about a dog who'd saved a little girl from drowning when Epic came out to find me.

"Hey." He rubbed his eyes. "Can't sleep?"

"It's the booze. Once the alcohol wears off, the sugar takes over, and I wake up for a while. Go back to sleep. I'm fine."

"But now I'm awake." He pouted. Reaching for my shoulders, he began rubbing them in lazy circles.

"Oh, that's heavenly."

"That's me. I'm positively celestial."

I laughed, and something he did made me drop my chin to my chest like my neck was a noodle. "Oh."

"You're tight. Do you ever get massages?"

I shook my head. "Nuh-uh."

"Mm. Maybe you should if you like it that much. My roommate, Bea, gives great massages. She's getting her esthetician's license in order to work at Pure Harmony Spa."

"Where's that?"

"About fifteen miles south of St. Nacho's on the 101. It's a newer hotel, spa, and wedding venue like this one." He frowned. "Well, not like this one, because seriously, this place is in a class by itself."

His fingers worked some kind of magic, unlocking each of my nerve endings and turning me into a puddle of goo.

"You okay?"

"I am." I sighed. "That feels so good."

"I guess you kind of got thrown into the deep end this trip. First, I made you play mini-golf, and then we bumped into your ex. That can't have been fun."

"No."

"Do you still miss him?"

I had to give that some thought. "Not him specifically."

"Oh. The idea of him?"

"That's it. The idea of that one person who really knows who you are."

"Did he?"

"Yeah, but I'm pretty sure he didn't like me. He spent a lot of his time campaigning for change."

"I know what that's like because Steven and Chloe are the same." I must have looked blank. "My parents."

Epic's hands drifted away, and he took the chair beside me.

"I like you, Ryan."

"Thank you, but it's not exactly as if you know me."

"I know what you care about." He was a smart kid. I guessed he probably did. "I know that you drive yourself."

"Of course I—"

"And don't make a joke about cars because you know what I mean."

I bit my lip. "Okay."

"I know that you came here expecting to pal around with a"

friend who could make you feel better about all this, and I'm sorry he couldn't make it, but I won't let you down."

"You couldn't, Epic. You don't have to do anything. I like you too."

He gave me a sweet smile and rested his head in his arms. "I'll keep you company until you want to go back to bed, okay?"

I shut down my computer, closed my laptop, and took his hand. "Come on. We need our sleep because we're going to have lots of fun tomorrow."

"We are?"

"I'm counting on it."

CHAPTER NINE

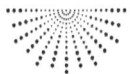

The following morning we dressed after ordering breakfast in the room—shakshuka for me and eggs Benedict for Epic, along with a fresh berry bowl and a large pot of coffee.

We sampled each other's dishes like we had the night before. His was rich and buttery with delicate ham and perfectly poached eggs. Mine was fragrant with garlic, covered in Lebneh cheese, served with a thin, herbaceous bread to soak up the spicy tomato sauce.

Despite the interruption to my sleep, I felt refreshed and ready to spend time doing…something.

"What do you suggest we do today?" I asked Epic. "It says in the hotel binder they have personal trainers, guided meditation, tennis, yoga."

"Oh, goodie." He rolled his eyes.

"What sounds fun to you, then?"

"What if we go into Santa Barbara? There are a ton of art galleries and shops."

"We could do that."

"I think it would be fun to look around."

I stood. "I'm in. I could use the walk."

"Cool." Once again, he slathered me with sunscreen—no wonder his skin was so pale. "You should probably get a hat."

"Maybe I should get black socks and oxford shoes, too? Or carry a big camera so there's no mistaking me for a local."

"You can get a cool hat."

"But I'll get hat hair."

"My grandmother looks forty even though she's sixty-eight and she says it's because she never puts a toe in the sun without protection. I intend to benefit from her advice."

"Fine. I'll buy a hat," I said to make him smile. "I'll buy you one too."

"But I'll get hat hair." He echoed me with more than a modest amount of mockery.

"That's the price of beauty, my dear."

He wrinkled his nose adorably.

After we got dressed, we ordered our car from the valet and headed into town. We found a place to park off State Street and started making our way from shop to shop, or rather Epic made his way from shop to shop, and I followed as his comic foil.

He kept up a running commentary, half of which was to express delight in everything he saw, and half was to keep me apprised of things he was certain that people in "my generation" weren't clear about.

"See this?" He pointed to a T-shirt with a long-haired man on it. "That refers to The Witcher."

"Oh really?" I let him enjoy his teasing.

"And this"—he picked up another graphic T-shirt—"is about Pokémon."

"Very funny." While our age difference rankled, I got the pop culture references. Epic didn't have a clue how much time I spent online.

We finally found a hat shop, and I think we tried on half their stock.

"Oh, this one is dreadful," I said about a black Fedora. "I look ridiculous, and it's hot out there."

"Yeah, no. Try this one," he said hopefully.

The natural straw Panama hat didn't work either. "Maybe I'm not a hat guy."

"Wait. Try this." He held up a two-tone trilby fedora with an olive plaid band. I tried it on, and I liked it.

"What do you think?" I asked.

"I love it." Epic clapped his hands happily. "It's perfect. Now help me find one."

I checked the price and gulped unhappily.

"Put it back on and just wear it for a second. It really looks good. It's the perfect hat for a summer vacation." He was right of course, but now I wanted retro sunglasses too.

Epic tried on a hundred hats and ended up with a straw fedora with a wider brim. He looked like he should be drinking Cuba libres and smoking a cigar, but it suited the shape of his face and his attitude perfectly.

I bought both of our hats, then we wandered until we found a sunglass shop where I could buy tortoiseshell sunglasses with green lenses. Epic already had classic Ray-Ban Wayfarers, so when we left the shop, we were as stylish as could be.

After we'd walked about another mile, I asked, "Are you hungry?"

He nodded. "I could definitely eat."

We found a restaurant, and of course, it being Santa Barbara, the menu advertised locally grown produce, grass-fed beef, and buns made with love, or good karma, or some such thing. We tried their home-brewed kombucha and snickered over the fact that the burgers tasted just like ones made from regular cows.

We had an entirely drama-free morning, unless you counted Epic, who was so animated and delightful and easygoing it felt like I had unwittingly entered a rom-com.

I kept waiting for the bad news, a time when he was petty, or thoughtless, or immature, but it never happened.

As we made our way to the beach after lunch, he practically skipped along, talking about everything that interested him, and I found myself reawakening to a world I'd lost touch with a long time ago.

"IT'S TOTALLY NO fair if I'm doing all the work," Epic whined from behind me.

"You're not."

"I am. My thighs are killing me. We'll never get back at this rate."

"I'm doing all the work here," I shouted. "Do you even have your feet on the peddles?"

I glanced back, and of course, he didn't. Cheeky bastard.

Renting a tandem bicycle had been all his idea. The last time I'd ridden a bike had been in a spin class years before. I thought I was acquitting myself admirably until I realized we'd been out only half of our rental time. By then, I was ready to abandon the thing on the side of the road.

"This was your idea," I reminded him.

"You went along with it."

"Because I like your smile," I admitted. He didn't say anything, and at that point I knew I was the only one peddling. Had he abandoned ship?

When I glanced back, it was to see him grinning softly. Beads of sweat glistened on his forehead beneath the tragically uncool protuberance of his bike helmet.

"What do you say we walk this bad idea back to the rental place and never tell anyone we did it?" I asked.

"No." He started pumping again. "At least let's ride back."

"Okay, but no more slacking."

He still slacked, but it was okay. We dropped the bike off

in plenty of time and continued along the beach for a while, letting the breeze dry our sweaty bodies. The air smelled of minerals, and iodine, and tar.

"That never happened." I raked my fingers self-consciously through my curls.

"Who am I going to tell?" Despite having been squashed under a helmet, Epic's hair seemed to sift into its normal style. Silky and dark, the late afternoon sun reflected off it like a halo. My calf muscles had tightened, changing my stride. My thighs burned with every step. Epic made me reapply sunscreen.

"Feel like a dip?" I asked.

"Just because I wanted to go bike riding?" Epic gaped at me. "No."

"I meant do you want to go back to the hotel and have a swim before dinner."

"Oh. Okay." He smiled slyly. "Sure."

As we drove back to the hotel, Epic turned on the radio. I had it tuned to a satellite radio station that played classical music. He pushed the *Seek* button.

As he listened to the snippets of each station, I wondered if this was going to be the thing that began the end between us. Epic's playlist had been great, but what was his normal taste in music? I'd driven over twelve hundred miles to get to Santa Barbara, and I could not have done it listening to country western or trance music.

"You don't like classical?" I finally asked.

"I like it. Just wanted to see what else there is. My beater hasn't exactly got satellite radio."

"Oh."

"Are there presets?"

"Why?"

"I'm snooping. I want to know what you listen to."

"What do you listen to?"

"Lots of stuff." He relaxed back into his seat. "Dance,

trance, hip-hop, heavy metal, techno, jazz, funk, new age, classical, you name it."

"Gregorian chant?"

"Totally. You?"

"Oh sure," I said wryly. "I get down with my bad self to Hildegarde von Bingen too."

"That racist bitch? No way. She's cancelled."

I glanced over, surprised. "How do you know Hildegarde?"

"Well, unlike you, I didn't go to school with her." He shot the playful jab with a grin. "I know a very little bit about a lot of things. That's part of my charm."

"Indeed." I liked his explanation. "Is there anything you know a whole lot about?"

"You mean like…tantric sexual practices?"

My mouth went dry. "Mmhmm."

"Not really. Who was it that said, 'deep down, he's really very shallow'?"

"Oh, I know this one." I raised my hand. "Dorothy Parker for the win."

"Seems like you know a little about a lot of things too." He glanced my way with approval.

"It's my stock in trade."

He went back to the classical station—Joshua Bell playing Chopin's E-flat Nocturne—and put his seat back a few inches.

His hand rested on the console beside mine, and I had the most absurd urge to take it in mine. There was something about Epic, the way he moved, and laughed, and sighed when he was utterly, completely content that touched me in ways I never could have foreseen. It was as if we'd walked together but separately all along and closing the distance between us would feel as natural as breathing.

"Ryan?" he asked.

I had to clear my throat. "Mmhmm?"

"Are you happy I came along on your trip?"

"Very." I did take his hand then. A blanket of warmth swept over me when he laced our fingers together.

"Me too."

At the hotel, we left the car with the valet and went to our room to shower off and change. I wore board shorts. Epic returned from the bathroom in a microscopically small Speedo with a pair of swim goggles around his neck.

Smooth as silk, I fished my tongue out of my throat and stood up as though I was ready for this. "They'll have towels poolside."

"Okay, let's go." He took the towel he'd slung over his shoulder and flung it onto the bed.

As I watched him walk across our suite, I fought the urge to grab my fluffy hotel robe.

I'm not a vain man, never have been. I run, but that's pretty much it. Biking today had cost me the use of my ass and legs, and honestly, I didn't expect to do much in the pool besides float. I'd planned to take a healing dip in the hot tub as well as maybe grab a sauna—most of which were definitely medicinal.

Now, before me walked my young Adonis. Nearly my height but leaner with a cut swimmer's body he hid beautifully beneath his clothes. He didn't swagger, but he didn't have to. His body was...breathtaking. Honed.

I'd noticed his broad shoulders and lean hips, but now I could see each muscle was defined down to six-pack abs and a V-cut. His body didn't come from a gym but was the product of a lifetime of activity.

Before I even took off my flip-flops, Epic dove in, cutting through the water like a knife. He swam to the other end of the pool underwater, surfaced, and swam back to hang on the pool's edge.

He raked water from his hair. "The temperature is perfect."

I slid in beside him and decided it was cold. Keeping a smile on my face occupied the next few seconds of my life until I could breathe again.

"Want to race?" he asked.

"Not a chance." I wished I had thought to bring Epic's floaty. Instead, I pushed off the side with my feet and back-stroked around like a lost turtle while Epic did a few more laps.

A few minutes later, he punched through the water by my side and slipped his goggles to the top of his head.

"Let me guess," I said. "Competitive swimmer?"

"Kind of," he hedged. "Not in college. What about you? What's your sport?"

As if everyone had one. "Track and field in high school."

"You still run?"

"Yes, but if you ask me if I want to do that this weekend, the answer's no." No way would I embarrass myself like that. "My pace is probably slower than you're used to.

He splashed me. "I like a man who paces himself so he can go the distance."

Despite the cool pool, his words had a pretty predictable effect on my dick. I sank and swallowed a lot of water. That was the exact—and weirdly metaphorical—moment I found myself in deep with Epic Alsop.

So deep, in fact, that Epic towed me to the shallow end.

"You okay there?" His grin wasn't just cheeky, it was positively evil.

"Yeah," I sputtered. "Just got...a little something..."

"Not so little, even though it's cold." He snorted and took off.

Jesus. I got out and retrieved towels for both of us, then slid onto one of the loungers to dry. The sun warmed my skin, and the fragrance of plumeria, ginger lily, and climbing ylang ylang filled the air. I'd drifted into that perfect tipping point where sleep seems inevitable when I felt someone sit beside me.

"Let's get out of the sun." Epic tugged on my hand.

I opened my eyes to find him looking down at me with a

perfectly amiable, playful smile on his lips. Backlit, his shoulders sparkled with droplets of water. Slicked back, his hair gleamed glossy as a seal's fur. He held out his hand.

I took it. "All right."

He helped me up and didn't let go on the long walk back to our suite. The usual worries didn't plague me like I thought they would. Work was a thousand miles away along with the rest of the things that made this a bad idea.

Epic walked ahead of me, strong and certain, and I followed because wherever he was headed, wherever *this* was headed, I wanted it.

We got back to the room, and I waited while he slid his key into the reader. Inside, his foot landed on a parchment envelope.

I recognized the studied, spidery writing as Luis's. My full name: Mr. Ryan Taylor Winthrop.

"What's that?" Epic asked. "Looks like an invitation."

Our moment shattered like glass.

CHAPTER TEN

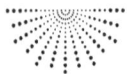

A*morcito,* the note read, *You and your guest are cordially invited to attend an informal gentlemen's evening of tapas and music, seven tonight at the Ty Warner Bungalow. If you require directions, please contact the concierge or ask one of the staff to direct you. I hope you will honor us with your presence. Respectfully, Luis and William.*

"Amorcito," Epic scoffed. "What do you suppose his fiancé thinks about that?"

"Mm."

"Are you going to go?"

"We, you mean. The invitation is for both of us."

He gave an eyeroll. "Sure. What could go wrong?"

"What do you mean?" I asked.

"For one thing, this feels a little Machiavellian." He laid his key card on the table and headed for the bathroom. "I don't know the players, so I'm not sure I trust the game."

"Luis does like a bit of intrigue." My hair was almost dry, though I needed a shower to rinse off the chlorine. "You want to shower first?"

"On it." He stepped inside the bath, and seconds later, I heard water running.

I slipped my trunks off, tied my towel around my waist, and studied the note. Expensive paper as always. Exquisite penmanship as always.

Luis teased me about my handwriting, which was as unlovely as it was serviceable. Anyone could read it, but it wouldn't win any prizes. Luis's writing was the result of years of painstaking practice. He wrote with a fountain pen. Even if he was writing on a Post-it, his notes always seemed like mementos of a bygone era.

Lost in the past, I didn't realize Epic was near until he was standing over me again.

"What?" I glanced up.

He smiled softly. "Shower's yours if you want it."

I met his gaze. "Do you really think we shouldn't go?"

"I'm not sure I'm the one who should decide." He picked up the note. "He writes like it's a royal decree."

"It's not. We always have a choice."

"You could go on your own."

"I'd prefer not to." I could just imagine how much fun that would be. I'd be relegated to sitting in the corner, barred from interacting with some of the guests, who I knew from experience pretended not to understand my Spanish. To William the fiancé, and others, I'd simply be the ex, to be studied and found lacking by comparison.

"It's going to be super bougie, though, isn't it?"

"Beyond bougie and into the absurd probably. The food will be outstanding."

He rubbed his hands together gleefully. "You'll help me pick an outfit? I don't want to look like I'm trying too hard, but I don't want them to look down on me."

"They'll probably look down on both of us no matter what we wear."

He shrugged. "I've been thrown out of better places."

"Good to know." There was the irrepressible boy I'd met outside Nacho's Bar. "Me too."

WE ENDED up wearing variations on the same theme. I put on a white linen button down that was so translucent it was almost like gossamer, while Epic wore a French-blue oxford cloth that suited his schoolboy looks. We both wore jeans and loafers.

Ordinarily I didn't wear jewelry, but I put on a watch, rings, and a chunky silver chain. Epic accessorized with leather and steel. We stood side by side in front of the mirror.

"I feel like we've armed ourselves to dine socially," he murmured.

"A necessary evil. There will probably be cigars."

He made a face. "Of course there will."

"What does that mean?"

"This sounds like it's going to be an old-dude thing."

"Yes, I think it's sort of a boys' night out, only in."

"Why only men?" Epic asked. "Where will the ladies be?"

"Luis is probably taking this opportunity to spend time with the older men in his family and his groomsmen."

"Like a bachelor party?"

"Yes and no. Much more reserved is my guess."

"This should be fun." I doubted he believed that.

"This is a good thing for Luis. His family is traditional and Catholic as fuck, yet they've come to celebrate his wedding. I don't know much about William's family, but for Luis this is a very big deal."

Epic softened. "It's nice they support him."

"Very." I'd found a map. The Ty Warner bungalow had a gated entrance past the putting green and the croquet lawn. "Ready?"

"As I'll ever be."

We walked from our suite along brick paths strewn with tropical plants and through a second building to get to Luis's luxury accommodations. I had nothing to compare it with in my experience. A butler answered the door and led us to the patio, past a buffet of rich-smelling, spicy dishes. On one side of the lap pool, a guitarist played flamenco while a couple in traditional dress danced on a small portable dance floor.

On the other side, a group of men sat around a long table arguing, drinking, and being served tiny plates of food by two discreet servers. Family got table service. The rest of the guests made use of the buffet.

Luis detached himself and came to greet us.

"Ryan, I'm so glad you decided to join us this evening. Epic, was it? Good to see you again. Come, join us. What will you drink?"

"Amontillado," I answered.

Epic said, "Same."

"I don't need to ask for your identification, do I?" Luis teased.

Epic grinned. "I have it if you need it."

"Of course not. This is a private party. At any rate, I have diplomatic immunity." He waved us over to the table.

"You do not," I pointed out.

"I should, don't you think?" He winked. "If I want to serve wine to my family, I should be allowed."

I should have probably googled the announcement of Luis's wedding, but it felt like ripping off a scab at the time. William wasn't what I expected. He was tall and svelte with the coloring of an elf from *The Lord of the Rings*. He had the grace of a dancer and a thin, sweet voice, but I didn't like his smile when it turned on me. He wore a barrister's smile.

"How do you do, Ryan? Luis has told me so much about you that I know we're going to be great friends."

"I'm sure. Pleasure to meet you, William."

He turned to Epic. "And you must be Epictetus? Such an interesting name. I'm very pleased to meet you."

Epic shook hands with him. "Thank you. Pleasure to meet you too."

"Enjoy the evening, gentlemen. I'm sure we'll have the opportunity to chat again." He drifted away as if he wore skates.

Luis led us down the family table to introduce his brothers, Jorge, Jaime, and Salazar, and his uncles Juan and Jose Miguel. We smiled at everyone and nodded as we made our way to two empty chairs at one of several four-top tables set up for dining.

Though I tried to keep up, I lost half of the groomsmen's names to the music. Epic seemed to pay closer attention.

Someone handed me a glass and a plate so I could pick and choose from any of several tapas-style dishes on the buffet.

At last, William and Luis stood at the head table, and we all toasted to their health.

I got a shock when, after the toast, Luis's brothers Jorge and Salazar came to sit at our table. Jorge had always been a little standoffish, but Salazar was the baby of the family and prone to shenanigans.

"Good to see you again, Ryan." Salazar lifted his glass to his lips.

"Nice to see you too." I took two fiery prawns from my plate and passed them to Epic. "Your family is well I hope."

"Very well, thank you." He set his glass down. "I hope it's not awkward for you to attend the wedding. There was some contention over whether to issue an invitation, but Luis and indeed William were insistent."

"That's very kind."

"William puts up with much from my brother. The man is a saint."

He might need to be. Epic offered me a saucy little meatball.

"The food is to die for." His whispered words next to my ear sent shivers straight to my groin.

Once the party got underway, servers replenished each table with plates of tidbits. Epic smiled warmly at our server, who handed each of us a small glass of what I assumed to be gazpacho.

Epic said, "Thank you."

The waiter winked.

"Are you still in Vancouver, Ryan?" Jorge asked.

"Yes, still with StolenLives."

"Don Quixote with your windmills. I admire your fight."

I sipped my soup. "You've always been a very generous benefactor, and I thank you."

"Will you never settle down? Marry and build a family of your own?"

"It's not in the near future," I answered politely.

He turned his gaze to Epic. "And what do you do, young sir?"

"I wait tables at a restaurant called Bistro in St. Nacho's."

"How very American. Do you attend school?"

"Not right now."

I watched and waited for Epic to mention that he'd finished school with an MFE, but he didn't. He ate a meatball, smiled serenely, and turned to me.

"This is delicious. Try yours."

I did as he asked. The meatball tasted wonderful—smooth, moist, flavorful meat in a spicy sauce. "You're right. These are divine."

"And the gazpacho is so yum."

"My brother always serves the finest dishes." Salazar picked up a meatball and popped it into his mouth. "He's an incurable foodie. William indulges him, but soon he will be as fat as Jose Miguel."

"Shh." Jorge laughed with him. "Uncle won't appreciate hearing you say that."

"Luis is very disciplined." When I was with him, he worked out first thing every morning, rain or shine. "He'll always be fit."

"Let's hope he keeps his hair." Salazar offered me a plate of papas braves with an aioli sauce for dipping. "William is too lovely for a bald husband."

The evening went on with waiters bringing out different dishes, croquetas—meat and potatoes rolled in breadcrumbs and fried—fried peppers in crusty sea salt, octopus, and bundles of peppers wrapped in sardines with green olives.

"Now I totally understand why tapas is a thing." Epic definitely enjoyed the food. He studied every morsel as he ate it, savoring each one. "Every little bite just sings."

Flush with wine and spicy food, he looked delicious himself. I hadn't forgotten what had almost happened before we'd received the invitation that had changed our evening's trajectory.

Not being twenty-something, I filled up long before Epic, so I kissed his cheek and went to relax in one of the loungers. I watched the dancers for a while, mesmerized by their vitality and passion.

A severely dressed dark-haired woman, the guitarist's fingers moved so fast at times they were barely visible. Sometimes, they plucked so slowly and passionately it evoked the long hot nights when Luis had played my body just so.

Every expressive, emotional note took me to another place, another time, when Luis and I had been happy together. For a few minutes, I enjoyed the memories, but then I remembered other less pleasant days, and it came back to me that I was glad things had ended between us.

I only wished we'd been quicker to realize that love couldn't last—not if I continued to pursue a demanding career, not if he wanted to live a jet-set lifestyle. There was a lesson there, and I'd almost forgotten it that afternoon. Romance wasn't in my cards, not while my true passion lay elsewhere.

"Is the amontillado putting you to sleep?" Luis asked from beside me.

I'd been so lost in my thoughts I hadn't noticed his

approach. "No. I'm enjoying the music. This is a wonderful party. Thank you for inviting us."

"I'm glad you came," he said.

"William seems wonderful." I would probably never know if he was or was not, and I found I didn't care. "You're both very lucky."

"William is perfect. Despite his many gifts, he wishes to take care of me."

Because after all, I'd expected Luis to take care of himself. "I'm glad."

"They say there is someone for everyone."

"They do say that, don't they?"

"Yet you bring a boy half your age to my wedding. I wonder if you're even seriously looking."

"I'm not," I said. "And Epic is delightful, I'll have you know."

"I'm sure," he said dryly. "But he's tapas. Not a meal for a grown man."

"*Luis*. Don't be an ass." Epic had finished eating and was standing behind him.

"At least with tapas, he'll never be bored." Epic shot me a smug smile.

Luis's lips tightened. "Of course, you are right."

Epic's blue eyes sparkled. "Congratulations again on your upcoming marriage."

"Thank you."

"Mind if I join you, Ryan?" Epic asked as he sat on the side of my lounger.

"Of course not."

"I must make the rounds." Luis rose. "Good to see you, Ryan. We'll have more time to talk later, I hope."

"I hope so."

I made room for Epic, and we stayed like that, spooning, drinking amontillado, watching the dancer and the flickering firelight while conversation in two languages eddied and flowed around us.

"So this is how the other half lives?"

"More like the one percent."

He turned to me. "Really? You dated a one-percenter?"

"Oh, yes. There are more billionaires on this patio than waitstaff and minions."

"Oh my." He relaxed against me. "You'd think I'd want to stay awake for that, wouldn't you?"

"Mmhmm."

"Sadly," he said with a yawn, "I won't be able to, I don't think. Those meatballs were so yummy. I don't suppose you could get a recipe…"

I lit a cigarette when the others began the ritual of cigars. Epic had fallen deeply asleep by then, and the music was no longer live but piped in.

Clouds drifted across the starlit sky, and the sound of waves reached us like the low rumble of distant thunder.

Epic had turned toward me in his sleep. His breath teased the skin of my neck. Contentment swept over me like the cool ocean breeze. For the first time in a long time, I didn't want a party to end. But parties do that. They end. Weary stragglers had to head home.

I had some decisions to make with regard to Epic.

What did I want from him?

What did he want from me?

And if we took what we wanted now, what would it be like to walk away?

CHAPTER ELEVEN

Epic leaned heavily against my side while we walked back to our room. He was still a little drunk and a lot tired. He talked, making expansive gestures I'd come to recognize as pure Epic.

"That was exactly like the wedding scene in *Pretty Woman*." He indicated the party we'd left with a windmill of his arm. "I can't wait to tell Bea all about it."

"How was that like *Pretty Woman* again?"

"Well, there were all those rich people, and they all knew I was just a waiter, so they—"

"Because you declined to mention your master's degree."

"I know, right?" He stifled what I suspected was a drunken giggle. "To them I'm just a waiter named Epic at a bistro called Bistro. That's hilarious, don't you think?"

"I'm not sure I get the joke."

"I was like a spy." He lifted his finger to his lips. "Shhh."

"I'm beginning to think you enjoy it when people underestimate you."

"Hell yeah, I do," he said. "I love it."

"How come?" I thought maybe I understood. I didn't mind being underestimated myself.

"Because you can do whatever you like when people expect nothing from you. My parents—" He bit his lip.

"Let me guess. It was difficult to live up to their expectations?"

He frowned. "Well, yeah. Okay. That's true."

"So a little preemptive exploding of expectation probably served you well."

"Yeah. You got me." He clasped my arm. "What about your family? What are they like?"

"Dad owns a kitsch little hardware store in Boulder. Mom teaches math. I have two brothers and a sister. Randy, Ransom, and Regan. Regan's the baby."

"All those *r*'s. Wait. Were your parents pirates?" he snorted. "Sounds nice, though. Are you very close in age?"

"We are. And in temperament. Randy and Ransom are both married, and Ransom has two kids already. I suspect I'll end up with a great many nieces and nephews. Regan's engaged. I like all their significant others. We video chat all the time."

"A big family must be so fun at Christmas. It snows, right?"

"Yes."

"That must be heaven," Epic said dreamily.

"I rarely make it home for the holidays."

"You what?" He turned to me. "Why not?"

"I don't know. There's a lot of work to be done, and winter is particularly good for fundraising."

"Winter is good"—he smacked my arm—"for *fundraising*?"

"It is." I rubbed the spot. "What's with you?"

"I'm beginning to see what Luis meant when he said there is your work and what it takes to support your work and little else."

"You have a flawless memory."

"Shh." Epic stifled another giggle. "That's another secret."

I filed that away.

"Why'd you break up with Luis?"

"Our lives went in different directions."

"Nuh-uh. That's the sanitized version. What really happened between you?"

"Luis felt I wasn't giving one hundred percent to our relationship."

"Were you?" He led me to a bench in the tropical garden near a cluster of plumeria and plunked himself down.

"Not even close." I sat next to him, leaning forward, hands between my knees.

"What do you think of William? Do you think they work together?"

"It certainly appears that way," I said carefully. "William seems to enjoy spoiling him."

"I'll say."

"Multitasking is an ability I wish I had." William never took his eyes off Luis while gliding around the party making every guest feel special. Whatever Luis wanted, whatever he needed, William had anticipated and simply manifested it.

"I enjoyed the party very much, Ryan." He took my chin and tilted it so we were eye to eye. "May I kiss you?"

I...didn't know what to say. The question—despite the heat between us at the pool earlier—caught me off guard.

My heart sped up. "Why?"

His eyebrow lifted. "It seems kinda self-explanatory at this point."

Yeah, okay. But I'd imagined that when our first kiss happened, Epic wouldn't be the one to initiate it. Did that bother me? Surprisingly, no.

"Okay." It would be a damn shame to waste a pretty glorious moment. Fragile moonlight sifted over the fragrant garden, gleamed off banana leaves, limned delicate trumpet flowers, and made pale polka dots of the scatter of pebbles beneath our feet.

Epic used both hands to cup my face. He leaned toward me and pressed his lips to mine, a kiss so gentle at first, chaste even, that I barely felt it. Then he licked my lips, seeking to deepen our contact.

I opened my mouth to his, tasting the wine and spices he'd eaten and the flavor of newness and hope and wanting.

Needing more of that, I relaxed against the bench and let him lead, which he did—would have done, I thought—whether I'd yielded or not.

Perhaps that was another of Epic's secrets. It was for damn sure I'd never foreseen this sexy, take-charge side of him. Nurturing? Yes. Dominant? I didn't expect it.

I gripped the bench with one hand, uncertain whether I was ready for sexy Epic.

"Okay?" he asked.

"Mmhmm."

He rubbed his nose against mine playfully. "Then why are you clenched up like an opossum."

"Am not," I scoffed while I tried to unclench.

"Am I moving too fast for you?"

I wanted to scoff again, but I knew how I'd sound. "No?"

"Oh my god, you're adorable." He stood, clasped my hand in his, and started walking while I tried to figure out what it meant that he found me adorable. He was the cute one, the young one, the one who wasn't a workaholic with alcohol issues who was taking his first vacation in six years.

How did he keep turning things upside down for me?

WE ENTERED our suite and turned on only the most necessary of lights. I brushed my teeth while he changed into boxers and a T-shirt, then he brushed his teeth while I changed.

"You have a preference for breakfast? Do you want to eat here or go out?"

"Let's go out." He set his phone on the charger by the bed. "Maybe we can find someplace cool along the beach?"

"Sure."

"Are we really not going to talk about it?"

"About what?" I stalled.

"About what just happened between us. I know you're older, but surely you remember that kiss?"

"I remember."

I sat on the side of the bed. "I don't want you to get the wrong idea, Epic."

"I'm in a billion-dollar luxury resort with a gay man I find super attractive. I don't think it's me who's got the wrong idea."

I grasped my knees with both hands. "I didn't invite you here to hook up."

"But you have to admit the idea has merit."

I laughed. "You're absolutely incorrigible."

"Ryan, it's okay if I'm not the right guy or—"

"That's not it."

"Or if it makes you uncomfortable. I just want you to know that I like you. I feel good about things when I'm with you. So I'd be down."

"Just like that." I scooted up so my back rested against the headboard.

"Exactly like that." He knee-walked toward me but stopped when he was about a foot away. "Either way, it's all good."

I had to clear my throat. "I'm a little tired and a little drunk right now."

He nodded, though I knew he saw through the lie. "Maybe you're right. It'd be better if we were both sober."

"Sleep well, Epic."

"You too, Ryan."

I lay awake long after Epic fell asleep, thinking about him.

The thing I regretted most was lost contact. Because even if hooking up was off the table for me just then, I missed the warmth of casual touch. I missed the way his back had pressed to my chest in the lounger and how he'd turned over and tucked his face into my neck. I missed holding him.

I'd gone so long without touch, Epic's had ruined me in a single night.

He made me want.

He made me relive coffee-flavored kisses and long walks in the sunshine and someone who cared whether my ribs showed or I smoked too much. He made me miss Luis, whose lips I would swear still had a smile he shared only with me.

I relived lost days—lost dreams—with Luis, whom I'd met at an ordinary fundraiser in a posh hotel. I'd walked past him to get a drink in the bar, but I never got there. He'd grabbed my hand and simply never let go. Not until he realized there was nothing to hold on to, anyway, but by then...

By then we'd broken each other's hearts.

When I finally drifted off, I dreamed of that hotel, and the look Luis gave me in its gilded mirrors, and the clench of his fingers around my wrist as he'd pulled me into the shadows and kissed me without introducing himself first.

I dreamed of his room, and the view, and the way we fed each other breakfast the next morning and how I'd believed I'd never be alone again.

"You feel too deeply," he told me time and again. "You think too much."

Whether it was my job—my *windmills* as he called it—or him, he was never comfortable with the way a news story or a casually caustic word from him could blow my world apart.

I didn't like it either, so I'd retreated inside myself and my work, little by little, until we paid the price.

For some reason, I never dreamed of the bad times.

Instead, my stubborn, idiotic heart held on to the best times, the golden hopeful moments, the sweet smiles, the rain-soaked kisses, the way he woke me in the morning with coffee and pushed inside my body at night.

When I woke beside Epic the following morning, there

were tearstains on my cheeks. The persistent ache in my gut I'd been so certain was some kind of ulcer had turned out to be grief. Only grief.

I lay there crying, unable to help myself. Unable to hide my tears. I started to rise from the bed, but Epic reached for me.

"Hey." He pulled me to him. "Hey. Oh, sweetheart. What's all this?"

"It's nothing." I turned away, half-afraid he was going to try to dry my tears and half-afraid he wasn't. "Bad dreams."

"I'm so sorry."

"Please let me go. It's really nothing." I tried to pull away, but he cupped my face between his palms. I felt absurd. It was absurd, being handled by a man so young.

"My grandma says as soon as you tell someone about a bad dream, you'll never have that dream again." He pressed his cheek to my forehead and kissed my brow. "Tell me, Ryan."

"It hurts."

"Mm." He kissed my temple. My eyes. The tip of my nose. A spot under my ear. "You'll have to be more specific. What hurts?"

I clenched the T-shirt over my heart. "Here."

"Oh." He pulled me to him, and that was worse by far. I'd been trying to arrest the flow of tears, but his kindness just… broke the levee.

Unforgivably, I wrapped my arms around his neck and cried helplessly over things I'd stored away for years without real awareness. Epic smoothed soothing circles into my back but said little. He murmured mostly, making sounds that said he identified with me, little noises of approval, or solidarity, or comfort.

Losing Luis had hurt me. His decision to leave had gutted me. I'd walked around like a living corpse for months while I'd thrown myself into work, convinced it was all I'd ever be good at—all I was good *for*.

Yet all this time that anguish had built inside me until

inevitably, Luis sent me a wedding invitation. He hadn't done it to gloat. He was genuinely happy, and I believed he wanted me to share in his joy.

The problem was me. I was such a petty, vindictive man that I couldn't wish him well.

"Shh," Epic crooned softly. "Shh. I've got you. It's okay."

I shook my head because it wasn't okay. It never could be.

Luis was right. My work was the only redeeming thing about me, and just like I had with Luis, I'd lost sight of that with Epic. I might be happy for a while, distracted for a while, but in the end, I'd always go back to the work I had to do.

But Luis had been wrong about one thing. I didn't do my job because no one else could do it, or for my ego, or for any kind of personal gain. Those were other people's reasons, not mine.

I worked as hard as I could because anyone who could help fix even the smallest of the world's problems had no business walking away from them.

Even if their hearts shattered under that workload.

CHAPTER TWELVE

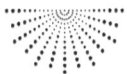

I took a shower while Epic sorted out breakfast. Steam filled the glassed-in space, but I couldn't get warm. I didn't have the strength or desire to get myself off, even after spending the night next to Epic who was...just luscious.

I don't know how long I stood there with hot water pounding my back, but eventually the door opened, and Epic turned the water off.

"C'mere, you," he muttered as he rubbed my hair with a towel and buffed me dry everywhere else. "You're all red. How hot did you have that water?"

I blinked at him trying to gage that. *How would I know?*

This—being tsk'd over and fussed at—was so new I barely comprehended it.

"Breakfast is on the patio. Come on. Get dressed." He caught my hand and towed me to the bedroom where he'd laid out a pair of jeans and...a band T-shirt?

"What's that?"

"That is a little thing we like to call casual wear. You didn't have anything but plain white T-shirts, so I'm loaning you one of mine.

"Panic at the Disco?"

97

"It's a band."

"I know what it is. I'm just afraid by wearing it I'll lose my adult card."

His smile lit the room. "What do you need that for?"

He had a point.

Today he had a point, I amended.

I dressed and followed him outside. In-room dining had delivered an array of healthy options—yogurt, fresh fruit, oatmeal, and green tea. It all tasted the same to me, but I ate what he put in front of me.

Not satisfied with that, he picked out the choicest berries from his stash and practically said *here comes the train.*

"C'mon. Eat. It's good for you." He picked the berries up with his fork, one by one, and I ate.

"Thank you."

"You're scaring me a little this morning," he said seriously.

"I think the twelve-hundred-mile drive finally took its toll."

"Because man was never meant to go over twenty miles an hour," he said dryly. "It couldn't possibly be because last night you were faced with the inescapable truth that your ex has moved on with his life."

"Of course not," I lied. "We were over ages ago."

He spooned up some of his oatmeal. "I know you can hear yourself, so I won't be a jerk and point out the obvious."

"You just did." I put my cup down. "What's the object of saying you aren't going to point out the obvious when you go right ahead and do just that?"

His eyes fell to his bowl. "I'm sorry."

I glared at him for another three seconds, then felt ridiculous for starting a fight. "Me too."

He checked his watch. "Exactly one hour from now, we're going swimming."

"Oh, are we?" I asked with a defiance I didn't feel. Yet somehow, I ended up hanging onto the side of a rainbowmaned unicorn pool float while Epic, in his Speedo, sprawled on it like a porn star.

"How is this helping?" The ball of grief in my stomach hadn't diminished. Sadness continued to surface on waves of memory like bioluminescent foam.

"It's perfect. It's early yet, but the sunshine will still do wonders for your mood."

"Can the sun even get in after you slathered me head to toe with SPF 50 waterproof sunblock?"

"I know you're not trying to tell me I shouldn't take care of you."

"Maybe I'm telling you exactly that?" I would have sworn I couldn't pout anymore, that *petulance* wasn't in my closet of coping mechanisms, but there we were. "I can take care of myself."

"But you're in luck, baby cakes, because you don't have to. What shall we do this afternoon? I know. Let's get your ears pierced."

"What?"

"You'd look hot with pierced ears."

"Why don't I just go bald and grow a ponytail?"

He frowned at me. "I don't think you're taking me seriously."

"It's not you. It's piercing my body parts. Pierce your own ears."

"They are."

I edged around the float to look. "How come you're not wearing earrings?"

"I forgot to pack the ones I like."

I rested my cheek on the warming white plastic. "You could pierce something else."

"We could get matching tattoos."

"No, we couldn't. You could get one."

He put a finger to his temple. "I'm sensing a theme."

I led him straight there. "I *hate* needles."

"That was the theme." He smirked. "Afraid of a little boo-boo?"

"Absolutely," I said. "And I'm not ashamed to admit it. Next suggestion?"

"More art galleries?"

"Next?"

He sighed, "There's always Solvang."

"What's that?"

He overset his unicorn in his eagerness to tell me, which was how, three hours later, I found myself walking the cobbled streets of a Danish-themed town that did double duty as a living history museum and secretly led the life of a tourist trap.

"Wow, another store full of wooden shoes and candle-powered whirligigs," I said, after the fifth shop exactly like it.

He sped off to another display of hand-crafted wooden toys. "The magnetic kissing cow salt and pepper shakers you got will be a great Christmas gift for someone."

"No one I actually know."

"Don't be such a downer. This is fun, right?"

"Of course." I wanted to say no, but a lifetime of honesty prevented it.

"You know you want aebleskivers."

"I know no such thing." What sounded like an incurable rash turned out to be round pancakes flavored with cardamom. I read the menu, and they didn't sound bad. "Do I want them stuffed?"

"Trust me, they're the one thing you don't want stuffed this weekend." Heat flooded my face when Epic put his arm around me. "Real aebleskivers are plain with raspberry coulis and powdered sugar. Stuffing them is gilding the lily."

"I think I saw a potholder with that saying on it three stores ago."

"We'll make a convert of you with these. I promise."

He ordered plates of medisterpolse and round, fried pancakes. "You've got something." He pointed to his face, so I'd know where to wipe, but in trying to correct it, I guessed from his expression I'd made things worse.

He covered his mouth with his napkin. "No. Um. You just—"

"I know." I dunked my napkin in my water glass and tried again. "Now?"

He shook his head.

"Better?"

"Almost." He reached out with his thumb and wiped something off the corner of my lips. When he lifted his thumb to his mouth to suck off the jam and sugar, I couldn't tear my gaze away. My breath shortened. My heart rate picked up. There were busloads of disapproving seniors around us eating brunch, but that didn't stop my train of thought from heading straight to Sex City, population two.

I put my fork down and sat back as turned on as I'd been in years.

I swallowed hard. "I think I might be having...mood swings."

"You think?" He looked at me with such empathy I wanted to drown in the blue of his eyes.

"I might have put being sad on hold for a while," I admitted. "After Luis left."

"Sadness can be like that. You bury it in the ground and then someone builds a suburban housing tract over it. Next thing you know, all your shit is flying around the house and your kid is trapped in a television.

"No, I think that was the plot of *Poltergeist*."

"I'm sorry." He didn't offer more sarcasm. How did someone so young know exactly when to push and when to nurture? "The wedding is bringing buried grief to the surface, isn't it?"

"It is." I reached across the table and laid my hand over his. "I'm so grateful you came with me. I honestly don't know what I'd have done this morning without you."

He glanced at our hands. "You'd have probably turned right back around and gone home."

"Exactly." I acknowledged the truth of that. "And you won't let me do that, is that right?"

"I won't stop you, Ryan." He turned his hand palm up and clasped mine. "If that's what you really need to do."

I had thought about leaving. "It's the coward's way out of a necessary situation."

He waited while our waitress filled our coffees before speaking.

"It's not cowardly to protect yourself." He picked up his fork with his free hand. "Or your heart. Only you know what's in there."

"How'd you become an insufferable know-it-all?"

"Ravenclaw." He lifted his shoulders as if that should answer everything. "It's kind of our thing."

Did he realize the chasm that put between us? He'd grown up with Harry Potter. I almost couldn't take it in.

"I grew up when there were only hobbits, elves, orcs, and dwarves."

"Oh, you're definitely none of those."

"I'm not an elf?" I asked, horrified. "Not even a little bit?"

"Ha. No." He shook his head. "Can you see yourself with pointed ears?"

Reluctant to lose contact, I ate the last of my food with my free hand. "Speaking of ears, let's find you some earrings."

"That'd be a great thing to look for here. Maybe some little delft shoes."

"Those are from the Netherlands, you know. The tulips, the blue and white china, and wooden clogs. I don't know why it's here, but it's like having Japanese things among Chinese things and assuming it's all 'Asian.'"

"Well, technically—"

"Asia and Africa aren't countries, they're continents with many discrete countries that have entirely different landscapes, cultures, religions, and economies."

"You're right." He lowered his gaze. "I know that. I was being flip."

Oh God. I'd turned into a monster. "No, I'm sorry. Certain things are prima facie, though. Unless and until people stop sorting each other into comfortable bins—"

"You're right. I understand. I won't do that again."

Now I was thoroughly ashamed. "You're the last person I need to be lecturing about anything, Epic."

His gaze lifted hopefully. "Meaning?"

"It seems to me that despite the spurious MFE you carry, people mean more to you than numbers. Your heart is just...good."

He gulped. "That's awfully nice. How can you be sure?"

I wished I knew. But I was absolutely, positively sure the world was a better place with Robert Epictetus Alsop in it. I shrugged. "I just am."

The waitress brought the bill. I let Epic get it. I didn't want to fight him over that—not when I planned to buy a twelve-pound cast iron aebleskiver pan and ten pounds of mix because I expected him to lug my packages around for me.

"Come this way," I said when I got my bearings outside. "I saw a shop earlier and I want to go back."

He let me take the lead while he carried all our purchases in three doubled up jute handled shopping bags.

We'd passed a number of jewelry stores, but several had been run-of-the-mill places with the usual sparkly engagement rings and expensive watches in the window. What I'd been on the lookout for was a place with an on-site designer, someone who made art pieces that happened to be jewelry—things you wouldn't find anywhere else.

We found what I was looking for down a stairway in a cool,

brick courtyard surrounded by tiny shops. It reminded me a little of entering a Middle Eastern caravanserai. Colorful, one-of-a-kind scarves hung in one boutique, and hand-crafted leather goods were featured in the window of another.

The one I wanted carried jewelry made from precious and semiprecious stones that evoked both modern and ancient design sensibility. Unlike the other stores, this one wasn't crowded with wares. The walls had been painted a deep ocean blue, and the floors were black marble. LED lights from the ceiling highlighted simple black plinths on top of which related jewelry items might be set on driftwood or in ceramic bowls. New age music floated in the spaces between.

The shopkeeper invited us in, offering Epic a place to put down our packages. She was young, blonde, and dressed all in black. She told us they were her pieces, this was her show-room, and she worked out of her home. I felt Epic's eyes on me as we walked around the store, listening to her low-voiced answers to my questions about her work.

"What I try to do is evoke the feel of ancient ideas without directly copying them," she said.

"Your pieces are lovely. I noticed them when we walked by earlier, and I wanted to explore the shop further."

"Thank you."

"I'm particularly drawn to your inlay work. I'm looking for earrings. Something understated that a man might wear —"

"Ryan, you really don't need to buy me earrings."

"What if I want to?" I asked.

A delicate blush crested his cheeks. "They don't have to be art pieces."

"Don't worry." He liked the idea; it was probably the expense that made him balk. I had expected to spend a large chunk of my savings on the hotel, but Laurie's machinations took care of that. "I'm good for it."

"But —"

"I want to buy you earrings. Will you let me choose them? It would make me very happy."

He tilted his head. "All right. Just don't go crazy."

"You don't want giant dangly pearls?"

He rolled his eyes.

"What are you wearing to the wedding again?"

"I have a black vintage tux. White shirt, black tie."

"Bow tie?"

"Regular necktie."

"Mm." I turned back to the shop owner. "What do you think?"

She looked at Epic. "What's your birth month?"

"October."

"Opals...perfect." She returned with a handful of black boxes, each bearing earrings in geometric shapes with opal inlay.

My instant favorite was a pair in black onyx about six millimeters round with an inlay of ocean blue and milky white opal.

"I created these," the owner said, "to be reminiscent of a taijitu, the symbol for yin and yang. Rather than nesting commas, I placed the white and dark opals in the shape of a lunar eclipse. The two earrings are different, see? On this one the light overlays the dark, but on the other, the dark overlays the light."

"I like them very much." I stepped behind Epic and held the box next to his ear so he could see them in the mirror. "What do you think?"

Epic sighed. "They're amazing."

"You think so?"

"I love them." He leaned toward me to whisper. "But they look really expensive. Don't you think we should look for something a little less...high end?"

"I like these." I told the designer. "Can you tell me a little about the backs?"

"Yes, sir. I use surgical-steel screw backs on all my pieces because I'm allergic to nickel and even more allergic to losing an earring."

She took one out and explained her process for attaching the findings to the stones, but just looking at them convinced me of their quality.

"I'll take these. Thank you." I handed her my credit card.

She gave me an impish smile as she rang up our purchase. "Thank you for your business. There's a secret inside the box. I sometimes do that with pieces that mean a lot to me. If someone is willing to buy, then I tell them. There's a catch in the box. See?"

I looked more closely at what I presumed was a simple wooden box. Epic saw the mechanism first and pressed it. A tiny drawer slid out, inside of which was a third piece—a round tack pin in onyx like the earrings, but instead of the moon, the opal inlay featured the earth. The craftsmanship was amazing. It looked exactly like photos of the earth from space.

"The extra piece goes with the earring set?" I stared at her.

She laughed at my expression. "Yup. It can be part of the gift, or it can be for the gift giver. I see the earth and the moon as entities locked in gravity's dance. The moon creates the tidal force, the earth's shadow determines the moonlight. As an artist, I wanted to represent the idea of their partnership."

"Oh, now it's even better." Epic pinned the earth piece to my lapel with no small amount of determination. "Thank you so much."

"It's wonderful. Can I get your card so I can remember where I got them? Do you sell your work online?"

"Yes and yes." She held out a card with both hands. "I'm so glad you're happy. You made my day."

"Mine too." Epic beamed at her.

After we left the shop, neither Epic nor I seemed to know where to look.

"I really am Cinderella this weekend. Gonna be a shame when the carriage turns back into a pumpkin."

"I think you'll be okay."

"Of course I will." He slipped his hand into mine and laced our fingers together. "I'm more worried about you."

"Me?"

"Yes, you." He glanced at me then away. "Never mind. I'm probably deluded, and you'll go back to work, and it will be like you never left. But you might find it harder than you expect."

I didn't know whether to be insulted or to laugh. What would be so hard for me? I spent most of my time analyzing data in the office or traveling to negotiate for information with law enforcement and other NGOs—the things I was actually good at.

Occasionally, I had to spend time eating delicious food and explaining why people should care as much as I did that sex was consensual and laborers got paid fairly.

Though there wouldn't be time for mini-golf, or tandem cycling, or long walks in the moonlight with gorgeous, exasperating men like Epic, I had a pretty good life.

As we walked back to the car, I dragged that great big lie behind me like a strip of toilet paper stuck to my shoe.

CHAPTER THIRTEEN

The immense patio of the Bella Vista glittered with the light from a hundred candles. Lanterns hung in the wind-twisted trees. We'd been seated near the brick fire pit which added much needed warmth, but I was glad we'd both worn jackets. The waiter came over with water — much needed after the long hot day spent shopping.

Epic wore his new earrings to dinner. They caught and held my gaze every time the light hit them. I studied the gemstones whenever he moved his head. They winked fire, like magic, and every time I felt as if I'd marked him. The feeling was good.

"What are you getting?" I asked Epic. "I'll probably have the snapper."

"Mm. Have you ever eaten duck?"

"I have. The roasted duck breast on the menu looks very good. I thought about it, but duck's a little rich."

"That's what I was thinking. What if we share again?"

"I'm game. You okay with half my snapper?"

"Sounds delicious." He handed the waiter his menu.

When it came to wine, I asked for recommendations. We ended up with a bottle of pinot noir the waiter assured us would pair well with both meals.

After dinner, I sat back and let the stress of my emotional day slide off my shoulders.

"You okay?" He slid his hand over mine. "I could use a cup of coffee."

I signaled the waiter and got us both some. "Would you like dessert?"

"No, thank you."

A dreamy relaxation had swept over me, probably wine related. Epic moved his chair closer so we could both look out at the water. He put his arm around my shoulders.

I studied his profile. Watched as candlelight made shadows play over his features. It would have been too easy to lean over and kiss him. Too easy to take his hand and lead him back to our suite, to our bed, and the unknown but much-anticipated places after that.

Yet Epic was so real to me. So vividly human. I couldn't think of a good way to gage whether taking advantage of the situation would hurt him.

I had only my feelings to go by, and I...I was falling for him. Maybe because I was older, and I'd been hurt, I'd made peace with giving up the things he rightfully had ahead of him —a partner, a family, a long happy life with someone who had time to devote to making him happy every day. I didn't expect that anymore, so I was able to take what I could get and let go.

But I didn't think Epic would ever accept such a fate.

I hoped he never would.

So I steeled myself to leave his heart intact for the man who would someday deserve it, and I hoped by caring but not pushing anything further between us, I could reach the end of the weekend having achieved my goal.

Then he'd demolish my good intentions with a smile, or a wink, or the clasp of his hand over mine.

"How much do thoughts cost these days?" he asked.

"I don't know. You're the master financial engineer." I blew on my coffee before I sipped because it steamed in the cool air.

"I can do sufficiently math-heavy and cerebral finance stuff, but pricing someone else's thoughts? Not so much."

"Well, mine are free. I'm tired. I think I'm floating along on a current of good wine, food, and exhaustion."

He leaned over and kissed my cheek. "Best place to be. Ride the wave, sweetheart. It's great to see you so relaxed."

"Feel like a walk after coffee?"

"Yeah, maybe." He studied my face. "You just want a cigarette."

"I won't lie."

"Fine." He took another sip of his coffee. "We can sneak back to your favorite guilty pleasure spot."

"You have no idea what my favorite guilty pleasure is or my favorite spot, for that matter."

He lifted his brows. "If that's a dare, I bet I could find out in about fifteen minutes."

"It's not. Brat."

"You're the bratty one."

"No, you are." I grabbed the check wallet, signed the meal to the room, and slid my chair back to stand. My spine cracked one vertebra at a time like popcorn.

I hoped Epic hadn't heard, but he snorted. "Sure you have another walk in you?"

"Shut up."

"I could piggyback you to the suite."

"No."

"I could have security bring one of their golf carts. You could ride back."

"No."

He got to his feet as if he were grace personified, damn him. "In that case, let's go take that walk so you can light up because what good is arthritis without some sort of lung disease to go with it."

EPIC FOLLOWED me through the gardens and out onto the beach without speaking. Normally, I'd have felt it necessary to make small talk on the way. With anyone else, I'd have remarked on the temperature or the stars, but with Epic, it wasn't necessary. He was taking it all in too, and he had his own thoughts.

When his hand wrapped around mine, it felt natural and right. I had to swallow the fear of how I'd feel when I went home again because I knew the closeness we shared couldn't— wouldn't—last.

At the end of the long beach pathway, I lit my cigarette. The flame briefly illuminated Epic's features. I worried he was thinking the same things I was. I wondered whether it would hurt him when we parted as much as I feared it would hurt me.

Perhaps that's why we weren't speaking, and it wasn't comfortable at all but simply a way to put off the inevitable.

We sat on the seawall together while I smoked. Our shoulders brushed. From a few feet away, I heard footsteps, and sure enough, as though some dramaturge had staged it, Luis materialized from the shadows again.

"I'd say you planned this if I didn't know you better," he said.

"I didn't."

"I know. Admit it, you'd have broken your leg to avoid running into me by chance."

I stubbed out my smoke. "I'd have pretended to break my leg, maybe. Not now, though. It has been good to see you again, Luis."

"That's nice to hear." He shoved his hands into his pockets. "Sorry to interrupt. I was taking the evening air and saw you sitting here."

"We were just going in." I stood.

Epic squeezed my hand. "Thank you again for inviting me to the party last night. I really enjoyed it."

"You're welcome."

Awkward, running into Luis on the night before his wedding. I tugged Epic to his feet. "We should probably—"

"I'll walk with you." Luis spread his hands amiably. "I need to get back anyway."

If the walk to my smoking spot was natural and free of anxiety, this was the antithesis. The three of us walked together stiffly, followed by a hundred invisible thought balloons—things we could say, things we shouldn't say, things I might have been foolish enough to get off my chest, except for the warmth of Epic's hand in mine.

At the place where our pathways should have diverged because he was in the Bungalow, and our suite was nearer the front office, Luis followed us into the dense garden. I had only a few moments to realize he had some ulterior motive before William stepped into the pathway before us.

"Hello, Ryan." He smiled widely. "I knew Luis would find you. Do you have a minute to talk?"

I hesitated. "About what?"

William turned to Epic. "May we speak to Ryan privately?"

Epic eyed me, and I knew he wanted me to refuse. But Luis and William had gone to a lot of trouble to make this happen, and I frankly wanted to know what they were up to.

"It's all right, Epic. I'll meet you in our suite in a few minutes."

"Are you sure?" Epic eyed me with concern.

"I'm sure." Because what could they have to say? Luis probably wanted to clear the air about some past nonsense, and who was I to begrudge him that?

The grief I had acknowledged that morning was for what might have been, not the reality of what Luis and I had had when we were together. I knew that now.

Epic hesitated another few seconds, then he nodded, squeezed my hand, and walked away.

I turned back to Luis and William. "What is it, Luis? I've been shopping all day, and I'm tired."

"So brittle." Luis moved next to me. "You never did enjoy shopping."

But I had today. "I suppose that depends on what I'm shopping for."

"Luis has spoken about you quite a bit," said William. "I admit I've been very curious to see you for myself."

"Is that so?"

"Oh yes." William's voice was silky and sweet with just a hint of soprano saxophone. It probably helped in his work. He could doubtless seduce a jury if he used the tone he was using with me. "I always wondered what it was about you that he simply couldn't let go."

"Obviously he let go a little."

"Nevertheless, I am very intrigued." He moved from blocking my way to walking in a slow circuit around me. All the while, he seemed to study me. I felt distinctly uncomfortable under his scrutiny and began to wonder why we were really there.

"What is this?" I turned to Luis.

"I'm jealous of you, Ryan," William said baldly. "I have been since Luis and I met."

"Luis is the one who broke things off, not me. He didn't want me then, and he sure as hell doesn't want me now. He's marrying you tomorrow. This is ridiculous." I made to step around him, but he caught my arm in a viselike grip.

"Is it?" William asked. "Do you know why I asked him to invite you?"

"Not really." Dear God. This had all the hallmarks of Luis's deep intrigues. I'd have put it down to reading the classics at an impressionable age, but of course, I had too, and I didn't like any kind of drama. This was one of the things we'd fought about.

"I asked him to invite you so I could get a good look at the man he can't forget."

"I think that's my cue to leave."

Luis stepped into my path. "Just hear him out, please."

"If he lets me go." I met William's gaze until his fingers loosened.

"I didn't mean for this to be confrontational." William changed tactics, now choosing a more conciliatory tone. "I hoped I'd get to speak with you privately at the party, but you brought your little waiter."

"My—"

"Really," Luis laughed. "I was prepared to meet Lawrence Dunbar. He was your original plus-one, was he not? Our wedding planner was beside herself."

"Yes."

"Pity he couldn't make it." William and Luis exchanged glances. "That would have been interesting."

"Did you simply ask the first man you found to accompany you? Or did you choose Epic because he's young and pretty?"

I hated his tone. "This is beginning to feel very insulting."

"It's not meant to be. Not at all." William leaned against Luis, who wrapped him in his arms. "It's meant to...well, to assuage my curiosity."

"And how can I do that? You've seen me. I'm not all that interesting."

"But I'll always be curious about the man in his past, don't you see? So we made a bargain, Luis and I."

"Oh?" I didn't like the sound of this.

"Spend the night with us," William offered coyly.

Speechless, I turned to Luis.

"I know that look. It's your puritanical-American shocked face."

"I'm not—"

"But hear us out." Luis put a finger on my lips. "You can't imagine how overwrought William has been in regard to my past with you. When he asked if he might meet you, I couldn't refuse. He likes what he sees, Ryan."

"And if Luis and I were to *share* a past with you," said William, "I don't think I'd feel so defenseless against his feelings for you."

"Oh hell no." Beside us, a wall of undulating hibiscus flowers expelled Epic into our path. "That is the dumbest idea I've ever heard."

Privately, I agreed, but I wanted the satisfaction of hearing them defend it. "No, no. Let's hear them out."

"Come on," Luis cajoled. "One night. We'd love to spend one night, just the three of us, making memories that could last a lifetime."

"I...uh...probably..." On the face of it, two of the most handsome men I'd ever met had just propositioned me for a three-way. That was probably the only reason I hadn't immediately told Luis where he could shove his stupid idea. I wasn't actually thinking about it. Not *doing it*, anyway, but imagining a threesome with those two took up a lot of my bandwidth.

"Okay, that's it." Epic took my hand. "Maybe you don't understand what's going on here, but I do. No way am I going to let you do anything this degrading."

"Let me?" I said with a gasp. "You're not going to let me?"

"No." He suddenly seemed to tower over me, although there was little difference in our heights. "I am not."

"Epic—"

"Because this is not okay. I get that on some level you seem to enjoy doing things that aren't good for you, but this? This is dumbassery of the highest order, and you"—he pointed to Luis—"should be utterly ashamed of yourself."

Luis narrowed his eyes. "Your waiter has pretensions, Ry—"

Epic took my hand. "I don't even know why we're having this conversation. *You,* come with me."

"Wait—"

"Nope." Epic yanked me away. "This man did enough to erode your confidence in the past. If you do this, it will destroy you. You are coming with me. Now *move.*"

This was a side of Epic I'd never seen. Sure, he'd taken charge a couple times and given me sass, but as for actually ordering me around? That was new.

And, oh God, I liked bossy, implacable Epic a lot.

I moved.

CHAPTER FOURTEEN

E pic hauled me along the path, muttering every so often
about the scene with William and Luis.

"I can't believe you. Why did you just stand there?"

"I was too shocked to move," I admitted.

"Were you too shocked to tell them no?"

"No."

"Oh, so you can say that word." He glanced my way. "I was
beginning to wonder."

"I wouldn't have gone along with their scheme, you know."

"Could've fooled me."

"Believe it or not, I was looking for a way to extricate
myself when you burst through the flora to rescue me. You're
bleeding by the way."

"I know." He put a hand to one of the scrapes on his neck.
"The bushes were denser than I thought."

"And there you were without Excalibur to hack through
them."

"Shut up." He softened his tone finally. "I thought maybe
you were going to take them up on it."

"Who knows? At another time and in another place, I

might have. But not the night before their wedding. That makes things awkward."

"I think William really wanted a shot at you. Maybe he didn't think Luis would go for it after the wedding."

"Whatever. It's not like I'd go through with it at all."

"Wouldn't you?" Epic asked. "You sure the hell weren't fighting them off."

"One moment of hesitation—"

"I swear, you looked like an armadillo about to be hit by a semi."

"Hush." When we got to our suite, I opened the door and led Epic to the bathroom where I made him sit on the side of the tub. "Let me get my first aid kit."

"I don't need you to—"

"You saved my maidenly virtue. It's the least I can do."

He huffed unhappily but stripped off his shirt and let me clean him up.

He had a lot of scratches, mostly on his hands, neck, and chest, but there was one on his cheek and one on his forehead. As I dabbed healing ointment onto each, I wished I could kiss them better.

This boy.

This sweet, silly, loving boy was going to be the end of me.

I kissed his unscratched cheek. "Thank you for saving me from what probably would have been a very hot but ultimately degrading three-way with my ex and his uber sexy husband-to-be."

He took my shoulders and held me back a bit. "Is that something you and Luis used to do?"

I didn't answer.

"No, come on. Tell me." He let me go and went to the sink to wash his hands. "Did you guys used to bring in a third?"

"Sometimes."

"Sometimes?" Epic turned to lean against the sink with his

arms crossed over his chest. "Because I don't see that as a 'you' thing."

"You're right," I admitted. "It's probably more of a Luis thing. I still wonder why I went along."

"I think that's sad." Epic sighed. "Now I'm going to feel weird at their wedding."

"It might work for them. No need to pass judgement."

"No, that's not it. What do I care what they want?" His gaze hardened. "But if you were mine, I wouldn't share you with anyone. That's...not worthy of him or you."

"Mm." As I rearranged things in my first aid kit, I allowed myself to poke at emotions I'd believed I was well past allowing to hurt.

I thought about the times Luis's eyes strayed. The clubs where he pulled a third into a dance or a drink, then coerced me into bringing him home with us to "share."

I thought about the ugly mornings after when he'd lost interest and I had to gentle some stranger out into the street with a few kind words and a solid goodbye—the ones that were hopeful and the ones who felt ashamed. Luis didn't disappoint them; that was always my job.

The attempted seduction put a damper on their wedding festivities for me, especially since I now suspected that their three-way idea was the sole reason I'd been invited.

What would have happened if I'd come with Laurie? Would I have gone along with their plan? Passed it off as an adventure and gone home feeling like one of the strangers we'd given no more thought to than a sex toy?

I glanced up to find Epic's eyes on me.

"Come here," he said simply and held his arms out wide. I went, determined not to cry, and yet...shit.

"Hush." He stroked my hair. "Shh."

"Fucking Luis"—I sniffed—"and his fucking games."

"Shh." Epic took my weight and rocked me gently. "They're a pair, aren't they? Leave them to it."

"I should have known he had some sort of ulterior motive."

"You couldn't. It's not in you to think like that."

That made me laugh. "I spend almost all my time trying to think like human traffickers."

"That's not the same as wondering if your ex has some douchebaggery in store for you the night before his wedding."

"Right?" I had nothing to grip but the muscles in Epic's arms, which — *wow* — were pretty firm. "Sorry."

"No reason to be sorry." He slid his hands up my arms and over my shoulders to wrap them gently around the back of my neck. "You and I had a great day, didn't we?"

"We did."

"And we're going to have a great day tomorrow," he said, "despite the wedding. Then it will be all over, and you'll never have to think about the two of them again."

I still felt a little dewy eyed when I nodded. He handed me a tissue.

"Dry up."

"Okay, but I'm ordering alcohol from room service. You want anything?"

"Don't."

I turned. "What?"

"That's not going to make either of us feel better."

"C'mon. What if I order a very nice bottle of champagne and one of each of their desserts?"

"Well, dessert." He frowned. "When you put it that way…"

"So that's a yes?"

"Could be a yes." He eyed me thoroughly. I tried to look stable and unemotional. "Okay, yes."

I picked up the phone next to the couch to place an order. Epic strolled over, and I invited him to sit next to me. He slid beside me and put his arm around me. Next thing I knew, he was kissing my neck.

In-room dining answered, and I managed to tell them what I wanted. It wasn't easy, what with Epic's lips and teeth and tongue finding all the secret spots that made my skin sizzle.

"Mm. What are you doing?" I asked after hanging up.

"I'm kissing you."

"But why?"

He shot me a look that made me feel fifteen again. "Well, when I like a boy very much, I usually try to put my tongue in his mouth and my dick in his ass, and that's called—"

"Shut up. I meant, why now, at this moment."

"I saved you from a fate worse than death." He gave my cheek a little pinch. "That means you're mine now."

"Epic—"

"No. We've danced around this...thing between us for a couple days now. It's fine if you're not interested, or you don't want to, or this isn't the right time for you. If you don't consent, it's fine."

"But?" I wanted to hear him say it.

"But I want you, Ryan. I don't know how many ways you need me to tell you or show you how much I want you, but I will jump through whatever hoops you need me to. I'll be good to you. I'll be good *for* you. I will never let you feel less than or look at another man when you're around—"

"Epic—"

"And I don't want to hear that you aren't going to be around for very much longer because I knew that going in." He turned and lifted his leg over mine so he straddled me. "I know this is temporary. Don't waste any more time. Do you want this?"

"Yes," I whispered because it was all I wanted.

All I could think of.

All that mattered.

Epic met my lips in a bruising kiss and took charge from there—cupping my face and turning me this way and that so he could deepen the connection between us.

He plundered my mouth, then trailed hot kisses over my

cheeks and neck while I pecked at whatever part of him my lips could reach and simply tried to breathe him in.

He smelled delicious — a heady mixture of flowers and sea air and healthy male sweat. He tasted of the sweet sauce that had accompanied his duck breast — cherries and black pepper. Before I realized what I was doing, I'd dug both hands into his thick dark hair. The strands slid through my fingers like silk.

"Mm. I like that. Pull it. I enjoy things a little rough." He pulled back and switched his attention to one of my nipples. "What about you?"

"Some." That's what most people wanted to hear. I needed to be drinking or totally in the heat of things to endure any kind of pain while making love, but lots of people bit, or pulled hair, or scratched mindlessly, and so I told a little lie to smooth the way.

I gasped when Epic lightly bit my nipple. He studied my face.

"Maybe you'd like me to be gentle with you? You like that better, don't you?"

"Maybe?"

"All right. You don't have to be careful with me because I don't mind a bite here or there, but when I worship your body, I'll be careful." He whispered, "I'll treat you like blown glass if you want."

"Blown is good." My face heated with some kind of shame. I was a man after all; I could take a little manhandling. "Glass not so much."

"If that's what you like, that's what I want to do." He unbuttoned my shirt, and as he did, he placed tiny, gentle kisses on my throat, my chest, each nipple, and down my treasure trail. My belt came next, then my zipper. "Okay?"

"Yes." He took my cock from my briefs and gave it a long stroke. *"Oh."*

"Lift." I did as he asked, lifting my hips so he could pull down my jeans and briefs. Next came shoes and socks. He smoothed his hands over my thighs, his touch so light it gave me goosebumps. "Do you want me to suck your cock, Ryan?"

Lips pinched shut, I nodded.

Why couldn't I say it out loud?

Probably a combination of fear that speaking would spoil the moment and fear that I'd blurt out something shrill like *Now, do it now!*

"Mm." Epic licked a line from my balls to my glans. I shivered all over and sank farther into the seat. My back arched, making my dick slap my belly like a seal asking for a fish.

Epic did a poor job of hiding his smile.

He cupped my balls with one hand and held my cock in the other. When his tongue caressed me again, I was ready for the sensation. My thighs tightened in anticipation and my cock leaked in preparation.

"You're so responsive." He buried his nose in my ball sac. "And you smell so fucking good."

As I smoothed his hair, I willed him to get on with it, but Epic would not be rushed. He explored every inch of my cock before ever taking it into his mouth, coming at me with long swipes of his tongue and kitten licks and nips with his lips.

When at last he took my cock, he slid down the entire length of me in one agonizing descent, and then hollowed his cheeks to suck hard as he withdrew.

He drifted his clever fingers lower to massage my balls and then my taint as he did that long slow glide and suck, over and over, until I was ready to beg, or cry, or scream for him to speed up, suck harder, do more. Then he pressed into my hole with one finger, and I flew apart.

"Oh God...yes. Oh my God. Epic. I'm—"

He stayed where he was, swallowing my spend to the very last shiver.

"Epic." I cradled his head between my hands in a tight grip. He rested his cheek on my thigh.

"Mmhmm?"

123

A polite knock at the door startled us both.

"Stay." He put his hand on my chest. "I've got it."

When Epic stood, the outline of his thick, erect cock showed clearly beneath the fabric of his jeans. He turned a terrific shade of pink while he adjusted himself. I couldn't be seen from the door, but I slipped my shirt over my lap anyway.

"Back in a second." He winked. I caught and held his hand. He turned back, one eyebrow lifted. "Something you need?"

"Thank you. I—"

The knock came again, slightly louder.

"Hold that thought." Epic kissed the top of my head. "We're not anywhere close to done."

CHAPTER FIFTEEN

E pic expertly opened the champagne and poured two glasses. Dessert turned out to be banana pudding, lemon pot du creme, cheesecake, and a decadent chocolate layer cake with chocolate buttercream frosting.

Each dessert sat on a perfect plate accompanied by fruit, powdered sugar, raspberry sauce, or in the case of the pudding, a vanilla wafer crumble.

Because I'd ordered emotionally, all the lovely sweets left me feeling a little *meh*. I wanted a single bite of each and a glass of champagne but later.

Epic handed me a champagne flute. "What shall we drink to? New friends? Missed opportunities?"

"How about we drink to you? The best fake boyfriend and knight in shining armor a guy could have."

"Shut up." A pleased flush accompanied the slight shake of his head. "I'll drink to the best fake boyfriend, though."

I nodded and we touched our glasses together and drank.

Epic laid our desserts out on the coffee table. He arranged them with forks and napkins and placed the champagne in its ice bucket. Because he wasn't wearing a shirt, it was pretty

obvious he was still hard, especially since his cock had damp-
ened his jeans.

"Oh, Jesus." He reddened with embarrassment. "Sorry."

"What do you have to be sorry for?" I took the glass from
his hand, picked up my own, and stood. "Come with me."

He raised his brows. "Where?"

"Bring the champagne, will you?" I left him for the
bedroom where the sheets had been turned down invitingly
and the maids had again left chocolate on our pillows.

He came in a few seconds later with the wine. "Oh, I see
how this is going to go."

I stretched out on the bed and put my hands behind my
head. "I'm pretty sure you weren't done with me. Or was that
my imagination?"

"Oh no. I'm definitely not done with you." He gave me a
little peep show while he slid off his jeans. "In fact, I'm having
trouble deciding which of my evil plans to undertake. What
would you like to do?"

"Fielder's choice. Fuck me, make me suck you. Take me
any way you want." My cock had already plumped up at the
thought of him fucking me. At Epic's age, he probably never
even got soft. I hoped I could give as good as I got. "If you
want me to fuck you—"

"Not tonight." He came forward, cock standing proud in a
nest of dark hair. "Tonight, I'm tapping your sweet ass, Ryan
Winslow."

I shivered. "It's all yours."

"Yeah?" He started from the bottom of the bed and crawled
over to loom above me. "Whatever I want?"

"Anything."

"Mm." He swigged champagne straight from the bottle and
leaned over to kiss me. When I opened my mouth, the crisp
dry wine flooded in, bubbles bursting between our tongues.

"Warn a guy, will you?" I gave a little cough.

"You are so sweet." He held the bottle for me to drink

more. I sipped slowly; my head already swimming. When I was done, he licked stray droplets from my lips, then slid lower and lower still. He tongued my navel, which tickled, and lifted my knees over his shoulders to plunder my cock, balls, and taint where even his breath drove me crazy with lust.

I never expected Epic to be so...fearless, so confident and knowing, yet there we were. He licked over my hole a couple times and then his thumb followed, gently rubbing the rim.

"Lube and condoms are in the drawer there."

Surprised, I rolled my torso to take a look. "Really?"

"I like to be prepared."

"Pretty sure of yourself," I muttered as I handed them over.

"I'm a sure thing. I hoped you'd be."

"Cheeky."

"Who's talking?" He squeezed one of my butt cheeks and then did something with two thumbs that made my whole body come alive.

"That's...amazing."

"You're really tight." He lifted his gaze to mine. "Are you worried about something?"

"It's been a while." I clenched the sheets.

His blue eyes narrowed. "Okay."

"It's fine. I'm not made of glass."

"I can take my time." Even though his cock leaked strings of precum onto the pale linen sheets, I believed he'd take all the time in the world.

I was the problem because my brain wouldn't shut up.

He did wonderful things to my body, but I couldn't help picking each tiny annoyance apart. It was too quiet. The lights were still on. If he looked down at me, he'd see every flaw, hear every creak of my aging bones and every groan and grunt I made.

Maybe when you're twenty-three you don't mind getting fucked in a room lit like a surgical suite with no sound besides your gasping breaths, but at my age, I preferred a little camouflage. Some music, maybe. Candlelight. A partner just drunk enough to forgive me for a blemish or a scar.

I definitely wished we had music, and then I remembered I could program the system in our suite from my phone. I picked my phone up, and Epic froze.

"I must really be doing a great job if you're checking your messages."

"I'm not," I reassured him. "Just looking for music."

"Oh."

As I'd hoped, soft jazz played through hidden speakers. "Maybe you could dim the lights a little?"

He sat back on his heels. "What's wrong?"

"I don't know." I couldn't look at him. He was so *perfect*. "You don't have to have all the lights on, do you?"

His eyes widened. "Are you nervous?"

"Not necessarily."

"When was the last time you did this?"

My cock wilted. "Why are you interrogating me?"

"When?"

"I don't know. Last year some time."

He sat back on his heels. "Jesus."

"No, I think it was just some guy in a bar."

He gave my knee a playful shove. "Dude."

I rolled onto my side, effectively shutting him out while I gathered my nerve.

"So it's been a while," he mused, "and you're not feeling it?"

"No, that's not it. I'm totally feeling it."

"Oh, yeah. I can tell by the way your cock deflated." His head came over my shoulder, bangs tickling my skin as he kissed under my ear. "Didn't I say the secret password?"

"Stop."

"Okay." He went still. "What do you need."

"Just dim the lights."

"Because it's too bright in here?"

I nodded.

He rubbed my shoulder and the top of my arm. "How will I be able to see every part of my very hot lover if it's dark?"

"When he arrives, you could turn the lights back on."

He pulled me to my back again. "You total tool. Do you think I can't tell you're comparing again?"

"I'm not," I lied. "I'm…more comfortable in flattering light."

"Oh. I see."

"So…"

He got up and adjusted the lighting. There was a dimmer switch on the wall and a remote that controlled flameless candle sets around the room. The result was so much better. Romantic.

That was being a fake boyfriend with style.

He came back to bed and kissed me until I relaxed that fractional bit more. After, his thumb slid inside me easily.

"There's my boy," he said from between my legs. "Relax now, sweetheart. I've got you."

Hell yeah, he had me. I gave a shuddering sigh. "Mm."

He used more lube, and more fingers, and his mouth on my balls and dick to make me so ready I could have cried. Foil rustled. He lifted my knees.

"This okay?" he asked. "You want this, Ryan?"

"Yes." I never knew how sexy consent could be until now —until Epic made me articulate how much I wanted him with each step. I was down to words of one syllable. "Yes, yes, *yes*."

He breached me slowly and with aching tenderness. I felt no pain, not even the usual pinch and burn, just the inexorable glide of his cock deeper and deeper into my body.

I clenched his shoulders because he felt huge—so much bigger than I expected, although I'd seen his cock, so I didn't know why I was surprised. He filled me, going so deep that when he bottomed out, I spasmed around him, giving a weird sort of all-over shake like a wet dog.

"God." He simply stayed there, sort of gathering me to him,

and everything between us vibrated with excitement—each breath, each shiver, each muscle, the bones of his hips against mine.

His hands clasped my ass, and my feet brushed his thighs, and when he pulled out and shoved back inside me, everything went a little haywire from there.

He fucked me, and I bucked against him, and this time no one was treating anybody like glass. The way he moved squeezed my cock against his belly with each thrust, ratcheting up the tension in my balls and dampening my skin.

His hands went everywhere, gripping me, gaining purchase and leveraging all his strength for the single purpose of going deeper, and mine had to touch him everywhere. Worship him. Smooth and soothe the hot skin of his back, over his ribs, down his buttocks while he used me.

It couldn't last, and it didn't. My orgasm started in the center of my being and radiated outward, vibrating every part of me, raising the hair on my skin and letting loose in a slick frenzied series of jerks against the taut muscles of his belly.

"Good boy. Oh God. So pretty." Epic cupped my face in both hands and kissed me while I shuddered with pleasure. He ground his hips against mine, dragging out more electric tingles inside me. Then he stiffened and blew apart in my arms.

I don't know how long we lay there panting, kissing, and laughing until he whispered, "Steady. Pulling out."

"Mm." That time I did feel a bit of a burn, but that was all I could feel. The rest of my body floated somewhere where nothing could touch me. I couldn't feel my legs. If there'd been a fire, I couldn't have gotten to my feet if I'd tried.

Epic rolled to the side and tossed the condom somewhere. I didn't care unless I ended up stepping on it. He could be pretty fastidious. I doubted he'd let that happen.

I rubbed my dry lips together and rolled so I could stare at him. I thumbed sweat from his forehead and swept his bangs aside so I could read his expression. He turned his head toward me, lip caught between his teeth.

"Okay?" he asked.

"Perfect."

"I know I am." He shoved a pillow under his head. "But thanks for saying so."

I gave his shoulder a push. "Goofball."

He pushed back lightly. Mostly for show.

Somehow, I managed to sit up and get the champagne. "Sip?"

He blinked. "Sure."

I passed the bottle to him. He took a swallow and passed it back.

"Give me a minute"—he groaned and sat up—"and I'll bring you a dessert picnic in bed."

He didn't look like he wanted dessert. He looked ready to fall asleep.

Was Epic one of those guys who dropped off after sex?

He stifled a yawn.

Oh my God, he was. He could barely keep himself awake, but he was trying to fight it.

"Or you could put the plates in the fridge, and we could eat them later."

"No, you ordered all those desserts—"

"And now I'm telling you to put them away." I laughed sheepishly. "I'd go, but I can't feel my legs yet."

He gave a pleased smile. "Okay. Going."

He threw the covers off and left. I heard plates clatter in the living room. A few seconds later, he came back into the room.

"All tidy." He crawled in beside me and pulled me to him. "Just give me a sec. I'll get something for us to...um..."

Then it was lights out for Epic, just like that.

Each deep, even breath he took puffed the hair at my temple. He didn't snore. Didn't move. I thought of about a

Z.A. MAXFIELD

hundred things I should be doing, but the pleasant ache between my legs and the warmth of his body made doing them feel like a hurdle I couldn't begin to get over.

I did manage to get to the bathroom where I took care of business, washed my hands, and cleaned myself with a damp cloth. I took another cloth in to wipe sweat and jizz off Epic. He didn't wake despite the cool air on his skin. I found the condom, tossed it into the trash, and left the damp towels draped over the lip of the tub.

Once I was back in bed, there was nothing left for me to do but study the half-moon shadows Epic's eyelashes made on his cheeks and run my finger down his adorable nose and kiss the full lips that still looked swollen from use.

I made sure he was covered, and dry, and warm, and more because I could never fuss enough over my gentle, caring fake boyfriend.

Not when he treated me like I was precious to him.

Sure, there were problems on the horizon.

Enumerating them wouldn't change anything. The most important thing was how we fit together here and now.

The little jewelry shop we'd visited that day seemed a million miles away. The moon earrings and the earth pin mere trinkets—pricey, well made, but essentially only objects, not portents.

Even so, like the earth and the moon, Epic and I were gravitationally predisposed to be in each other's orbit, in spite of the long distance life placed between us, in spite of our age difference, in spite of...well...us.

Whatever one of us did would affect the other from now on. I knew it in my heart. I felt it deep in my bones. Was there any way at all for me to hold on to him?

For the first time in my life, the questions I had couldn't be answered by working harder or denying myself. For the first time, I wanted something I couldn't *earn*, and I didn't know what to do.

CHAPTER SIXTEEN

I snaked beneath the sheets to wake Epic with a blowjob. It had been a while, but it was like riding a bike. I knew what to do once I got going.

After last night, there was no going back. Epic and I spent the morning—after we ate a healthy breakfast and had a nice dip in the pool—finding new ways to sex each other up. This was how I'd ended up naked with my hands loosely tied to the arms of a padded wicker chaise longue.

At least I was in the shade.

"I can't believe you brought cuffs." Epic's furry restraints had Velcro closures.

"They were still in my duffel bag from the last time I went to Comic Con."

"Do I even want to know?"

"Probably not." He grinned like a kid. "I could bind your feet, but I want you to be comfortable. "You're going to be here a while."

I didn't have a clue what time it was. Noon, maybe? One? "Don't forget, we came here to attend a wedding."

"Which isn't until six."

"We'll need time to shower and dress."

"Don't you worry about a thing." There were crocodiles who looked less predatory than he did right then. "Just know that whatever happens next, I'm in charge. Is that okay?"

"Will I need a safeword?"

"You can say stop, and I will. Or red if you like to say stop when you don't really mean it."

"I'll use red." Although I wasn't certain if there was anything I'd stop him from doing to me. "Yellow means slow."

"Got it." He left for a minute and came back with a small nylon sack from which he pulled out rope, a couple of plugs, some microfiber cloths, and toy cleaner. I watched while he cleaned things and laid them out beside the chaise.

"Okay, now you're just scaring me."

"How come?" He turned his boyish blue eyes my way. "Are you afraid I might hurt you?"

"No. I'm afraid I don't know you well enough for this."

"Then let me introduce myself." He kissed my cheek. "I'm Epic Alsop, and I like being in charge."

"Aw, no, really?"

"You can always say no. Or red."

"How far are you going to take this?"

"I give you my solemn word that I won't hurt you physically. You said you don't like that."

"I don't."

"I don't much like hurting people either. But what if I control your orgasm?" He bit his lip. "Because I thought since we have some time…"

When he didn't finish, I asked, "How would you do it?" I imagined some kind of cock and ball torture device, given he packed rope in his suitcase for Comic Con.

"Why don't you give me your permission and find out?"

I hesitated. "You really won't hurt me?"

"Never." He crossed his heart. "But I also won't let you come."

"That's...okay, I guess." At my age, I should save up orgasms anyway.

"You know what to do if you want me to stop?" he asked.

"Say red."

"Perfect." He pumped a little lube onto his fingers. "You know you're absolutely gorgeous like this, don't you? Bound and helpless for me."

I glanced away because if last night's lighting was harsh, hello daylight. Every quirk of my aging ass was probably visible, clear, and in super HD.

At first Epic touched me so gently I barely felt his fingers on my skin. He began with one hand stroking my balls while the other lightly touched the head of my dick. He slid a finger over the slit, circled the crown, rubbed at the sensitive place just beneath. If at any time I gasped, or moved my body, or arched to get more friction, he simply took his hands away and got more lube.

A fresh breeze off the ocean cooled the sweat beading on my skin, making me shiver.

This went on and on. Light, barely there touches, deliciously on target every time, drifted over my most sensitive skin. I don't know how long I lay there before he moved the hands cupping my balls to my ass, but he went through the same torturous, teasing process with my hole until he loosened me enough to slip a plug inside.

That pressure in my ass drove me to a whole new level of arousal.

Now, his fingers weren't just teasing my cock. It felt like there was an invisible string tied to my balls and my ass, like a spiderweb of pleasure, and every time he did anything to one part of my anatomy, it alerted the others to his presence and the possibility of more.

One hour went by. Two. Sweat dripped down my face, my chest bloomed fiery red, my skin felt fever hot. He gave me water whenever I asked for it. Slowed the stimulation when I begged him to. But he never entirely stopped, and he didn't allow me to orgasm, and by midafternoon, I babbled mindlessly, sobbing for release.

He still didn't stop.

I arched in frustration, and Epic took his hands away again.

He stroked the inside of my thighs, my knees, my calves. He rubbed my feet. He didn't put his hands where I wanted them—where I needed them—until I'd backed off the precipice.

"Oh God. Come on," I howled like a beast.

"Look at you," he said. "So thirsty for my cock."

"Please. Please, *please*." When was I going to get the fucking I needed so badly?

"The sun is changing. Soon we won't have shade." He pulled his phone from his jeans pocket and checked the time. "Oh. It's almost time to get cleaned up and go."

Finally. Oh God, finally he was going to put me out of my misery.

I sighed with utter relief. "Thank God."

"You want to go to the wedding that badly?" He started putting things away.

"Not really, no."

He untied my arms. "I won't be able to take my eyes off you tonight. I'll picture you just like this, all hot and soft and ready for me."

"Okay, well...you can finish me any time now." Even though I'd been begging for hours, I thought a little hint couldn't hurt.

"That's not how it's going to be." He shot me a fond smile. "You go shower first. Keep the plug in. If you even touch your cock, I'll know, and I will be very, very cranky. You don't want that, do you?"

"Haha. Cut it out," I said, still going along. "It's been *hours*."

"And you were fuckably gorgeous the entire time."

"And?"

"And, I changed my mind. Let's shower together. I want to play with you some more before we leave."

"No."

"No?" he asked carefully. "Do you mean red?"

"No, I mean no. You don't get to tease me for — How long have we been out here?"

He looked at his phone again. "Four hours, thirty-six minutes, and twenty seconds. That's a new record for me. You're so hot, Ryan. Oh my god, I can't believe you're my fake boyfriend. *Squee!*"

"Under no circumstances have I given you permission to *squee*," I muttered unhappily.

"No? But this is beautiful. Tonight, while we're watching your asshole ex and his dick fiancé get married, your mind's going to be on a totally different asshole and dick. I promise. This will be the best wedding you have ever been to."

When Epic was right, he was right.

There was no way in hell that, under current circumstances, I'd feel anything more than mild annoyance over my ex and his stupid wedding.

"There's going to be dancing, isn't there?" he asked.

"There will probably be an orchestra. Maybe a DJ later in the evening after the oldsters fade out."

"I'm not very good at dancing."

"Don't worry. I am." I tried to stand, but my knees buckled. "Usually."

"Whoa there." He caught my arm and wrapped it over his shoulders. "Steady, big fella."

"Fuck. You." I let him help me inside because I could barely walk on my rubbery legs. "How am I going to do this?"

"One step at a time, sweetheart." He helped me into the bathroom and turned on the shower. "I'm going to get you cleaned up and help you dress. By that time, you'll feel fine."

"I doubt I'll be fine for a week."

"Flatterer." True to his word, Epic soaped every inch of my body and helped me rinse. I got a scalp massage when he washed my hair. I couldn't think when I'd last been treated so gently—so carefully—by anyone but my mom.

He left the plug inside me.

I had to give him props. There seemed no better way to say fuck you to Luis than to be wearing Epic's plug, thinking of Epic's gentle fingers, dreaming of his sweet mouth on my cock while I suffered through Luis's nuptials.

The only problem was my constant state of arousal. The cut of my jacket would hide it, but I had no illusions about what it would mean to traverse a receiving line that included European nobility with a boner.

"I am so going to hell for this."

"I'll be right beside you." Epic kissed my neck and ruffled my hair with a towel. "It's okay if I wear my earrings, right?"

"Of course."

"You'll wear your pin?"

"I already put it on my lapel."

The rest of our preparations passed by in a flurry of warmth and kisses and Epic everywhere. I dressed in a lust-drunk haze.

For the first time in my adult life, I had to rely on someone else for every little thing. Helplessness made me uncomfortable, and yet...this felt bearable. I'd gone long past needing to come and arrived somewhere entirely new—down a rabbit hole of Epic's making.

I trusted Epic to take care of me at Luis's wedding.

The rest of my worries simply dropped away.

We shaved side by side. Combined products and styled our hair. I spritzed on cologne, and he used his own scent. We spent ten minutes telling each other how delicious we smelled.

I tied both our ties, having a better command of the Windsor knot.

Epic's retro tuxedo turned out to be a sixties mod, four-button, black wool jacket with black velvet piping around the collar and lapels. Underneath, he wore a notch-collar waistcoat that came up all the way to the knot of his tie. Impossibly slim trousers stopped above his bare ankles. He completed the look with patent leather oxfords.

"You look like a Beatle."

"Grandma bought it for me. She says the mod boys used to make her swoon."

Same, Grandma. *Same...*

After we fussed and preened and took selfies—which he sent to all his friends and I stored like some demented squirrel hoarding acorns for a long, cold winter—we were ready to leave. At the last minute, he remembered our sunglasses. He set mine on my nose with care.

"Are you still feeling a little spacey?" he asked.

I nodded. "Is that normal?"

"I think I played with you a little too hard for your first time."

"You think?" His worried frown made me want to reassure him. Kiss him. Smack his ass for putting me in this position.

"I want you to know I'll be right by your side. I know what you need. Do you trust me?"

"Yes." Unequivocally. I trusted Epic with a certainty I'd never known before.

He handed me a bottled water. "Drink some on the way."

"Thank you."

He took my hand as we let ourselves out of the suite. The wedding invitation contained a map leading to the Mariposa Garden where the ceremony would take place. After, there would be dinner and dancing under the stars.

We were halfway there before I remembered to worry about wearing a butt plug. For the first time since I'd received the invitation in the mail, I didn't dread the wedding itself.

Epic pulled me along with confidence I didn't feel. His step was jaunty. He wore a dazzling smile. At the venue, the sunset had begun in spectacular style. The moon hung on one side of the wide watercolor sky while the sun seemed to balance it on the other.

It took me a minute to realize the unusual configuration was due to a selenelion—an event where both the sun and moon could be seen above the horizon during a lunar eclipse.

I'd wondered why Luis and William had scheduled their wedding for a Sunday. Only Luis would rope in celestial bodies for a command performance like this.

Luis and William were getting their once-in-a-lifetime wedding.

I wanted to hide the tears stinging my eyes—to pass my weakness off to the bright dazzle of the setting sun. But Epic had torn me open in a hundred physical and emotional ways. All my pent-up emotions surfaced and there was no hiding them anymore, especially not from myself.

The dream of a partnership or marriage with Luis was one I'd held close to my heart for so long. What Luis and I once had, had died out, but I'd never let the dream go.

Now, here was its funeral, under a glorious sky complete with a celestial anomaly.

I could be happy for Luis. I *would* be.

I simply couldn't hide the grief of letting it all go.

Epic drew me into the shadows where he cupped my face with both hands.

"It's okay," he whispered. "It's okay to feel."

"I know." I glanced toward the sky, willing my tears to stay in my eyes but feeling them slide down my cheeks. "I've played this same tune for far too long. It's only an earworm now."

"Grief is weird." He kissed my forehead. "Grief is over when it's over. Are you sure you want to do this? We could go back."

"I'm fine." I would not let my emotions dictate to me like this. "And the food is bound to be spectacular."

He took both my hands in his. "And you promised me dancing."

"Plus, I'll get a boner every time I remember I'm wearing your butt plug."

"I doubt you'll forget even for a second."

True that. I felt it with Every. Step. I. Took.

"There will be payback someday."

"Bring it." Epic laughed and shifted onto the path again. The wide white wedge of his grin battled the brilliance of the sun. "Come on. Let's do this thing."

I'd wanted to avoid Luis's wedding, but I'd sucked up my courage and done everything I could to mitigate the fallout from it. Now the wedding was upon me, and I only wanted it over with.

Except the parts with Epic.

Epic was worth a lot of fallout.

Smiling, I let him take the lead.

CHAPTER SEVENTEEN

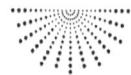

With over one hundred guests in attendance at the ceremony, Epic and I were seated so far toward the back I spent more time people watching than listening to Luis and William make their vows.

The grooms looked spectacular in matching morning suits —black tailcoats and trousers, white vests, white butterfly-collar shirts, and red-and-gold ties—a nod to Luis's family colors.

The wedding party echoed the color scheme. Luis's mother wore a crimson gown, his father, a vest in gold with a red tie. The wedding party consisted of siblings and relatives, all of whom bore the dark-haired, olive-skinned beauty of Luis's family or the almost fae-blond locks and pale eyes of William's Norwegian forebears.

Epic and I made the long trek down an excruciating receiving line. I had to remind myself that some of these people were still my friends. His mother had liked me. His father had often counted on me as a partner when the family played bridge. Of course they greeted me graciously. They welcomed me like a long-lost relative.

We found our place cards at a table with a group of men

and women I didn't recognize, but I was used to gala fundraising events, and I knew how to ingratiate myself with people I didn't know.

I had to shift every now and again to get relief from my silent companion. I'd actually never had the pleasure before. I'd certainly never considered wearing a butt plug outside the bedroom. Epic's eyes tracked my each and every movement.

He hid a feral smile through the entire dinner.

***

AFTER DINING, the grooms danced with their mothers. Luis and William led their first dance with Tchaikovsky's Sleeping Beauty waltz, which I thought was a pretty interesting choice. For one thing, it had a certain Disney-princess vibe, and for another, Tchaikovsky was kind of a reprobate and not because he was gay.

But whatever. It wasn't my wedding after all.

I pulled Epic onto the dance floor.

"I need you to know something," I told him.

"Yeah?" He'd had too much champagne and had taken to peopling with a vengeance.

"When we're on the dance floor, I lead."

"Fair enough." He blushed sweetly. "You'd better. I know zip about dancing."

"Come with me, dear boy, and all will be made clear."

Oh God.

Nothing had prepared me for holding Epic close in formal wear. He moved stiffly at first. He didn't trust himself not to step on my feet. He didn't respond to the pressure I put on his hips to turn him or the way I subtly changed directions, but my mother had pretensions, and she'd enrolled me in cotillion during my first year in middle school. Since then, I'd found ballroom dancing to be an enjoyable—if slightly ridiculous —pastime.

"You're really good at this." Epic beamed at me. "I wish we'd thought of getting in some practice before the event."

"I didn't think this far ahead."

"I didn't think it'd be fun." He'd relaxed enough to let me reel him out and pull him back with a tiny flourish. "Do you dance a lot?"

"If there's dancing at a fundraiser or something. When I travel abroad, it's considered a plus to be able to dance. Being gay, I've often taken the role of unattached male. I can't count the number of wealthy donors—men and women—I've quick-stepped around a dance floor."

"It's kind of a dying art, isn't it?"

"People are learning again because of *Dancing with The Stars*. I've noticed a real uptick in younger men and women partner dancing at events like this."

"My sort is better at grinding."

"Don't remind me." I had never done anything at all with a butt plug seated in my ass. Dancing proved to be torture...and yet. The illicit thrill of it was reflected right there in Epic's knowing gaze.

"Feeling okay?" he asked.

"I'm so turned on right now, I don't know whether to laugh or cry."

"I'd like to stay until they cut the cake."

"Of course you would."

"And they probably have those little bubble bottles so we can wish the grooms bon voyage when they leave."

I gasped with actual horror. "You can't possibly be suggesting we stay that long."

"I don't know. It's a lovely night."

"That doesn't mean we can't enjoy some of it in our room."

"Is someone anxious to get back?"

"Maybe I should see if some of Luis's aunties would like to dance."

"Nuh-uh. You're all mine, Ryan Winslow." He tightened

his grip on my shoulder. "Enjoy this moment. You *only* lead on the dance floor."

I laughed. "Fair enough."

I spent the rest of the evening teaching Epic how to follow my lead. When the DJ started, we threw off our jackets and reclaimed the floor to grind and tease each other until the cake was cut and the happy couple said their goodbyes.

I went to the bathroom to piss and splash some water on my hot face. Epic followed. He stood behind me at the sink, crowding me against the marble.

"How thirsty are you for my cock right now."

"Jesus," I managed, mouth suddenly dry.

He pressed against me, cock thick and hot in those tight suit pants. "Ready to go yet?"

"Beyond ready."

"Then come on." He bumped the air dryer with his elbow and held up my damp hands, rubbing them between his. "All done."

I stared at his mouth. "Okay."

He kissed my throat. "Do you need to say good night to anyone?"

"No." I doubted anyone actually cared I was there, much less if I'd left. We got our jackets and said goodbye to the few people we'd talked to earlier.

Epic took my hand and led me back across the resort grounds. Here and there, guests chatted in small groups. They took advantage of the comfortable patio seating and the resort's many fire pits to drink and reminisce and gaze at stars.

A few said hello, but I couldn't say who they were.

The only thing on my mind at that moment was Epic and how he looked windblown and wild, jacket slung over one shoulder. His grip on my hand felt firm and sure. He didn't need to read the many signs to know the way.

It was Epic who opened the door to our suite. Epic who ushered me inside like a man on a mission. He helped me out of my jacket and tie and slipped my shirt off my shoulders. While he worked on my clothing, I made my way into his. I toed off my shoes while he unbuckled my trousers, and then I was naked, aching with need built up over what seemed like days.

He pushed me into the bathroom and stood behind me again, eyes on mine in the mirror.

"What do you see?" he asked me.

"Us."

"Mm." He tapped on the butt plug. "Who is 'us'?"

"You and me."

"How do you feel, Ryan?"

"Needy."

"You thirsty for my cock?" He wrapped his hand around my throat with just enough pressure to be noticeable but not enough to choke. "You want my cock in your ass?"

I shuddered all over. "I'm gasping for it."

"Ask me."

"Please, Epic. Give me your cock."

His fingers slid between my ass cheeks and whatever he did with the plug sent a wave of pleasure through my body. "Ready for this to come out?"

"Only if you promise you'll fill me with your dick." My knees buckled, and I gripped the sink to stay upright.

"Ready for me to fuck you?" he asked.

"*Yes,*" I begged. "Yes, please fuck me."

I braced myself on the counter while foil rustled and lube slurped behind me, and then he pulled the plug out and pushed his cock inside me in one long, slow move.

"Ah God, Epic..." I gasped. "Oh God. Yes."

"You like this?" he asked. "You like my fat cock in your ass, Ryan?"

"Yes." I didn't take my eyes off his. "Yes, God. Yes. Harder."

I groaned with each heave of slick skin as he pumped

146

inside me. I groaned with each brush of his cock against my sweet spot.

"*Fuuuuuck,*" I whimpered. "Not gonna last."

"Let go." His breath ghosted over my ear. "I've got you."

And he did. My God, each stroke struck like lightning inside me.

I opened my mouth to breathe and out came these helpless, guttural cries. I should have been ashamed to let them go. I should have been taking back some of the control he'd wrested from me all day. Instead, I jerked, and bucked, and twisted, and sobbed his name, and when I felt the first faint tumbling sensation of orgasm wash over me, I went limp and helpless in his arms.

"Yes, Epic," I cried out. "Yes. God *yes*..."

We stiffened and came in a thunderclap of pleasure, and then I fell against him, and he fell to the floor.

"Oh, whoa." He gathered me in his arms. "You okay, sweetheart?"

"Think so." I lay with my back to his chest, my head on his shoulder, covered in sweat and jizz. "That go as planned?"

I felt him chuckle. "More or less, minus the free fall at the end."

"Couldn't hold my own there."

"No worries." He palmed my damp hair off my forehead and planted tiny kisses up and down my neck. "Bones intact?"

"I think so. Yours?"

"Can't feel 'em."

He slumped against the side of the tub and wrapped both arms around me.

"So that's edging?" I said the words conversationally. He laughed against my back. "Good to know."

"Let's take a quick shower and lie down somewhere."

"Somewhere?"

"Anywhere." He hauled me to my feet and turned me to face him. "Christ, you're beautiful."

"Me?" I scoffed. He was the beauty. My bossy Adonis with his cuffs, and his plugs, and his unexpected tenderness.

"Yes, you." He towed me to the shower and turned the water on. "You're gorgeous. You know this."

I stood propped against the tile wall while he cleaned the plug carefully and wrapped it in a towel. "Come over here."

"All right." He wrapped his arms around my waist, and I put mine around his neck. We turned, sharing hot water and kisses until we were clean enough for bed.

LATER, dry, warm, and impossibly relaxed, I slid between the sheets as Epic hung up our clothing. He brought me water to drink, then slid in beside me.

"You should definitely hydrate."

"Okay." I removed the cap from the bottle and took a couple big swigs.

"How do you feel?" Epic rolled to his side with his head propped on one hand, his exceptional blue gaze burrowing into my very soul.

"Like an empty suitcase."

He brushed my hair behind my ear. "That good or bad?"

"So, so good." I thought about it. "One kind of empty is when something is missing, but another kind is when you're ready to be filled with something new."

"Good to know."

"Mm." I pressed my cheek to his.

"What's tomorrow?" he asked.

"Been thinking about that. Originally, I'd planned to stay until next weekend."

Epic's eyes widened. "I need to get back for work."

"I figured. I would have driven you to St. Nacho's then come back here. It's not that far."

His features clouded with disappointment. "That'd be okay."

"Yeah, but I wonder..."

He stilled. "What?"

"What if I spent the rest of my vacation in St. Nacho's? Think you'll have some free time? We could hang out. Do whatever it is people do there."

"Really?" He seemed pleased by my suggestion.

"If it's something you'd like."

Suddenly, I had armfuls of Epic—happy, kissy, giggly Epic. He smashed into me so enthusiastically that we accidentally slid off the bed.

"Are you kidding me?" I complained when I stopped laughing. "Old men are delicate, for God's sake. You want to break something?"

"Sorry," he gasped with laughter. "Really sorry. I swear to God."

He stood and dragged me to my feet.

"This time," he said, "maybe get in the middle instead of hugging the edge like a frightened virgin."

Epic Alsop was the last person I'd expected to burst into my life, but he was also the person I'd needed at exactly the right time.

I did what he told me and got into the middle where he wrapped both arms around me. I laid my head on his chest.

He stroked my hair. "Night, Ryan."

"Night, Epic."

I fell asleep smiling.

CHAPTER EIGHTEEN

Birdsong woke me around six. Early morning sunlight filtered through the gauzy drapes. At some point during the night, Epic and I had moved apart. Probably I'd moved away. I didn't have a history of sleeping with people, and I instinctively turned from the surprise of hot skin next to mine.

That didn't mean I had to stay away now that I was awake. I used the bathroom to piss, brush my teeth, and wash up, and when I slid back between the sheets, I cuddled against Epic the same way I had the night before.

His lips curled upward softly in sleep. On waking, happiness painted an expansive smile on his face. His warmth gratified me greatly. How wonderful to be on the receiving end of his delight first thing in the morning.

"Hey." He combed his fingers through my hair.

"Hey." I propped my chin on his chest, careful not to dig in. "Yesterday was perfect. Thank you."

"Thank *you*." He kissed my temple. "I had a great time."

"Me too."

"Though that was the bougiest wedding I've ever been to, and that's saying something."

"Luis likes things nice."

"I'm still in awe of the sky. Who has the sun and moon perform at their wedding."

"It was most auspicious." I smothered a yawn. "I hope they live happily ever after."

He caught my chin and turned my face to his. "You really mean that, don't you?"

I nodded. "I've said those words before, but I didn't mean them. Not without reservations. Now, I feel capable of wishing Luis and William well from my heart."

"Why, do you think?"

"On some level, I never let Luis go. You know that. You've seen the emotional roller coaster I've been on."

"Yeah."

"It's okay for him to get what he wants. It doesn't mean all my dreams are dead. The choices I made…they're the right ones for me. You reminded me that taking a little time out to enjoy life won't kill me."

"Mm." He lowered his chin so our foreheads pressed together. "What time do we have to leave?"

"I'll call down and tell them I won't be staying. Maybe they'll give us a late checkout, but if not, probably around eleven."

"Plenty of time to eat breakfast and bend you over the table afterwards."

"Oh God." I would feel him for a week as it was. "You'll have to take a rain check I think."

"Oh, Ryan." He looked appalled. "Did I hurt you? I—"

"It's fine," I reassured him. "I'm just not used to spending that much time with something in my ass."

"Right." He nipped my shoulder. "Old men are delicate. I forgot."

"Keep it in mind," I teased. "My body aches all over, but it's a wonderful feeling. I wouldn't trade last night for anything, but maybe we should hit the spa."

"Ooh. Could we get one of the fancy couples' massages?"

The idea tickled me silly, but it wasn't a bad feeling. "Is that something you'd like to do?"

"Uh, yeah. Duh. Aromatherapy, candles, maybe there's even pan flute music." He mimicked the sort of wailing, new age music that belonged in spas. The sound made me shiver.

"You're so weird. Phone down and see if the spa can accommodate us. I'm sure it's exactly the kind of thing Laurie had in mind when he booked us the suite."

"Done and done. You won't regret it. You're such a Disney prince. This is going in my super-secret diary." He cupped my face to kiss me then scampered away to use the phone in the living room.

I let my head fall back on the pillow.

I loved how easy it was to make Epic happy. Knock a ball around a mini-golf course, ride a bike together, eat lunch, hold hands. I'd spoiled the hell out of him with the hotel, the quality of the food, the jewelry, and a possible trip to the spa, but I was sure that if I'd had nothing but a carton of McDonald's French fries to offer along with a walk on the beach, he'd have been just as happy with that.

While he talked to the spa, I began shaving. I was about halfway through when I heard the *thwump* of a body hitting the bed.

I poked my head into the bedroom. Epic sprawled flat and dejected across the mattress.

"What's up?"

"Bad news. There's no availability at the spa today at all."

"Oh, I'm sorry. Give me a minute to finish shaving and we can make another plan."

I turned back to the mirror. After a couple minutes, Epic slid up behind me.

"Turns out, the spa has a limited staff on Mondays, and they're all booked."

"We could try somewhere else if it means that much to you."

"No. It's okay. It just sounded like fun. What if we leave early and get brunch in San Luis Obispo?"

"That's fine with me."

"I hate giving up this awesome room."

"It is nice, isn't it?"

"Imagine cleaning all this grout though." He sat on the lip of the tub. "Where would you even start?"

"No clue. At home, I use a cleaning service," I said. "I spend so little time at my apartment, if I didn't, the dust bunnies would take over."

"You need to take better care of yourself."

I swiped my face with a towel. "I will consider your advice."

"And you need to eat better."

"I'll certainly try."

"And drink less. Quit smoking."

"Holy cow. My fake boyfriend is a closet life coach. Speaking of which, let me get a last smoke in on that beach."

"Okay." He snorted. "Because having a smoke where the air is fresh and delightful isn't cognitively dissonant or anything."

"Are we having a big word day?"

"Just saying."

We stacked our things by the door and strolled through the grounds one last time. Memories of our stay were everywhere. The bench where we sat and talked by the plumeria. The pool where we swam and relaxed. The tropical garden where William propositioned me.

On this very walkway, Luis and I met for the first time in six years.

I had yet to wrap my head around them wanting me to be the cream in their sandwich cookie. How could Luis think I'd go along with something like that? Perhaps he knew I wouldn't but had let William test me for his own reasons.

I would probably never know.

Epic didn't say anything as we ambled along. I wondered if he was playing our stay over in his imagination and what his thoughts would be. Whether we had a "spot" or if there was a moment that was particularly memorable for him.

When we got to my clandestine smoking spot, I withdrew my cigarettes and lighter and simply looked at them. They felt like a relic now. Like something from a time capsule that belonged to someone else.

I must have hesitated for a long time because Epic tapped my shoulder.

"Something wrong?" he asked.

"It's nothing. Just...I've only had two cigarettes a day for the last few days. First thing in the morning and last thing at night."

His eyes twinkled. "Is that so?"

He was going to make me work for this. "It seems like I don't actually need to smoke."

"How odd. Why might that be?"

"Don't laugh, you fucking brat." Deliberately, I lit one to take that first drag of the day. My head swam pleasantly for a second. I lifted my hand and stared at the lit end. "Maybe I'm past it."

Epic slipped behind me, close enough to put his arms around me. One hand went over my heart and the other smoothed over my hip where the slight ache of pleasure-pain told me I'd bruised the night before.

"You know what I think?" he asked.

"Tell me." I took another drag.

"I think that for the last six years, every time you opened a fresh pack of cigarettes, you thought about Luis. Every time you pulled the foil, you saw his hands. Every time you flicked your lighter, you saw his face. Every time your lips touched the filter, you pictured his lips touching the filter of his cigarette, and that was how you kissed him."

My throat closed over some instinctive denial, but it wasn't for Epic. I'd stopped lying to him a day or two before.

"So maybe I don't need them anymore?"

"Maybe you don't."

There were other reasons to smoke besides metaphorically kissing Luis, for God's sake. I'd probably have to slap on a nicotine patch for a few days. Taper off. I stubbed the cigarette out and threw the butt—and the rest of the pack—into the trash.

We stood there for the longest time watching the waves roll in one after another. The tide had gone out. Seaweed and other detritus lay on the beach where a half dozen men in green groundskeeper's uniforms combed the sand for trash. A pricy private beach must always appear pristine to guests—paradise untouched as long as one didn't bother looking beneath the layers of carefully cultivated plants and behind the scenes maintenance.

I much preferred St. Nacho's—what little I'd seen of it— with its coarse sand and weathered wooden fishing pier.

For six years, I'd been numb. I'd barely noticed my surroundings, whether I was in an office, an airport, a swanky hotel, or a packed clothing factory in a country where I didn't speak the language.

Now I noticed everything—every cloud, every change in the light, every seabird, every breeze that lifted Epic's dark hair.

And Epic. I noticed every single Epic, from bratty Epic, to happy Epic, to surprised Epic, to sad Epic, to the Epic who experienced wonder with every new thing he saw.

Epic, who only ever let me lead on the dance floor.

He held out his hand. "Let's go home, Ryan."

"Okay." I took his hand and let him lead me back.

155

AT CHECKOUT, they wouldn't take my money.

I left a suitable bonus for the housekeeping staff and tipped the men who carried our things and retrieved my car, but beyond that, Laurie had picked up the tab for everything.

There would definitely be an attempt to pay Laurie back in the future—partially, anyway. He would no doubt refuse, but still I'd try.

I'd also continue to feel relieved that I didn't *have* to pay the bill because I could hold two separate ideas at the same time.

Epic held his hand out for the keys. "I'll drive."

I handed them over—not because he was bossy, but because I felt wrapped in some sort of psychological batting. Even with my sunglasses, the light was too bright. The colors too vivid.

Every sign we passed, every building, every farmstead and roadside attraction seemed to have some message for me. When I reached for a bottled water, my hand trembled as if I was having an internal earthquake.

My thoughts raced. My priorities seemed to be rearranging themselves.

I had changed, and I didn't know how.

I had changed, and now I felt like I was taking my very first steps again, unsteady, uncertain, unable to find something to grab hold of because my old crutches were gone, and I didn't have new ones yet.

I glanced over at Epic, and for a single brief second, I hated him.

All of life's painful lessons—all its agents of change—practiced destruction before creation could begin.

I'd known the truth going in.

I'd pulled the pin on the grenade myself.

Was I sick with remorse, giddy with anticipation, or both?

I already had whiplash, and this was just the beginning.

In San Luis Obispo, we had made-to-order omelets on the terrace of a crowded farm-to-table restaurant. After, we decided on a stroll in the botanical gardens. Of course, we had to stop for sunscreen.

"Let me," Epic ordered.

"I already did it."

"You missed a spot." He was determined that not one ray of sun would reach my skin, ever. "You don't want to have polka dots when you go back to Canada. They won't let you in."

"Right. I'll be too colorful," I teased.

"Here." He settled my hat on my head and handed me my sunglasses. "In case no one told you, there's a hole in the ozone layer."

"The news did catch my notice a time or two."

"You liked the gardens in Santa Barbara, didn't you? We spent a lot of time on the grounds at the hotel." He took my hand. "Is this a thing for you? Are you a closet horticulturalist?"

"I keep an African violet on my desk, but I live in a high rise, so no."

He covered his face with both hands. "Don't tell me. You rent furnished."

"Yes," I admitted. "What's your point?"

"You know where I want to live?" He made an expansive gesture with both hands. "A huge tumble-down Victorian house with creaky stairs and a poison garden."

"Ad astra, I guess. If you want that, you could probably get it."

He kicked at a rock in the path. "Not waiting tables."

"Probably not. But you have a first-rate education, and whatever you do, a house with a poison garden is probably within your reach."

"Would you come and visit me?" He shot me a wicked smile.

157

"Hell no. You'd probably offer me tea, and how would I know it's safe to drink?"

"I wouldn't poison you." He held up three fingers. "Scout's honor."

"Were you a scout?"

"No."

"Hm." I leaned over to read a plaque next to a pretty blue-flowered shrub. "*Nipomo Mesa Ceanothus*. Say that three times fast."

He did.

"Show off."

"Am not." He casually bumped me with his shoulder, then took my arm. It brought us closer than handholding and placed us squarely into the couple category. Two motherly women on the path ahead of us *aw'd* discreetly.

Our difference in ages brought us totally different perspectives on PDA. At his age, I would never have so casually signaled a partnership in public.

There was plenty of vitriol left in the world against LGBTQ individuals, but when I was his age, gay people were casually discriminated against in churches, on the street, in businesses, bars, and restaurants. There was no protection for employees, no respect from most police.

I was torn between envy of Epic's confidence and exasperation with it. It had taken me thousands of dollars' worth of therapy and twenty years of exhausting uphill battles to get to the place of "no fucks given" Epic took for granted.

No. That wasn't right.

Good for him.

Good for him and still good for me. *We all stand on the shoulders of giants.*

"You're awfully quiet." He wrapped his arm around my neck and pulled me even closer. "Deep thoughts?"

I shook my head. "Just thoughts. Nothing deep."

"I don't believe that for a second, Thinky McOverthinker. All your thoughts are probably deep."

"Maybe."

"It's what I like about you." He leaned over to give some plum-sweet bearded irises a sniff, taking me with him. "You care about things that matter to me."

"Thank you. That's very nice. I like that about you too."

"What's next for you?" He broke away and jammed his hands into his pockets. "A few days in St. Nacho's and then what?"

"I go back to work."

"Better take it slow. You'll get decompression sickness after all this frivolity."

"I'll be sure to watch my ascent. Descent?" The laptop in my trunk was already calling me. "I'll probably spend a little time assessing where I stand from St. Nacho's. I wonder if Dan and Cam have broadband or FIOS?"

"You're staying with them? Cool. I mean you could stay with me, but it's barely better than dorm living. We have an actual brick-and-board bookcase, no lie, and Bea's got a bra perpetually hanging in the bathroom to dry."

"Not cool. I planned to stay a few more nights at a resort, not in someone's guest room, but if I must, at least Dan and Cam's place has a private bath for me."

"You could stay at the SeaView, but after the Four Seasons it might seem a little depressing. Why don't you see if there's an Airbnb? There are a couple of nice ones, probably."

Why hadn't I thought of that?

"You're gen whatever." I handed him my phone. "Pick me a nice one. My card's on file."

"Ooh." He tackled the task happily while I listened to the thrum of insects and the whisper of a breeze through the leaves of trees. We continued walking, but because he was so absorbed in my phone, I took a turn at keeping us on the path.

What I really wanted was to lie down on the grass and take

a nap. I had emotional jetlag—a kind of foggy, brittle exhaustion I could apparently get without going on a trip across time zones. Or maybe I had crossed one, from six years ago to now.

I'd let my emotions hibernate out of some misguided self-preservation instinct. Now they'd woken and nothing was what I thought it was.

I had changed.

"Got one." Epic announced. "You look exhausted. I'll drive. You can sleep the rest of the way.

"Sounds great." I could barely keep my eyes open.

He took my hand. "Let's go."

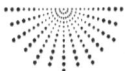

CHAPTER NINETEEN

E pic woke me after he parked outside the Airbnb. I looked
at the time. Three in the afternoon. I'd slept the rest of
the way back.

In the driveway, Epic introduced me to Ken Ashton, who
owned this place and several others if I understood correctly.

"Here are the keys." Ken handed them over and I let myself
inside. Briefly, he walked us through the house. "You'll find
your breakfast basket on the porch at seven tomorrow morning. Just fill out this form so I know what your drink prefer-
ences are."

He gave me a form and a pencil, and I leaned over the
counter in the kitchen and checked off the marked boxes.

"Food allergies?" I asked Epic.

"Nope."

"Regular coffee? Or do you want something else to drink?"

"Coffee's great. Cream and sugar."

"The basket comes with assorted pastries and muffins," said
Ken. "I have it delivered from Café Bêtise. I think you'll find
their pastries are superb."

Epic nodded enthusiastically. "We serve them at Bistro."

"Of course. You're the waiter." Ken rubbed a hand over his forehead. "I recognized your face. Jeremy, right?"

I snorted.

"Well, that's one of the name tags I wear, but my name is Epic."

"Is it?"

"Mmhmm."

Ken waited.

I'd seen this coming, sooner or later, and sat back to enjoy the show.

"Are you going to tell me your name?" asked Ken. "Or should I guess? Rumpelstiltskin."

"It really is Epic," I answered for my fake boyfriend, who looked blank. "Not an epic name, but the name, Epic."

"Oh." A sweet blush flooded Ken's cheeks. "Who's on first?"

"That's right."

"What just happened?" Epic's face scrunched up adorably.

"Old joke," I explained.

"Ah. Got it." He backed away slowly. "I'll just bring in the bags while you reminisce."

We watched him go.

"You'll both be staying with us until Friday?" asked Ken.

"Yes." I hesitated. "No. Epic lives in town, so I don't know if he'll be here or at his place."

"No worries. We'll assume two for breakfast if you don't let us know ahead."

"Sure. Thank you."

"My pleasure. What brings you to town?"

"I attended a wedding in Santa Barbara, and I'm taking a few extra days. I have friends here."

"Anyone I know?"

"Dan and Cam Livingston?"

"Oh, I know both of them very well. Dan and I do business. I helped his brother start Café Bêtise as a matter of fact."

"Small world."

"You don't know the half of it."

Epic returned. "Did you see the yard yet? The ad said there's a hot tub."

"There is. I'll show you." Ken led us out French doors to a nicely landscaped back yard with a redwood deck, a gas grill, and a four-seat, above-ground spa.

"Looks like heaven," I said. "I look forward to spending time in there."

"Enjoy." Ken shook my hand. "If you need anything, my number is on the fridge."

"Thank you." Ken took the form I'd filled out and left.

"Well, this is really nice," I said. "Thanks for the idea."

Was it weird that I felt awkward now that we were back in St. Nacho's? After all, Epic could return to his normal life if he wanted to. He didn't have to stay with me.

Since I was only halfway home, the transition hung over me like a black cloud.

"What's your work schedule like this week?"

He checked his watch, then blew out a breath that made his hair fly up before falling over his eyes.

"I'm scheduled to catch the early dinner shift in an hour." His eyes brightened. "But that means I don't close. Why don't you meet me at Nacho's Bar for drinks? Some of my friends will probably be there. Ten o'clock?"

"Sure." I'd get a nap and still have plenty of time to set up my computer and wade into work before then.

"What will you do for dinner? You should come to Bistro."

"I'll find something. I want to call Dan and Cam to let them know I'm back. Maybe they'll want to go out."

"If so, sit at my table and tip me well." He reached out to kiss me. "I've gotta go, though."

"I'll drive you to your place."

"I'm only three blocks away. I'll walk."

"You sure?"

"Of course. You still look dead on your feet." He took my mouth again, unhurried, tasting...teasing. "Mm. See you tonight."

"Sure." Since when did I go all warm and squishy over a kiss? "See you then."

With another sly glance my way, he slipped outside and hurried off. I closed the door and leaned my forehead against it, willing my body to act like a mature adult. My body seemed to think that idea was overrated because when I stripped to my briefs, I was still hard.

In the bathroom light, I appeared paler than normal. I stifled a surprised gasp when I saw how Epic had marked my skin. He'd kept his word that he wouldn't hurt me, and yet I had scratches on my back and love bites all over my chest. Bruises dotted my hips where Epic's fingers had clutched at me. It was exciting, in a way, seeing how desperate we'd been for each other mapped out on my body like that.

I was still smiling when I tumbled between the crisp, clean sheets on the bed in the master bedroom. Second nap of the day—that had to be some kind of a record.

There was no doubt my body needed the sleep. I never slept enough. Only this time, my mind seemed not just resigned to the fact but more than willing to let go. In no time, I drifted like a baby in a Moses basket along the currents of mostly nice dreams about my fake boyfriend, Epic.

Epic, I decided, was the nicest dream of all...

I WOKE AT DINNERTIME. Since I didn't feel hungry, I decided to create an office of sorts at the kitchen table. I brought in my laptop and set up a printer. I don't know which of the tech giants first decided that paperless was the way to go, but I liked making notes on paper. I doodled and scribbled. If I printed out an article, then I could clip it to other articles. At the office, I had what my workmates referred to as a "wall of crazy" to link my ideas together.

I'd tried using many different mind mapping software apps, but in the long run I'd watched too many detective shows. I liked a white board with pictures and colored markers, and failing that, I made do with any handy wall, painter's tape, and yarn. But Epic had a point about decompression sickness. I got a headache when I tried to wade in as if I'd never been away.

I spent the afternoon rereading my notes and reacquainting myself with several news stories I'd been watching. From 1980 to 2012, a staggering sixteen percent of female homicides in Canada were indigenous women and girls, even though they represented only four percent of the entire Canadian population. Native American women were murdered every year in the US at an equally high rate per capita.

Many of these women and girls were being lured into a lifetime of drugs and sex trafficking, if not outright kidnapped and beaten or tortured into it, only to be thrown away like garbage if they were too rebellious, or strung out, or sick to be profitable.

There were grassroots organizations attempting to publicize this fact, but marginalized people got little traction. You had only to look at the cases of LaToyla Figueroa and Natalee Holloway to see where the media put its attention.

When StolenLives went after traffickers, I liked to believe we were doing something positive before the fact, not after. But for every trafficker we caught, every pornographer or sexual slave trader, there were ten more people waiting to step into the vacated shoes. Marginalized women and children were easy pickings in every country in the world.

I didn't end up eating dinner at all. When Epic called to find me, I was already late.

"Did you fall back to sleep?"

My mouth was dry. Jesus. Even my water bottle had gone untouched.

"I think you may have been right about me getting the bends."

"Oh no. You still want to meet up? If you're tired—"

"Yes. I'm so sorry. I lost track of time. I'll be there in a few, okay?"

"We're drinking and having fun, no worries. Glad I called though."

"I should have set an alarm."

"Just haul that sweet ass of yours down here and all is forgiven."

That boy. A hot flush crept over my body while I changed into something decent. I turned to give my ass a look.

"Not bad for an old guy." Great. Now I was talking to myself.

There wasn't parking on the street, so I used the veterinary clinic's lot again. I walked the rest of the way.

Low clouds had swept in, blanketing the coastline. Visibility wasn't a problem, but a translucent mist hung in the air, creating spheres of light around the streetlamps and moistening my skin. Salt laden air competed with the aroma of frying tortilla chips and roasting meat.

I itched for a cigarette. I should have gotten a patch if I was really going to quit. As I approached, I saw Epic on the boardwalk and waved.

"There's my guy. Come and kiss me before I do something rash." He bit his lip. "Hi."

"Hi." I said the word too fondly. There was no lying about this anymore—not to others and not to myself. Epic was a perfectly pristine lagoon on a tropical island. Every time I saw him, I happily drowned in the cool blue of his eyes.

"You ready to drink?" he asked.

"Um—"

"You didn't eat, did you?" He caught my chin. "I knew I should have taken you something on my break."

"I should have set an alarm."

He took my arm and towed me to the restaurant. "If you're going to be Batman, you'll need to get yourself an Alfred. You have a cleaner. Hire a chef when you get back or at least subscribe to a meal service."

"That's a pretty good idea, actually."

"Duh." He opened the door of Nacho's Bar for me. Live music thumped through my chest as we walked inside. He pointed out his friends, who had pushed two tables together. The waitress was serving drinks, beers, and shots, and the mood was raucous already.

"Hey, guys." Epic clinked his glass loudly with a fork. Every eye turned his way. "This is Ryan Winslow. He's the one I went to the wedding with."

"Hello." I waved my hand.

"Oh my God, he is a Disney prince. Too bad Cinderfella had to come home. I heard the resort was amazing."

Epic grinned. "It was."

"And you know Lawrence Dunbar?" one of the girls squealed. "Oh God. Why couldn't you have been looking for a fake girlfriend?"

"That's Bea," Epic said, pointing. "She's my roommate."

"Nice to meet you." I put my hand over the table to shake hers.

She shook it and then pretended it burned. "So hot."

Epic got me a chair from somewhere. "Bea's friend over there is Muse."

Muse wore several piercings in her ears, eyebrows, and nose. Her hair was black and silky, cut in a fashionable bob. "Hello, Muse. Nice to meet you."

We shook.

"And that's Lonnie." A younger, dark-haired man waved from the other end of the table. There were three other young men—Kellan, Zaid, and Max.

I waved at all of them, suddenly and acutely aware I was the oldest person there by at least thirteen years.

"What are you drinking?" asked Bea.

"He's not drinking until he eats something." Epic called the waitress over and ordered a couple of appetizers from the bar menu. "Is Oscar still here? Can you ask if he can make me a salad, pretty please?"

I tried to argue. "Epic that's—"

"If he can't, he can't," Epic argued.

"It's fine. I'll ask," she assured him. "Anything to drink?"

I glanced at Epic, who graciously allowed me to order that for myself. "Maker's Mark and a Moosehead if you've got it, please."

"I don't think we have that."

"Get a Corona," Epic muttered. "Thinks he'll get a Moosehead in a Mexican restaurant on the central coastline."

"Hey," I complained. "It's the first brand I thought of."

"We need to expand your horizons." Muse eyed me. "Get you out of your comfort zone."

I glanced around the table. "Mission accomplished."

"You're a friend of my brother, right? Dan Livingston?" Lonnie leaned forward, hands wrapped around a glass of soda. No way was he old enough to be drinking.

"Yeah. You're the youngest?" The kid nodded. "You're in school, right?"

"I'm a freshman at Cal Poly."

"What are you studying there?" I moved empty glasses toward the middle of the table.

"Sustainable agriculture practices."

"That sounds great. Do you enjoy it?"

Lonnie nodded, but a whoop went up at another table, and I didn't hear what he said next.

Our food came fast. I had the waitress put it into the center of the table. Epic grabbed a plate for me and loaded it up. Apparently, his salad plea had found favor because I got a nice garden salad to go with the mostly fried foods.

"Eat." Epic narrowed his eyes. "Or I'll drink your alcohol."

"Can't have that." I'm sure Epic's friends thought I was humoring him, but the way he micromanaged my health hit me like a blast furnace right in the solar plexus. Whether Epic pushed food on me, or slimed me with sunblock, or reached out in the middle of the night to drag the blankets over my shoulder, I could not get enough of his warmth or his kindness.

Epic leaned over to whisper, "Why are you looking at me like that?"

"I like looking at you."

"But you're staring."

"No, I'm gazing," I corrected him. "Right now, you are the object of my affectionate gaze."

"Really?" One eyebrow lifted. "Is that what people did before television?"

"Oh, son, that's what people did before *porn*."

He nodded, all innocent. "Okay, we're kicking it old school. I like it."

"I live to serve."

I guessed I said that too loud because Bea's eyes widened. "Nice."

"Now, have I eaten enough that I may drink?" I showed him my empty salad bowl.

"Oh, good job. Yes, now you may drink." Epic inclined his head regally.

I heard a throat clear. "Ryan. You're back."

I turned to find Dan and Cam standing behind me. "Hey."

I stood up, and people hugged each other in as many permutations as it took for the whole table to acknowledge one another.

"Lonnie," Dan said. "Muse. Seems like Ryan's hanging out with the cool kids. You got room for us?"

"Pull up chairs." Lonnie's happy expression made me miss my brothers. I resolved to take more time for family.

"I thought you said you weren't coming up this week," said Dan.

169

"Changed my mind at the last minute." Lonnie shrugged. "I was gonna crash at your place."

Dan frowned. "Ryan has first dibs on the guest room."

"That's okay. I took an Airbnb so I'd have a place to myself," I informed him.

"Okay, as long as you're sure," said Dan.

"Thanks for offering, but I need to spread out and do some work. I thought it'd be better."

Dan gave a nod. "God, I get to see you twice in one year. How was the wedding? You took Epic, right? Epic, how'd you get on?"

"The resort was amazing. I hate weddings, but this one was nice."

"You hate weddings?" I asked. "You never told me that."

"God yes." Epic wrinkled his nose. "If I had told you would you have taken me?"

"No."

He grinned. "That's why I didn't tell you."

"What is it about weddings you hate?" asked Cam.

"The atmosphere for one thing. And the expense. If I get bored during a wedding, I try to calculate the exact cost per minute based on visible clues and then divide that by the number of guests. I spend the rest of the time worrying that I'm not having enough actual fun to offset the bride and groom's investment in me."

"Math geek." I nudged him with my shoulder.

"That's the easy math. It's when you start to consider the cost over the statistical likelihood of the couple staying married that things get trickier. Among the weddings I've been to, very few people reach the point where a large wedding isn't a complete waste of time and money."

"Define waste in this calculation," said Dan.

"Well." Epic dimpled. "Marriage is thought to confer a number of benefits, including mental, physical, spiritual, and financial health. So in that light, you could look at weddings as the investment one makes in those things."

"Seriously?" Dan glanced at me.

I sipped my drink. "Science does show marriage can benefit those things in the long term."

"What about all the people who kill their spouses?" asked Muse.

"They're factored in," Epic assured her.

"Okay, so what about Luis and William's wedding?"

"The bougie brothers?" Epic rubbed his temples. "Even given the growing life expectancy among European males, they're statistically unlikely to live long enough for the benefits of marriage to offset the cost of that ridiculous fucking wedding. I mean, God, that was obscene."

"And?" I prompted him because basically honest Epic would have to admit he'd enjoyed it.

"And...I loved it." He moaned. "I'm a fucking whore. The food, oh my God. And that stupid lunar eclipse. Who has a lunar eclipse at their wedding?"

"They probably couldn't get Beyoncé," Muse observed.

"So you had a good time?" Cam asked.

"I had a spectacular time." Epic glanced meaningfully at me when he spoke.

"I didn't quite catch that, Epic," I teased. "What did you just say?"

"I had a good time," Epic practically shouted. "I had the best time, except when William jumped you in the bushes and asked if—"

I clapped my hand over his mouth. "Look at the time. Is it really that late?"

Epic's blue eyes sparkled with humor. "Mph, mphre mmph."

"Did you say something?" I lifted my hand cautiously.

"I won't tell."

Around the table, pleas to hear the story went unanswered.

171

I finished my bourbon and sipped my beer while I picked at the nachos and the rest of the table chatted, and drank, and blew off steam.

Epic didn't seem to notice how many times he reached for me. Except for the fact we were with his friends, I probably wouldn't have noticed it either. He liked touch. He didn't hesitate to reach for people—not just me, but obviously, the way he touched me was sensual. Tantalizing.

Occasionally, I met Cam's or Dan's knowing gaze and flushed with a hot mixture of pride and shame. Ego because Epic seemed happy to be with me and guilt because I didn't know what to do about that.

Epic's friends graciously welcomed me to the tribe. Whether that was because people came and went often in Epic's life or they simply took a chance I was okay, I didn't know.

"Okay, drink up and let's go." I guessed Epic had checked his phone and decided it was past my bedtime.

"All right." As we left, Epic flung his arm around my shoulders possessively.

Every eye in the place watched us go.

Because we'd been drinking, we walked to the rental. Epic promised to get my car in the morning.

We walked hand in hand, avoiding root-buckled sidewalks and crossing empty streets together. Each house we passed had a different level of wear. Some were dilapidated. Some were quaint. It couldn't be easy to maintain the older houses this close to the beach. Few had lawns, but there were several overgrown gardens. Ornamental grasses whispered as we passed. Moonlight spilled over fragrant jasmine-covered fences.

The porch light welcomed us to our rental. I opened the door and let Epic inside. He went straight to the kitchen where I'd spread out some paperwork, pens, notebooks, and Post-its.

"Wow. You really carry your office with you."

"I have to with the way I travel."

He smiled patiently. "As long as you don't bring it into the bedroom. Deal?"

"Can't make that deal. The job stays in my head."

"I know." He laid his hand on my shoulder. "I'll take your mind off it tonight."

Oh yeah, he would.

We took turns in the bathroom, got undressed, and brushed our teeth side by side. Epic was a habit already. More than smoking for sure, because I didn't give cigarettes a single thought until I was ready to slip between the sheets.

"Do you think you could help me remember to get a nicotine patch, or gum, or something?"

"Happy to." He burrowed under the covers like a cartoon gopher snatching a carrot.

I caught his body to mine—my surprisingly solid, surprisingly strong, surprisingly dominant boy-man. I'd seen and done a lot of things, and I thought nothing could surprise me, then along came Epic Alsop.

Surprise, surprise.

CHAPTER TWENTY

When I woke, the bed beside me was empty. I rolled out and hit the bathroom to piss and brush my teeth before looking for Epic. One of the fluffy bathrobes was missing. Presumably Epic had it. I put on the other.

I found him in the kitchen where he'd set the table for two with dainty mismatched china as if we were having Her Majesty to tea. An assortment of pastries and muffins sat in a wicker basket next to a very large thermal carafe.

He poured me coffee, leaving it black, and went back to reading the notes I'd made the night before.

"Morning." I kissed his cheek.

His impish smile called to something inside me I didn't have a name for yet. He'd arranged my notes in piles.

"So how does this work exactly?" He tapped one pile. "I see arrest records, applications for business licenses, news stories, missing person reports. How do you take all of this and find out anything?"

"Mm." I sat down opposite him and snagged a carrot muffin with—it turned out—a cream cheese frosting center.

"Okay. So..." I wiped crumbs off my lips to explain the string-pulling—how all the little points of data I'd gathered formed a darker picture that I'd trained myself to look for over years of trial and error. "It's best if I use an example of something that's already been uncovered because the picture is clearer, yeah?"

I picked up a legal tablet and started making notes so he could see.

"A few years ago, three girls went missing from the same general area in Northern California. One was from Redding, one from Castella, and the third lived in Red Bluff."

I pulled up a map of the area from Google on my phone.

"The three towns are along this particular stretch of the I-5 corridor."

Epic gave a shiver. "When was this? I didn't hear about abductions on the news."

"No, you wouldn't have. The cases originally weren't considered abductions because all three women left voluntarily with men they were dating. Two of the women didn't have family locally, so only their roommates and coworkers realized they were missing, but they had dead-end jobs. One worked as a waitress —"

"Hey." He smacked my arm.

"Sorry, sorry." I acknowledged his protests. "Forgive me. This woman worked in a casual-dining chain restaurant and was one of a large staff with lots of turnover. She was fairly interchangeable with other servers. One worked in a gas station convenience store."

"Who reported them missing?"

"Their roommates got worried after a couple of days, but the police don't hit the panic button over women who leave with a guy they've been dating for a while."

"And the third woman?"

"Her parents reported her missing when she didn't come home, but they'd had some pretty heated arguments with her about her boyfriend. It was assumed she'd left of her own volition."

"So not a lot of traction because people run away with bad boyfriends all the time."

"Right. And in each case, they'd been dating a while. Roommates both said the guy brought flowers, gave presents, took the girls out clubbing. The parents didn't like their daughter's boyfriend because he was a tattooed biker cliché, but they agreed he seemed to treat her well. On the face of things, it just looked like three girls had boyfriends their friends didn't approve of, so they took off."

"But I'm guessing that wasn't the case."

"It was in a way. Because in every case the "boyfriend" was the same man. Let's call him Jack Leary, but he has several aliases."

"Whaaaat?" Epic's eyes widened.

"And *bad boyfriend* was the least of Jack's crimes. He'd done several different stretches in prison—larceny, drug possession with intent to distribute, assault and battery, and kidnapping. Inside, he'd hooked up with the Aryan Brotherhood."

Epic winced. "What happened to the girls?"

"That's where the other data points come in. Once I connected all three women to one man, I started digging into him and his known associates. Several of his cohorts had arrests for weapons violations, assault and battery, attacks on women, rape, and kidnapping. I looked at where he and his pals lived, where they worked, any businesses they owned, bank accounts, vehicle registrations."

"Did you find anything? Seems a guy like that would use cash to stay under the radar."

"Right. That's problem one. Cash-based transactions are the norm in these cases. Dirty money needs to be cleaned though, and sometimes it's possible to find a trail."

He shook his head. "Wow."

"When I looked into businesses he and his known associates worked for or came into contact with over the years, we found a long-haul trucking company, strip clubs, card rooms, and massage parlors."

"Aw shit." Apparently, Epic didn't have to be told the nature of work a girl got in those businesses.

"This man lured the women legitimately. He probably seemed exciting and a little dangerous. He knows how to show a girl a good time. They think they have a boyfriend, but in reality, they're being groomed by a pimp."

"The women never suspect what's really going on?"

"Not until it's too late. He probably introduces them to recreational drugs, but by the time he's ready to start pimping them out, he's got them on heroin to maintain compliance."

"And you can tell all this from the things here? About the drugs and everything?"

I nodded. "I've uncovered arrest records on some of the women. After a few months, they're getting picked up for drug possession, or theft, or solicitation. These women are moved from place to place so often they're disoriented, entirely alone in a strange town, dope-sick with no one they can ask for help."

"And you find them?" Epic broke my muffin into bite-size pieces, which he hand-fed me while I talked.

"It's never that simple. All I can do is connect the dots around missing women, the men they were last seen with, arrest records, and businesses they're involved in. A lot of it is purely theoretical."

"Don't police detectives already do that when someone goes missing?"

"Yeah, of course. But they work on every case that comes down the chute, which means robbery, homicide, rape, and these missing persons. They'll put everything on the back burner for an endangered child, but their time and resources are limited in the case of a woman who may or may not have run away with her boyfriend."

Z.A. MAXFIELD

"I see, so because human trafficking is your area of expertise—"

"I poke my nose in. It's not always welcome."

"Yeah, well. They probably get a ton of cranks," Epic mused.

"I look for connections and I follow the money."

"How'd you ever learn, though?"

"Insatiable curiosity."

He covered my hand with his. "And passion."

"Yeah." I took a sip of bitter coffee.

"The whole thing is sick." Epic's grimace was pure empathy. He was easily one of the most compassionate people I'd ever known. This was why I rarely talked about work. It changed you, knowing this was going on in the background—everywhere—and there was no good way to stop it.

"What do you do when you find something?"

"I give any information I have to local or federal law enforcement, and that's where my involvement ends, but it's a hydra."

He got out of his chair to bring me a glass of orange juice from the fridge. "Drink."

"Thanks." I took a sip. "As soon as we identify and cut the head off the beast, more of these assholes pop up with the same business model. To them men, women, and children are disposable commodities—easy to manipulate and easy to throw away. They target minority women, not rich blonde girls for the most part, so there's less media attention. Given that the money fueling this trade comes from drug trafficking, illegal weapons, gambling—God knows what else—probably child trafficking and pornography on the dark web, there's never an end."

Epic was silent for a long time. Then he glanced up at me, eyes lit with the silver-lining brightness that was Epic's stock in trade.

"That one was solved though? The Northern California women?"

I nodded. "They found one of the women alive. The others are still missing."

"Jesus." He pushed his plate away and dropped his head to his hands. "I now understand why you're a workaholic."

"I'm the butt of a lot of jokes around the office, but none of us find it easy to let go when we're working on something hot."

"Wait. That's sex trafficking, but you look into forced labor too?"

"Yes. Employment schemes, mail-order bride schemes, student scams where kids end up working as slaves for years to pay for their so-called training. Immigration scams."

"This is happening all over the world all the time? How do you keep from getting crushed by the enormity of it?"

I didn't. *I couldn't.* That was the problem. "Knowing you might lose a war doesn't mean you stop fighting each individual battle. How can you?"

He studied me. "And you do this because you have a particular skill for connecting dots?"

I flushed. "I'm not the only one. Thousands of people do what I do every day."

"A lot of them do it on behalf of government, I'll bet."

"Gathering actionable intelligence in the war on terrorism or drug trafficking is theoretically the same job, yes. It's not rocket science. It's boring for the most part. Then you find the thread…"

"You've worked exclusively in the area of human trafficking?"

"That's right," I said dryly. "I positioned myself where the big bucks aren't."

"Hm." He tapped a pen on the table. "Do you really think this is your best recruiting speech?"

"What?" I sat back in surprise. My face got hot. "No, I'm not—I don't—"

He laughed. "Settle down. God, you're weird sometimes."

"I develop potential donors too, but that's not what I'm doing here."

"Penniless waiters need not apply?"

"That's not—"

"It's just that while you were talking, I realized I could probably contribute, given my education, which as you pointed out, is financial in nature."

"But isn't your area of expertise about theoretical mathematical modeling in the business sector?"

"Potato, potahto." He leaned forward and took my hand. "Seriously, Ryan. If you ever need an extra pair of eyes, or hands, or whatever, I'll do anything I can to help you put these motherfuckers away."

"That's very generous."

He leaned back in his chair. "I've got some free time since I'm taking this adulting thing slowly."

"But your parents are furious that you're not using your degrees."

"We made a deal after I graduated. I have time to figure out what I want to do. Plus, Grandma still believes in me, and she's no pushover."

"Well, since you so graciously offered me your help, if there's ever anything you think I can do for you, please don't hesitate to ask."

"Mm. I'll probably be able to come up with something." He gave me the bedroom eyes.

We finished breakfast while basking in the sunlight that filtered into the kitchen. I felt right at home, already attuned to the rhythm of the town and the scent of the ocean on the breeze. Unlike Santa Barbara with its ostentatious hotels and many upscale boutiques and restaurants, Santo Ignacio was a quiet kind of paradise—a legitimately peaceful place to take the time to think things over.

In Santo Ignacio, I could stay where I was and mark the sun's passage across the sky. I could go out to catch the sunset and walk along the beach with the locals, kids, and dogs. I could be as alone as I wanted or surround myself with friends.

"What are we doing today?" Epic stretched dramatically, allowing his lean body to arch off the chair with his robe open.

"What would you like to do?"

He wrinkled his nose. "We should get your car back. Want to take a walk?"

"Sure."

"Let me get the sunscreen."

"It's eight in the morning."

"The sun is visible, isn't it? I'm not letting my skin get old before its time."

I sighed dramatically. "It's already probably too late for me."

"You're gorgeous." He caught my chin. "I'm trying to preserve you."

My face got hot. "C'mon. You can slather me with anything you like."

"Anything?"

"Not really."

"You had me all excited there for a minute. I had a hundred ideas."

"That's what I was afraid of."

We dressed in shorts and T-shirts, but the day hadn't warmed up. I let Epic borrow an old Georgetown sweatshirt. It suited him perfectly, the preppy motherfucker.

"You look like every college boy who rejected me," I pointed out.

"Oh my God. We're going to have to do something about your self-esteem."

"My self-esteem is fine. Mostly." I turned away so he couldn't see I was still torn open by the honesty between us. "Now, anyway. Back then, my gaydar was a little unpredictable."

"Well, you're in for a treat, then, because I'm a bona fide homosexual, and I think you're hot. C'mon."

Epic ran, and I chased him down the street.

I felt twenty years old again, full of life and laughter and the intense longing to be with my really cute guy. The problems of the world even seemed far enough away that they didn't fill my heart with despair. I had the right to enjoy this moment. I had a right to enjoy Epic, and the gift he gave me with every smile, every kiss, every touch of his hand on my skin.

I had a wild want inside me to claim him and make him mine as well.

After feeling nothing for so long, the bittersweet ache of longing filled me up and overflowed, pouring out of me in tiny, emotional waves. Like raindrops disrupting a still pond, my reflection was blurred too much to see.

Who will I be after Epic? What will happen when I leave St. Nacho's?

In the short term, it didn't matter because it turned out fate had a few surprises in store for Epic too.

CHAPTER TWENTY-ONE

On our way to the beach, Epic decided to stop at home for a few things. I don't know what I expected; the sort of apartments I'd lived in when I was going to school, I guess. He'd called his place one step above dorm living, but the charm of the fourplex he lived in was unlike anything I was used to.

There were two units in front and two in back—each with its own welcoming little porch. Epic's porch was covered with potted plants in various stages of wet. Inside his apartment, there were more, along with the usual youthful bric-a-brac— Funko figurines, LEGO Star Wars toys, and beer bottles. The table in the kitchen was covered in computer equipment, and a gaming setup dominated the living room. His bedroom was little more than a place to rest his head. Full-size bed, chest of drawers, and hamper. All cheaply made.

After the vague little tour, I waited on the porch while Epic got what he wanted. He finally came out with a blanket, a beach umbrella, and a couple of kites. As he locked the door, a Lexus pulled up to the curb. When Epic saw the car, he paled.

"Shit." His shoulders fell. "Buckle up, buttercup."

"I don't understand."

"You will."

The woman in the passenger seat got out and everything fell into place. She was tall and dark-haired with fair skin and an unhappy expression—a frosty Snow White who let the huntsman take her heart because it was an inconvenience. She wore a stylish knit pantsuit with low-heeled pumps.

"Robert." She smiled at Epic, but it was a cool thing. The message? *Don't disappoint me.*

"Chloe." Epic took the visit like a punch to the gut. "I wish I'd known you planned on coming down."

"This is long overdue."

The driver's side door opened, and a man I assumed was Epic's father got out. He wore designer jeans and a billowy sort of shirt with a sweater vest. Though he had a full head of hair, the ponytail he wore made him appear as if he were balding. He wore sunglasses. His smile was bland and magnanimous. *Good cop, bad cop.* Christ, Epic's parents were only a few years older than me.

They took their time retrieving three massive suitcases from the trunk of their car. Each of them rolled one up to the porch and his dad went back for the third.

"Where are your manners, Robert?" demanded Chloe. "Introduce us to your friend."

Epic cleared his throat. "Ryan Winslow, may I present my mother and father, Chloe and Steven Alsop-Gray."

"Pleasure to meet you." I shook Steven's hand. When it came time to exchange a handshake with Chloe, she placed her hand behind her back. Oh, we were off to a solid start.

"So, you're Robert's...?" Steven seemed to run out of steam.

Chloe was much more direct. "How do you know our son?"

Biblically. "He recently helped me out of a jam."

"Is that so?" Chloe asked. "What kind of a jam would you need a twenty-three-year-old waiter to help you out of, I wonder?"

"I went as the plus-one to his ex's wedding," Epic answered truthfully. "His original date cancelled at the last minute."

"Ah. The wedding must be the source of all the pictures from Santa Barbara."

"Exactly." Epic locked the door to his place behind him. "As you know, my apartment is very small, and I have a room-mate. Where will you be staying?"

"We're not staying."

Epic looked pointedly at the suitcases. "You're a little over-packed for a day trip."

Chloe narrowed her eyes. "They're empty, dear. We brought them so you could pack your things."

"Me? What...?" He blanched.

"I'll help, of course."

"No way, Chloe." Epic's weary voice indicated long-term frustration. "I'm not going anywhere."

"I can see you're headed out right now," said Steven. "We'll leave the suitcases and meet back here when you have time. Are you working tonight?"

"At five." Epic looked at a spot in the distance, not at the man and woman who'd raised him.

"So we'll have time to talk if we come at three?" Steven pressed.

"I guess."

Family dynamics box you in young and keep you trapped for a lifetime if you let them. Just like that, the decisive, confi-dent Epic I knew became petulant Master Robert before my eyes. Could Epic break out of the role they'd assigned him? It shouldn't have mattered to me, but it did.

"Where are you headed?" asked Chloe.

Epic glanced at the things he carried—blanket, umbrella, kites—and said, "The British Museum."

His mother gave a long-suffering sigh as we passed them on our way to the sidewalk. For my part, I vacillated between whether to say something more or leave things at that. I could think of nothing besides apologizing for my presence in Epic's life, defending myself, or promising to go away and never come back, so I stayed silent.

We got a little way down the street before we heard the Lexus's doors open and close. The engine started. The car slid slowly past us with his parents staring straight ahead inside it.

"Awkward doesn't begin to cover that," Epic said. "I'm so sorry."

"Are your parents really planning to force you to leave?"

"Pretty much."

A sudden thought occurred to me. Aghast, I asked, "Were you lying when you said you were twenty-three?"

His eyes widened. "No, it's nothing like that. You heard my mom say it."

Relieved, I asked, "Then how can your parents make you move against your will?"

Epic chewed his lip. "They can't really, but it's complicated."

"They obviously think they can, though. Is it money? Did they pay for your tuition, and now they feel like they have a say with regard to your future?"

"Actually, no. I have student loans, but they're small compared to some of my friends'."

"So how can your parents control you?" Wind raked through my hair while I reminded myself I wasn't there to solve Epic's problems. I sighed. "It's none of my business, and I'm sorry if my presence made things more difficult."

"I'm the one who should be sorry. Chloe cast you in the role of defiler of innocents the minute she saw you."

"Right?" At least he didn't try to deny it. "That was a new experience."

He pouted. "This doesn't feel like a happy, kite-flying kind of day anymore."

"I'm sorry." I wrapped my arm around him as best I could,

given we both carried bulky gear. "I can take you out some-place if you'd rather. Shopping?"

"What I really want to do is mope."

"Moping isn't likely to help," I said carefully. "And given what I know about you, it doesn't feel like a thing you do."

"That's why it's so…irritating. My parents and I are oil and water. No matter what I try, we just don't mix."

"You need mustard."

He came to a halt. "Come again?"

"To form an emulsion. What you need is an emulsifying agent like mustard."

He smiled ruefully. "Grandma usually fills that role, I guess."

"Where is she?" I asked. "Can you call her to intercede on your behalf?"

"Maybe."

We'd arrived at a crossroads. We had to turn left if we were still heading for the beach or right if we wanted to go to my rental. Epic chose right, and I followed.

"Grandma and I talked about that the last time my parents got high-handed. We decided that if I didn't handle them myself, I'd never learn how."

"I'm sure even your grandmother didn't expect your folks to show up on your doorstep with empty suitcases."

"I like how you say folks. Do you have folks? I have Parents, capital *P*."

"I have 'folks.' My family is close-knit even though I don't have a lot of time for them."

"You should change that if you can." We entered my rental and dropped the beach things in the foyer. "Can we get in the hot tub?"

"Sure, if that's what you'd like to do."

"Do we have to wear clothes?" He waggled his eyebrows at me.

I shrugged. "I don't live here. Let's shock the neighbors."

He whipped off his shirt. "First one in gets a shoulder massage."

I let him win.

Ten minutes later, Epic leaned both arms on the side of the hot tub while I worked the knots out of his back and shoulders. He sighed happily.

"Three o'clock today," I reminded him.

"Hm?"

"That's high noon as it were. At three o'clock today, you're going to have to talk to your parents. Any idea what you plan to say?"

"What can I say?"

"Start from the beginning. Why are they here now?"

He dropped his head to rest on his arms. "We had a big fight after I got my master's. I wanted to live in St. Nacho's. Mom and Dad sent a blizzard of my CVs to all their business contacts here and abroad. Several companies would have offered me a job on the spot—midlevel finance stuff with an eye toward moving up in the world of fund management. In this economy, getting a job at all right out of school is huge, but I wanted time. We made a deal."

"Let me guess the rest. It's midnight, you're Cinderella, and now you have to leave the ball."

"Right. They called it a belated gap year. Gave me twelve months to 'get it out of my system.'"

"Did you give them your word you'd go home after a year?"

He shrugged. "I gave them my word I'd consider it if I didn't have a better option."

I wanted to laugh. It might be entertaining to watch Epic wiggle his way out of his parents' plans, although they looked pretty formidable. "You'll need to come up with that 'better option' fairly quickly then."

"Well, I was thinking about that when we were talking about your work this morning."

"Were you?" A cooling breeze blew across my neck.

"You have a foreign service and security background, but you're making an unconventional use of it. Just because I have a finance degree, doesn't mean I have to go into finance."

"Go on." I sat back, and he turned and floated to the bench facing mine. The spa jets made it harder to hear him.

"The thing is"—he raised his voice—"I'm a math geek. I've interned as an actuary in hospitals. I could pursue that route. But when I was a kid, I always wanted to be Charlie Epps from *NUMB3RS*. His character used math to solve crimes."

"I remember that show. I can see that being something you'd like."

"The women you talked about, the missing ones? There's definitely a way to model disappearances in the same geographical area to see if the cases are part of a larger picture."

"I know. That's what I do."

"But I could help you. Two heads are better than one, right? I could write an algorithm that tracks certain values like criminal associates and excludes others like prior runaway behavior"—he frowned—"although that could falsely exclude a lot of marginalized people, so—"

"So you plan to tell your parents what?"

He glanced up sharply. "That I want a consulting job with your NGO."

Shit. I blew out a breath. "Okay. Listen. You probably have skills we could use, but you get that it's a nonprofit, right? Nobody there makes a lot of money. And it's in Canada. I live and work there on a permit. You might be able to get a job there, but—"

"What I'd want is a consulting job where I could work remotely. I need to stay in St. Nacho's."

That got my attention. "You need to?"

"I'd prefer to." He caught his lip between his teeth. "Strong preference."

I opened a water bottle and took a sip. "Why St. Nacho's?"

"You probably don't need a lot of background to know my parents are perfectionists. It's virtually impossible to get their approval, so I grew up feeling judged every minute of every single day."

"I'm sorry, Epic. I know that must have hurt you very much."

"I had my grandmother. She made up for a lot of the bad things"

"I'm glad." I took his hands in mine.

He wrinkled his nose. "I have happy memories from childhood too. Despite our current conflict, I love my parents. But I love it in St Nacho's too. The minute I smell the ocean, I've come home. All my problems drop off my shoulders. I can be exactly who I am. Nobody judges me. Nobody tries to change me. What I do matters—whether I wait tables or invent the next iPhone—whatever my job is, only being my best self matters here."

"I understand." It would be awfully tempting to stay.

"The people here make me want to do everything better, but there's no pressure. Does that even make sense?"

"Yes." I'd felt the weight fall off my shoulders when I'd arrived in St. Nacho's too, though I had attributed it to having my first vacation in years.

What if it wasn't about the time off but the place?

What if I could finally find balance here?

"Will you go with me when I talk to my parents?" he asked.

"That seems like a bad idea." I couldn't imagine anything more awful. "Isn't it something you need to do on your own?"

"But I need them to understand what you do. I want them to meet you because then they can't say the job I want doesn't exist, or I can't make a living, or—"

"Epic, taking me with you to talk to your parents is the very worst thing you could do. It negates the argument that you're independent."

"I know, I know. But hear me out —"

"What would your grandmother say?" I stood, took the steps out of the water, and picked up my towel.

"She'd say, yes, it might make them think I'm taking guidance from you, and yes, that might seem like I'm not thinking independently. But she might also say that if I were going to talk about my future, I should consider making my case alongside people I want to be in that future."

I turned, heart pounding hard. "What do you mean?"

"You know what I mean." Epic came out of the water like some sculpture, all chiseled planes and taut muscles. He jutted his jaw at me belligerently. "You've become really important to me."

"I —"

"And I'm important to you. Don't try to deny it. I won't believe you."

"Even if that were true —"

"Oh, it's so true." He wagged a finger at me. "You think I'm adorable."

God help me, he had me there. "Even so, I live in Canada. I work a sixty-hour week when I'm slacking off. I travel for business about a third of the year. I'm not looking for a partner."

"But we're good together, Ryan." He held himself rigid. "Don't make it seem like we're friends with benefits. We're more than that, and you know it."

I did not want to have this conversation.

Not now. Not yet. Maybe not ever. But certainly not while his parents were giving him three hours to make good on a deal he'd made last year.

"Oh, Epic. I'm so sorry. This" — I gestured between us — "is a holiday. We had a fantasy weekend in a wildly expensive resort with fabulous food, alcohol, and great sex."

"Go on." He sounded smaller somehow. Deflated.

"I never meant for you to think that we could...that *I* was looking for more than that. I hope you can forgive me someday."

"Don't lie to yourself and don't lie to me."

"I probably have lied to you," I admitted. "I'm probably lying to myself right now. But things are what they are. Trying to make this thing between us last would only lead to unhappiness and regret later on."

"Fine." He swallowed hard. "I'll go to my parents without your support then."

"I think that's for the best."

"And I have work after. I'm closing late. I'll be exhausted between my parents and work, and...I might just want to sleep at my place tonight."

"That's fine." My heart sank because Epic saw what I was trying to hide. He had grown on me. I liked him. I *wanted* him —wanted to see where this would go between us. But the panic that had flared inside me when I was face to face with his parents... The guilt I experienced when his mother had asked what I needed from a twenty-three-year old caught me in all the raw places left behind from my work with exploited people, and I just couldn't give him this.

This was it. I knew it. If I didn't make an effort, meet him halfway, tell him I would try to make things work between us, I would not see Epic again.

"Call me and let me know what you want to do in the next couple days."

"Sure." He didn't sound as if he meant it.

"I'll be here until Friday around noon."

"Good." He squared his shoulders. "I'll just go get dressed."

———

I GAVE Epic a ride because he had all the beach things to take with him. It didn't escape my notice that he took his clothes and toiletries and pool float too.

"Taking everything?" I wanted him to say it.

"Nothing's clean. I need to do laundry." He refused to meet my gaze.

The bittersweet kiss he gave me after he finally got everything out of the car broke my heart. He imbued it with everything that made him Epic—all the emotion, all the joy, all the nurture, and empathy, and kindness he had to give.

He made all the right noises when he left. Smiled cheerfully. Tried not to make me feel like a monster. But our sorrow had a flavor—the metallic taste of my fear mixed in with sickmaking salty tears neither one of us acknowledged.

Everything had gone wrong. I shouldn't have walked away, and I knew it, but I couldn't stop myself—couldn't make myself choose Epic when I knew the consequences could harm us both.

"I had the best time." Epic kissed my cheek. "Thank you for everything."

"Thank you." *I love you. Love you, love you, love you.*

I was a fool to think I could walk away from Epic undamaged.

Like always, my heart tore itself into pieces because I wanted impossible things.

I WORKED THROUGH DINNER, which was not unusual for me. Later, I walked to a corner market for cup noodles and booze. I eyed the cigarettes for a minute. Had I really decided to quit smoking? Epic wouldn't be around to give me a hard time about it if I didn't...

Two things decided me. First, they didn't have Luis's expensive European brand—of course they didn't. Second, I was over everything *Luis*. Epic was right about why I'd started smoking in the first place. It had been a way to hold on to Luis after he left. An invisible kiss.

"Give me some nicotine gum as well, please," I told the cashier.

She showed me a couple brands, and I picked one at random.

I took my bag back to the rental where I ate salty noodles, drank whiskey, and got my nicotine fix.

Seems like old times.

I texted Epic at bedtime.

Me: How'd it go with your parents? Did you buy more time?"

But my text went unanswered.

Lying in bed with the spins later that night, I tried texting Epic again.

Me: What's the verdict? Are you going to stay in St. Nacho's?

That text went unanswered too.

CHAPTER TWENTY-TWO

The following day my breakfast basket arrived at seven. I placed it on the kitchen table next to my laptop and drank most of the coffee by eleven. Between the caffeine and the sugar from picking at pastries all morning, I decided I'd better get a salad for lunch.

Bistro was busy when I got there, but there was no sign of Epic. He often worked the dinner shift, so I didn't bother asking after him and no one said anything about him to me.

I walked back to the rental and spent the rest of the day going over some missing person cases in Eastern Canada. I made calls, requesting relevant information. It wasn't my first time calling the hotlines. Usually, the reception I got was positive.

More and more my thoughts drifted to Epic. He still hadn't answered my texts, and the longer the silence went on, the larger the possibility grew that he wasn't going to respond at all.

I tried again.

Me: Are you not answering because you don't want to talk to me?

Fifteen minutes ticked by before anything happened.

Epic: I need time.

Me: Can you at least tell me what happened? Because I'm concerned.

An hour without a reply was a reply in itself, wasn't it? I'd pissed Epic off and now he was ghosting me. There was nothing I could, or should, do about it.

Nevertheless, I went to Bistro again at dinnertime when I thought Epic would be on shift. Except I didn't see him anywhere.

I waited until someone came to seat me and asked, "Is Epic working tonight?"

She searched under the hostess desk and brought out a clipboard. Her brows drew together. "He's not scheduled to work for the rest of this week or next."

"Oh, really? Wow. That's odd." I ordered a meatloaf sandwich and a mango lassi to go. When it came, she offered it to me in a paper shopping bag with twine handles. "Thank you."

On the way home, I stopped by Epic's place.

Last thing I'll try.

I won't be stupid about this, but I have to try.

Bea answered my knock.

"Oh, hey. Hi." She opened the door with the chain in place. "Epic's not here."

"I looked for him at Bistro. They said he's not scheduled to work. Do you know where he went?"

"Didn't he tell you?" She flushed beneath a layer of worn-off makeup.

"I'm afraid not." I met her gaze. "Full disclosure, he's not answering my texts either."

"Well, he's not here." She pressed her lips together.

"Can I leave a message with you?" In the background, I heard the television. She moved to close the door, and I figured that was that, but she undid the chain and opened it wider.

"Text him again," she advised. "If he wants to talk, he'll get back to you."

"But do you know where—"

"All I know is that he went home. His parents came and got him. I have to look for a new roommate now." She didn't *exactly* say this was all my fault.

"I'm sorry."

"He and his parents had a deal." With the added light from outside, I could tell she'd been crying. "One year in St. Nacho's and then he goes out into the real world. I always knew he'd go, but I'm surprised how quickly it happened."

"Me too. Obviously." I didn't want our last kiss to be the end. I never meant to say goodbye this way. "Do you have a forwarding address for him?

"I can't give you that." She glanced down. "He has a phone. If he wants to talk to you, he will."

"Can you at least give me his email address?" I could probably find it, but asking was easier.

She went into the apartment and came back with a Post-it note. "This is the only one I know. I'm not sure he checks it very often."

I grimaced. "I have to try."

She shrugged. "Good luck."

"You too." I thanked her and left feeling, if possible, worse than when I'd set off on this journey.

THAT NIGHT, I got together with Dan and Cam at Nacho's Bar to say goodbye.

I was happy to see them, but I didn't feel like partying. The atmosphere in the bar was too loud. The beat of dance music thudded in my aching, hollow core.

"Disco night." Cam wrinkled his nose. "Sorry."

"No worries." I had to shout to be heard. I ordered a double bourbon and nachos with steak fajitas to keep me from getting too drunk.

"Tell me more about the wedding," Dan said. "What is William like?"

"The wedding and William were both very luxurious." I gave him a rundown of events—how I'd had fun with Epic, the tapas party, even the big proposition—as I got my swerve on.

"Wait. William did *what*?" Dan's eyes widened.

"Apparently they wanted to share me or something. William said he wouldn't be jealous of me if he got to fuck me too." Unfortunately, I shouted that information during a lull in the music, and several heads turned my way. I hid behind my glass.

Cam snorted. "What did you do?"

"I turned them down. What do you think? Epic nearly challenged William to a duel. That boy was so goddamned adorable the whole time. I'm going to miss him so much."

"Our Epic got angry?" Cam asked.

Dan said, "That answers my other question."

Of course he'd been curious whether Epic and I had come back more than friends.

I spun my drink mat. "I guess."

"He is an engaging kid," said Dan.

"He's a lot more than that," I admitted.

"Tell us," said Cam.

"Epic is a very smart, very confident guy. He's funny and silly—" The waiter set the nachos in the middle of the table and gave us each a small plate and napkins. "Thanks."

"So you got to know him well while you were gone?"

"You know how road trips are. Forced proximity adds intimacy. Laurie upgraded us to a really high-end suite. The whole trip from beginning to end was like a fairy tale."

"I can't imagine you playing mini-golf."

"Yeah, well, there's no evidence that I know of, although…" I took out my phone. "Epic's mother alluded to pictures."

A little searching turned up Epic's Instagram, and yes… there we were. I scrolled back through the last few days.

"I stand corrected." I showed them the picture of me trying to putt into the revolving drawbridges. My expression showed frustration but also a kind of indulgent humor.

"Oh my god," Cam said. "Look at you doing an outdoor activity."

"Why are you shiny?" asked Dan.

"Sunscreen." I scooped a mound of cheesy, beefy chips onto my plate. "Epic is a huge fan of sunscreen."

"Oh, you got a hat." Dan looked at each picture carefully. "Looks good."

"You did not ride a tandem bicycle." Cam did something to my phone that made his chime. "That's ridiculously romantic."

"Like I said…things just…sort of…"

"Clicked," Dan held up a picture of me and Epic in black tie. "Seriously. You guys look like you've been together forever here."

"No wonder his parents reacted the way they did," I said. "I am a *defiler* of innocent young men."

"You're not." Cam handed my phone back. "You're in love. Anyone can see it."

"I—" *I couldn't argue the point.*

"So what's going to happen now? Are you going to try to make it work? Long-distance relationships are tough, but—"

"Nothing's going to happen. Fairy tales aren't real."

Cam's face fell. "Oh, Ryan."

"Anyway, Epic moved back in with his family. He has to get a real job and start his life."

"I'm so sorry," Cam said gently.

"It's not as if it has anything to do with me. Moving back with his parents was the plan all along. I guess our trip was a last hurrah before he had to get serious."

"That doesn't sound like Epic." Cam sipped his beer. "I've gotten to know him since he started at Bistro, and I didn't think he'd ever leave Santo Ignacio. He really seemed to want to be part of the community."

I'd had just enough alcohol to loosen my tongue. "Yesterday, when his parents came, he started talking about my job and how he thought he could find ways to streamline my process through the use of mathematical modeling."

"What does that have to do with him leaving St. Nacho's?" asked Cam.

I picked at my food. "He made certain assumptions about me and my work that—"

"He thought you'd continue your relationship?" asked Dan.

"Apparently."

"What's wrong with that?" Cam waved to the waitress for another beer.

"Nothing. It's just impossible is all. It could never work between us. Especially not with his parents—who by the way are only a couple years my senior—breathing down our necks."

"You don't know that for certain." Between the two of them, Cam was the true romantic. Blunt as a fire ax, handsome, kind, and caring, Cam Rooney probably invented fairy tales. He was made of heroic stuff.

"He wanted me to go with him to talk to his parents." I pushed my uneaten food away. "And I couldn't do it."

"Why not?"

"What was I going to say? Yeah, I've been banging your twenty-three-year-old son all weekend, and I think he should come work for my company in Canada where I live?"

"Is that why he wanted you there? To make some kind of declaration about your intentions?"

I shook my head. "He said he wanted me to make the case that he could use his skills outside the financial sector. He thought StolenLives could benefit from someone with his skill set."

"So why didn't you go?" asked Dan. "That sounds very plausible."

I moved my chips around without picking one up. "It's a good idea actually."

"So why didn't you back him up?" Cam asked.

"Because I thought they'd accuse me of putting ideas in his head."

Cam scoffed. "Epic has tons of ideas of his own."

"No kidding."

"Admit it. You punked out over the parental thing."

"I did." I covered my face with both hands. "Oh my God, I did. You have no idea what his mother was like. She'd seen the pictures from his Instagram and had me pegged as some chicken hawk. I have never been so—"

"Guilty as charged?"

I poked at a spot on the table. "Look. I might have asked Epic to the wedding because he's young and beautiful—that's the type of guy you take to an ex's wedding—but you have no idea how utterly perfect he is in every other way that matters. He's an intelligent, generous, loving man. Compared to him, I'm a one-trick pony."

"You're not, though. And you can fix this." Cam put his hand over mine.

"How? I don't even know where he's gone. Plus, he wants to live here. Everything I have is up north."

"Does it have to be?"

I opened my mouth to say yes, but it felt like a lie. Certainly, my work was there. And my work was my life, wasn't it? It was the best part of me—the part I was most proud of.

How could I walk away and still be worthy of a person like Epic?

"I don't know the answer to that anymore."

"Then maybe you need to figure it out." Cam patted my

hand and went back to eating. The waitress brought his beer, and I ordered another bourbon and a draft beer to chase it.

Dan didn't say anything. Cam wasn't as laissez-faire. He eyed my empty glass.

"I hope you didn't drive."

"I'll walk," I said with more confidence than I felt. "I could use the fresh air."

"Dan will drive you. You might never find your place otherwise."

My eyelids felt heavy. "I'm at one of Ken Ashton's rentals. I kind of wish I lived in a place like that. I wish—"

"We know." Dan and Cam exchanged glances while I picked at my food. "Ken's my business partner. He's got a real estate license. He could probably find you a place here."

"I wish I could be two people." I bit into a chip. "One for work, another for home and dating and maybe someday, a family. But time isn't in infinite supply, and I believe the work I do with StolenLives is important enough to make certain sacrifices."

"That's bullshit," Dan said angrily. "Luis made you believe you had to sacrifice one for the other, but you could make it work. You could find balance if you wanted to."

"I can't see how." The waiter arrived with my drinks. "This hurts more than losing Luis. I feel like I've lost part of myself."

"Aw, bro." Cam patted my back. "St. Nacho's has a weird way of making things work out when you least expect it."

I snorted. "Everyone talks like this is some magical Christmas movie locale."

"It's not magic"—Cam took a sip of his beer—"it's fate."

CHAPTER TWENTY-THREE

The next morning, I gave up on texting and decided to try emails. Even if he didn't necessarily want them, even if he didn't read them, I found it sort of therapeutic to write them.

EPIC,

I know we said goodbye, but that was supposed to be for temporary. I wish you'd been more honest with me about things. There are goodbyes and goodbyes. I'd have liked the opportunity to say the right one, which is:

I'm so glad we met. I'm so glad I got to know you. I had a wonderful time with you in Santa Barbara, despite my misgivings about attending Luis's wedding.

You're an amazing person, and I can't wait to see all the important things you're going to do. I wish I could have done more to help the situation with your parents.

I hope you make your dreams come true. Fight for yourself—for what you want to do. If that doesn't exist already, then get out there and invent it. I believe in you.

Best,
Ryan

I HIT SEND, packed up, and left St. Nacho's at noon. The drive north on the cloudy coast gave me plenty of opportunity to think. I didn't stop for many breaks, but when I did, I checked my email for any sign Epic had written me back. By the time I got to Santa Cruz, he'd sent something. I read it eagerly.

RYAN,

I wasn't going to answer this. I went back and forth because we did say a kind of goodbye, which was:

I'm glad we met too. I wanted more. You didn't. The end.

That's fine, honestly. As you pointed out, I'm very young still, and things can't possibly be as meaningful to me as they are to someone with as much worldly experience as you have.

While I'm sure you already know this, you should probably take your own fucking advice.

Best,
Epic

STUNG BADLY, I replied right away.

EPIC,

It's a pity they haven't yet invented the sarcasm font. That would have made it easier to spot at a distance just how much of your note would hurt. You should wear several warning signs: "Caution, sharp

edges," being only one. Others might say, "Contents may be habit form-
ing," "Deep water," and the ever-popular "Slippery when wet."

I'm sorry, again. I know saying "I'm sorry" without resolving the
thing you're sorry for sounds like, "Sorry, not sorry."

How did we get here of all places?

Of course my feelings for you are more. And as Cam and Dan
rightfully pointed out to me, I punked out on you disastrously by not
facing your parents when you asked me for help. I should have had your
back, made the argument that you can—and should if it's what you
want—find work outside the financial sector.

Your math skills are useful in a range of applications, and you're a
competent adult. You don't need to go into the field they chose for you if
you don't want to.

I should have backed your play, and I'm sorry I didn't.

Instead, I got tangled up in what your parents might think of me.
How they'd treat me after I took you away for a weekend of tuxedo-clad
debauchery.

I let my ego take over my conscience, and I'm sorry.

I'm on my way north. I could meet you when I pass through the Bay
Area. If you want to give me a second chance to do the right thing, I'll do
my best to help you persuade your parents that places like StolenLives
would be lucky to have you. I'll also give you the direct line of our chair-
person, Lila Newcastle, and a great recommendation.

With warmth and best wishes,

Ryan

I STOPPED in San Francisco for the night a couple hours later.
Normally, it was one of my favorite cities. I traveled there a lot
on business. When I wasn't strictly on the job, I spent time
shopping, walking, or eating in the many great restaurants.
This time, I stayed in my hotel room, waiting for Epic's reply.

Dear Ryan,

I don't need you to persuade my parents of anything.

Now that you're being all nice and shit, I'm forced to admit I shouldn't have asked you to go with me to confront them in the first place. You'd have been a serious distraction. Things would more than likely have gotten ugly.

And okay, maybe you were right to press pause too.

I probably misread things between us. I can honestly say I wished for things that are just impossible if you aren't on the same page. I pushed too hard too fast. But you're mine. I know you're mine, and I guess I have to wait for you to figure it out too.

I love how important your job is to you. That's one of the things I find so attractive about you. I've never met anyone who feels so passionately about their work. Not anyone whose work is worth that passion anyway. But if you're going to be Sisyphus, then you have to understand the things we are supposed to learn from him. There's a reason for the myth. Yes, sometimes we're destined to fight a losing battle. You've obviously embraced yours. You need to pace yourself. You need to take care of your body, mind, and spirit if you're going to fight uphill all the time.

I love that your job is not just some rock you're rolling.

I love the possibility that you might be saving human lives.

I want to be part of that. I will find a way, just you wait.

I can't meet you while you're here. I don't need you to hold my hand with Steven and Chloe. This is my hill. My battle.

I have to invent the thing I need.

When I do, you'll be the first to know.

With warmest wishes,

Epic

P.S. Next you'll be trying to slide all up in my snail mailbox. Only boomers write actual letters anymore.

In the morning, I ordered an American breakfast, a fruit bowl, and a pot of coffee. I felt strangely good—relieved—

despite being on the road all day the day before. I guess the fact I didn't drink myself to sleep the night before had something to do with my positive mood, but Epic's willingness to forgive me and an open line of communication between us made all the difference.

Before I left the hotel, I sent another note.

Dear Epic,

You know I'm a millennial, right? There's nothing boomer about me.

And just because your kind can converse in one hundred forty characters or fewer with no punctuation doesn't mean you should.

There was a time when the manly arts included painting and poetry. Have you never watched Chinese palace dramas?

At any rate, I'm going to defend my email writing because I like feeling connected to you even in this small way. I hit Send, and then I stall out while waiting for you to reply. It's as if my heart comes to life when I see your name in my inbox.

Going to your place and finding you gone hurt. I'm not going to lie. I miss you. I miss us. That's the truth.

But I don't know what I could have done differently.

Whatever you do, wherever you are, at least take my words with you. Give me your words in return.

Yours,

Ryan

THE NEXT REPLY didn't come until I was back in Vancouver.

I keyed the lock on my apartment door. Inside, I found the same serviceable, monochromatic design scheme. Gray walls, charcoal couch, wood floors with a gray rug in a geometric pattern.

My place could have been a page in any furniture cata-
logue. Well lit, nice windows with natural light. Archeologi-
cally themed knickknacks were all that said *decor*. Without
those, my place could be interchanged with any other apartment on this floor.

The living room smelled of lemon cleaner and beeswax
candles.

In the bedroom, I placed my suitcase and garment bag on
the bed where I emptied them routinely. I filled a laundry
hamper, hung up the suits, and placed my toiletry kit under the
sink for the next trip.

The air tasted staler in there. Musty and smoky from my
clothes. The bedding needed changed. I opened a window to
let in fresh air.

In the bath, I sat on the lip of the tub, listening for the
longest time.

I don't know what I expected to hear. Plumbing sounds. A
door opening or closing in the hall. The occasional honk of a
horn from the traffic on the street below. Nothing human. No
children's laughter or barking dogs. No wind or waves. No
music drifting on the breeze from Nacho's Bar.

The world I lived in seemed sterile and uninhabited by
comparison. How had I never noticed?

I went to my home office and booted up my desktop
computer where I checked for messages from Epic. My unread
emails numbered in the high fifties, but the only one I cared
about was his. I opened it first.

Dear Ryan,

You miss us?

*Now you're going to say that? Now, when I'm a thousand miles
away?*

I told you so. I goddamn told you so. You're such a fucking tool

sometimes, I swear.
What do you want to do about that?
Epic

Oh, Epic. The moment we met I lagged a thousand miles behind you. Didn't you see me, always trying to catch up?

EPIC,

What do you want me to do? Obviously, shutting us down the way I did hurt both of us, but I honestly couldn't see a different path. I'm entrenched. My last serious relationship failed, not because I didn't love my partner or because he didn't love me, but because I couldn't walk away from my job.

It wasn't right for me to put my work before his needs.
How would it be any different with you?
Ryan

RYAN,

This is why I shouldn't have left the way I did.
I was hurt, and I wanted to hurt you back.
Still, I'm glad I didn't do things differently because distance is what makes this conversation possible. There's an economy to words in written form. I think about what I say before I say it. Plus, I can fake the mature-adult thing pretty well when I have time to edit. I probably would have kicked you in the shins if I'd stayed.

You said to find what I want to do and fight for it, and if that thing didn't exist, I should invent it.

Were you serious about that?

Because what I want is to live in St. Nacho's, dedicate my skills to

209

the work you do, and pursue you, even into hell if I have to.
    Tell me now if the answer is no.
    The rest is details.
    Yours? You are [still] mine.
    Epic

MY HANDS SHOOK when I read his message. I wavered between giddy and indignant. How could he be so brash? How was he so confident when I'd obviously tried the thing he was so certain of and failed?

He was young, so he thought he could have it all. And of course life would beat sense into him eventually, but I wished it wouldn't. I was ambivalent about him winning in the end—I wanted what he wanted, so of course I hoped we could find an answer. But I was keenly aware that if he was able to make things work, that would mean I couldn't because I was a failure, not because things were impossible.

I couldn't answer. I feared putting what I wanted—the things I deeply, sincerely, and with all my heart yearned for—into writing so goddamn badly that I worked through my other fifty-seven emails first.

Not only did answering those emails take me the better part of Sunday, the blank futility of their contents swept me into the undertow of my work mindset.

The following morning I was expected to be back at my desk, ready to wade into all the evils of the world. The time I'd spent away was already behind me. The magic of it dissipating like so much fairy dust.

Except for the deeply hidden place in my heart where Epic had carved his initials, things had already started back to normal, but for the first time in my entire life, normal wasn't going to be good enough.

I would never be content again, unless I asked for *more.*

CHAPTER TWENTY-FOUR

The office barely rippled when I walked in Monday morning. Cary at reception glanced up and smiled.

"Mrs. Newcastle wants you to check in this morning before you get entrenched, and there were several messages for you while you were out."

After having been in the US for a short while, Cary's accent was noticeable again.

"Thank you." I took the message slips from her and headed for Lila's office.

I knocked, and she called, "Come in."

Her office smelled of coffee and lavender. The seascape paintings echoed the distant sea view from her windows—bottle-green ocean with a cloudy gray sky.

"Welcome back."

"Thanks. Glad to be back. Anything major happen while I was gone?"

She wore a purple pantsuit today. The ensemble, along with a yellow scarf embroidered all over with violets, made her silver hair and gray eyes brighter by contrast.

"Get a coffee and sit. How was the wedding?"

"Ostentatious," I said while pouring myself a cup at the sideboard. "I'm sure you can imagine."

"Yes, knowing Luis." She sighed. "Are you glad you went?"

"Yes and no," I replied with honesty. "I got closure."

"And Laurie? Did he perform as expected? Were all the guests in awe?"

"Laurie couldn't make it. Something about having to film scenes over with a different actor."

She spread her hands on her desk. "Oh, how devastating."

I sat in the chair across from her. "I was upset at first, but I was able to get a last-minute replacement, and we had loads of fun."

Understatement of the year.

"That's good, anyway." She adjusted her scarf primly. "There's no going alone to an ex's wedding."

"Right?" I wanted to change the topic, so I asked, "Tell me about the missing drones? Have you heard from your contact in Mexico?"

Several minutes of drone footage had given us confirmation that a well-known cartel used kidnapping and extortion to attain forced labor to manufacture cocaine. The victims were mostly the children of peripheral associates. Some had been as young as twelve.

"My contact is safe, but she said the area is impossible to infiltrate now. After the drones were discovered, they doubled the number of guards and added booby traps in the area. But the original footage has generated a great deal of interest from law enforcement and government officials."

"That's good to know."

"A nine-year-old girl disappeared in northern Minnesota, but it's likely a custody dispute between parents. It's doubtful the case relates to the ones you've been working on there."

"I'll look into it."

"That's about all I can think of right now. You'll find the rest of the updates on our watch list. We'll scrum at ten."

"I'll be there."

She smiled, revealing her dimples. "Good to have you back. I've missed you."

"I missed you too." I took my coffee with me when I left.

IT TOOK all day to catch myself up on all the different tangents I'd been following in the weeks before my vacation. It was frankly sad to see how little things had changed. I measured progress in microscopically small units, and still, barely anything had happened that I could call progress while I was gone.

It only took a few hours for the real challenge of my job to subsume me. I saw a crime being committed—actual drone footage of a forced labor camp—yet there was nothing I could do about it but pass that information along and go back to gathering more.

For all my frustration, day turned quickly into night as I researched each tiny detail, each tidbit of information, in order to glean the next and the next.

I left when the cleaners came to vacuum my office and walked through the darkened building to my car alone.

On the way home, I got takeout from a Chinese place that stayed open late and ate it over my kitchen sink.

I realized that, in spite of everything I'd said and done while I was away with Epic, nothing had changed. Yet everything was different.

I had changed.

What I'd seen as a choice—to work because my work was the most important thing in my life—now seemed more like a hole in which I'd buried myself and all the hope I'd once had for a balanced, happy life.

Why couldn't I have that?

Why shouldn't I?

From the goddamned hole, it felt too dark to find my way out. I needed *clarity*. I needed help and nurturing and maybe a little tough love. I needed all the things Epic had offered me and probably a lot more that he hadn't. Those, I knew—in the depths of my ridiculous heart—he'd be willing to give if I only asked.

There was nothing new in my inbox from Epic that night. I hadn't answered his last email, and I could see why he'd waited for a reply. He had basically laid everything on the line, and I had to make the next move.

But blunt Epic—frighteningly brazen Epic—I was not.

I was more of a follower than a leader. He had to know that. He had to know that men who hide away in their lairs to analyze data are not the light cavalry of the modern day.

What was he really saying when he'd signed off, "Yours?"

... WHAT I WANT IS to live in St. Nacho's, dedicate my skills to the work you do, and pursue you, even into hell if I have to.

Tell me now if the answer is no.

The rest is details.

Yours? You are [still] mine.

Epic

I THOUGHT about how to answer for a long time. I thought about how it would feel to put my heart out there and fail. I thought about how I'd feel if we only ended up prolonging the heartache. We'd spent so little time together. There were so many hurdles between us. Yet I saw him when I closed my eyes at night. I reached for him when I woke.

Nothing could have prepared me for these feelings—longing, and wonder, and hope.

In the end, I went with my gut.

Epic,

God yes. I want that too. It took only one single day at work for me to realize I'm not likely to get what I want unless I ask someone like you to step in and help me out of this morass I've created.

I went to work this morning with an intact personality, and hopes, and dreams, and then I started pulling threads and couldn't stop. I left when the office cleaners forced me to. I ate takeout over the sink so I could shower, sleep, and do it all again tomorrow.

My life is never what I intend—it's only what happens.

I think I might actually be defective.

Is that why I couldn't make things work with Luis? Because I'm incapable of taking care of myself, much less another human being?

Am I only a bloodhound and my work the scent that makes me run? I think that would be fine, except that in this work, there are always a thousand unfinished hunts. A new one comes up every minute.

I can't tell whether this is an accurate depiction of my day or if it's just late and I'm tired and talking nonsense. I don't know if I can do this anymore.

I don't even know what I'm asking for. Or maybe yes, I need moonlight.

My answer is not—could never be—no. Not to you, Epic. Not to everything you are and everything you offer. Yet I'm afraid I may have to leave these particular details to you.

Is that wrong of me?

Can you forgive me for that?

Yes, yes, yes I'm yours if you want me, defective as I am. I want you to be mine.

I've figured out what I'm asking for.

You're so fucking young, and you have everything bright and beautiful ahead of you, but I'm asking you to claim me and save me, whether I'm worthy of you or not.

Of course I'm yours. You are [still] mine too.
Ryan

———

I DIDN'T HIT SEND RIGHT AWAY because after writing that I'd never felt so goddamn wrecked. I'd never poured my heart out like that for anyone, and it scared me. What if I was wrong about him? What if he and I were still fake boyfriends? What if I was taking the whole fucking thing too seriously, and he was simply stringing me along?

Please don't claim me, I wanted to say. *Please don't save me.* Because if things between us didn't work out, I didn't think I'd survive the loss.

Five minutes after I hit Send, my phone rang.

"Whoa, whoa, whoa." Epic's voice sounded tight. "Are you hyperventilating? Do you have a paper bag?"

"What are you talking about?"

"What the fuck? *Worthy of you? Claim you? Save you?* Did you eat?"

"Yes."

"Okay, so talk me through this. Wasn't this your first day back at work?"

I sighed. "Yes."

"So what happened to make you sound like I should climb your hair up a tower and fight a witch?"

I laughed; I couldn't help myself.

I laughed.

And laughed some more.

While I was prostrate with mirth, I heard Epic's voice, but I couldn't make out the actual words coming from my phone. The squawk-squawk sound made the situation more hilarious still, as if I was Charlie Brown, and Epic was Miss Othmar. *Wah-wah-wah.*

When I finally got a grip, I wiped my eyes and picked up

the thread. "...or are we having a little tête-à-tête with our friend Jack? Because you've totally lost the plot."

"Nope," I sighed. "No Jack."

"Jim? Jose?"

"Not even the Captain. That may be part of the problem, and it's all your fault. I've given up my usual coping strategies."

"Oh, sweetheart. You dope." His voice turned velvety soft and warm as honey straight from the hive in summer. "That wasn't coping."

"I know." I loved when he called me sweetheart. It made me weak in the knees. I left my office and lay down on my bed. "So, I guess we're talking now?"

He huffed. "Seems like."

"How are you?"

"It's a laugh a minute here, let me tell you." I could practically hear his eye roll. "Steven and Chloe keep sharing stories of their wild younger days."

"Why?"

"I don't know. Maybe to convince me they were once human? Whatever. You haven't lived until you've heard my mother describe naked psychedelic-drug shenanigans. I'm surprised my ears aren't bleeding."

"I can't picture your mom—"

"Be *glad*," he moaned. "Because there are actual pictures. I put my foot down hard there."

"Your family is so weird. Did you ever learn why your parents changed so drastically?"

"You know, honestly, I have no idea."

"Don't hate them for wanting what they think is best for you."

"I don't." he insisted. "They were pretty tough academically, and we're having a hard time now, but they were nice when I was growing up. They attended my soccer games and took me to Disneyland. We're going to be fine. Eventually. It's just tough going now because they're really entrenched."

"That's actually nice to hear. They seemed pretty cold."

"That's because I won't change my mind about what I want to do. I told them that. They're still trying to convince me a stint in some global asset management company holds the promise of happiness, but they're deluded. I have other options that are just as valid but not as lucrative. They'll have to adjust."

"I wish I'd had half your self-possession when I was your age."

"Guh. You sound like them with the *when-I-was-your-age* crap."

"Sorry."

"And you wish you were as self-possessed as I am at your age now. Don't lie. Jesus."

He was right of course. "I won't."

"Okay, so, now that we're talking, we should also be texting. I'll be expecting a good morning and a good night every single day from now on."

"Oh you will, huh?"

"I will. And if I don't hear from you, I will take drastic measures."

"What would those be?"

"I'll pay some random Canadian to tickle you until you squeal. Don't think I won't. The exchange rate alone—"

"Tickle me? You'd—okay. Wow." I actually shivered at the thought.

There was a long pause. "You like to be tickled?"

I hesitated before answering. "Maybe?"

"Christ. You couldn't have let me know that while we were in Santa Barbara?"

"It didn't come up." I ran my hand over my duvet, new ideas forming.

"*It* sure the hell would have if I'd known."

"You are so…fucking—"

"What?" he asked bluntly. "What am I so fucking? You? Because that's a yes."

"Er…dominating?"

"What was your first clue, sweetheart?" His voice thickened. "Was it when I rimmed your sweet pink hole? When I edged you out of your mind then made you wear a plug to your ex's wedding? When I fucked you so hard you probably still feel me inside you?"

"Um…yeah. Except no. Sadly, I don't feel you. Wish I did."

"Why do you live in Canada again?" Was that a whine? Was Epic whining now?

"Work."

"Fuck work," he said flatly.

"Speaking of, I do have to be in LA next month. Want to drive down?"

"LA?" he asked. "What for?"

"I'm being given a humanitarian award. First one, not that I expect to get more, it's just—"

"For what?"

"I compiled some information about a group trafficking sex work and child pornography in North Dakota. StolenLives is getting a generous donation from a corporation headquartered there too."

"North Dakota?" he asked quietly. "What corporation?"

"AIM Environmental Energy. Have you heard of it?"

"Yes, I have actually. North Dakota ranks tenth in the US as far as applied wind energy technology."

"Right. So the company's got these awards called "Greenies" but they're adding a humanitarian award this year. I'll be staying at the Bonaventure if you want to join me. It's not the Four Seasons, but that's where they're holding the banquet."

"Send me the dates, and I'll fly down."

"Will your parents—"

"They haven't got a say. Can you take a few extra days?"

"I'm afraid I only have Friday and Saturday. I need to be back to work on Monday."

He was quiet for a few seconds. "Did you hear that?"

"What?"

"We just made our first plans as not-fake boyfriends."

"Oh." I hadn't noticed. "So, we don't have to call ourselves fake anymore?"

I heard him sigh audibly. "Was it ever really fake for you, Ryan?"

"No," I admitted, throat tight. "It never, ever was."

"Well, my work here is done." Epic's light laughter was so sweet it brought tears to my eyes. "Keep in touch, sweetheart. Get some sleep."

"All right," I whispered. "You too."

CHAPTER TWENTY-FIVE

O ne Month Later

"You're here? Where?" I looked around the crowded lobby.

"I'm in the bar." The noise level around Epic's words was extra loud.

"Ooh, good place. Order me a Maker's Mark. Be there in no time."

The Bonaventure's massive lobby featured shops, a restaurant, a bar, fountains, and a dozen seating areas all built around and between elevator towers. I rounded the central tower and found Epic seated at the bar with his pilot case beside him. He had our drinks in front of him and a warm, welcoming smile on his face.

"God, it's good to see you." I didn't hesitate to pull him in for an embrace. Given the crowd around us, I left kissing for later. He took my hand.

"You too. Sit."

I sat.

"How is it possible"—Epic jiggled his drink so the ice clattered—"that you're even hotter than the last time I saw you?"

"Smooth talker."

"You look delicious." He covered my hand with his. "I have plans for you."

"I gained five pounds quitting cigarettes."

"You needed it. When we met, I could feel your ribs."

"You could feel them again right now if we go up to my room."

He flushed and glanced away. "I'm trying to be respectful here. Trying not to jump your ass in the first ten seconds."

"Then I hope you fail spectacularly." I sipped my whiskey.

"We have all night," he pointed out. "You need to treat me to a nice dinner at least."

"I'm at your service. Where would monsieur like to go?"

"I hear they have a nice restaurant here."

"I'm sure they do."

"And a revolving cocktail lounge?"

"Yup."

"Then we won't need to give LA traffic any more of our time." He slung his arm over the back of my chair. "The ride from the airport took forever."

"LA's a nightmare."

"I'll take St. Nacho's any day, thank you."

I agreed wholeheartedly. I would too if it were possible. "How are your parents taking your decision to move back there?"

"It's a slow process. You convincing Lila to hire me on as a consultant made things a lot easier."

"You're an asset," I reminded him. "And as you get up to speed, I'm sure you'll prove your worth in a dozen different ways. Lila likes you, by the way. She often asks about you."

"Have you talked to her about the possibility of working remotely?"

With a sigh, I shook my head. "It's not that simple in my case."

He patted my hand. "That's okay. Baby steps."

"I'm frankly worried how she'll take the idea. I've been there twelve years. It was my first real job after college."

"I know."

"I have it so good there. I don't want to shake things up and lose everything for what amounts to an experiment."

He stiffened.

"I meant working remotely, not being with you. You are a fait accompli in my book. No question."

"I knew that." He turned back toward the bar and his drink, which he studied as though it held answers. "Remote work is the future. I really believe that. Some employers think that if people aren't at a physical building, they'll work fewer hours, but several studies have found they actually work more."

"I've heard that."

"Besides, you practically work around the clock as it is. I'm sure Lila would have no fear of you slacking off to take up gaming or whatever."

"Everyone seems to think I should work fewer hours."

"True that. Especially tonight. Tonight, you'll have to let me do all the work."

My face burned because I could totally get behind that idea. I sat back and let him talk about his parents, about his flight, about looking for a suitable place to live in St. Nacho's and finding more contract work so he could afford it.

We laughed together. Ordered a second drink.

Eventually he wound down.

"Take me upstairs, Ryan." He bit his lip in a coy way that made me hard. "I brought you a present."

"Oh yeah?" I got our tab and left some bills on the bar before sliding from my chair. "Should I be scared?"

"You"—Epic eyed me—"should be tickled pink. Where to?"

"Green elevator. Fifteenth floor."

He led me there and pressed the Up button. We waited patiently with seven other people before boarding and stared at the numbers while the car rose into the sky. There's a point in the ride where the car passes through the roof, and then you're outside, with a view of the city. I only had eyes for Epic.

We made it to the room where I keyed the lock and let him in. He was on me before his suitcase hit the ground, peeling away my shirt and unzipping my trousers. My head swam as I tried to return the favor, but my hands shook so hard I couldn't do it.

I'd left the Do Not Disturb sign out so the maids wouldn't bother cleaning. The king-size bed was still unmade from the morning. He dropped me into its softness and fell on top of me, wrestling me out of my clothes.

"Gonna be hard and fast," he told me. "Can't wait."

"Me neither," I gasped. "Bring it."

I had lube and condoms ready, hoping he wanted this as much as I did. He telegraphed his need by the flush on his chest, his rapid breathing, his trembling fingers when he opened and readied me. He'd barely unzipped, and I guessed he planned to fuck me fully dressed, which added some hot new level of sexy I never imagined existed.

"This is so hot. Fuck me...*now*."

"Don't want to hurt you."

"You won't. Please," I begged him. "*Please*. You won't hurt me. I've waited too long for this."

He held both my hands with one of his and pushed inside me. It was perfect. He was perfect—graceless and needy. Each arch of his back and jerk of his hips drove me higher and higher. I wrapped my legs around him and clung like a sloth. He clenched my hands in his. I was helpless, but I took what I needed. I scraped my cock against his belly with each thrust, dragging it over slick skin and crisp hair while uttering helpless, shocked little noises with each push and pull.

Epic's movements grew frenzied.

He overwhelmed me—amazing, and savage, and solemn all at the same time.

"So gorgeous," he whispered next to my ear. "Who do you belong to?"

My orgasm built, and I let my head fall back with a cry.

"Say it. Who?"

"You," I cried out. "Yours. All yours. Oh God. There... Right. Fucking. There."

"Come for me. I want to see it. Come on my cock, sweetheart."

I let go and stiffened around him, clenching my legs to hold him tight and gripping his fingers with everything I had.

He milked my orgasm for as long as I could sustain it.

A noise I barely recognized as coming from me seared my throat.

"That's it, Ryan. That's it. Give it all to me." He stiffened and came with little halting jerks of his hips that brought me along for another few spasms of pleasure. "That's it. That's it, sweetheart."

My body felt boneless, weary, and energized at the same time.

As he almost always did, he blinked owlishly at me while he pulled out, then dropped the condom over the side of the bed. His eyes drifted closed, and he fell asleep.

That wasn't ever going to get old.

I got up to clean myself in the bath, then took a washcloth into the bedroom so I could undress and clean him. I covered him gently before pulling on a robe.

While he napped, I moved to the armchair to look at the sprawling metropolis that was LA. I couldn't remember the last time I'd felt as content—or rather, as content to sit without doing anything. A glance back told me Epic's power nap was ongoing, and I had nothing I wanted to do.

I didn't need to check my messages, or look at my computer, or worry about the future or the fate of the world. As I watched Epic sleep, the light outside faded into darkness. Headlights and traffic lights made the erstwhile ugly sprawl glitter like diamonds and rubies, emeralds and citrine.

A rustle behind me signaled my boyfriend was coming back to life. My not-fake, very real boyfriend rose from his sex coma like Dracula from the grave.

"What are you doing?" he asked.

"Looking."

"At what?"

I blinked up at him. "Just stuff."

"Sorry about that." He laughed. "That's my Achilles' heel. I tend to pass out for a while after orgasm."

"No kidding. Anyone could sneak up on you and do what they wanted with your person."

"You've got carte blanche. Were you waiting for me to wake up?"

"I guess I got lost in thought."

"Whatcha thinking?"

"Nothing, really." I rolled my neck.

"Come on." He reached out and started tickling me. "Tell me."

"It's not like that." I squirmed away, laughing. "Stop. I was just watching the traffic."

He stopped digging with his fingers to wrap his arms around me. "Hm. Sitting and thinking about nothing, huh?"

"I guess."

"Almost like you were totally relaxed?"

"Shut up."

"Like I'd fucked away all your worries and cares?"

"No, I'm not—" I sagged into him. "All right. You scrambled my brain. Yeah."

His blue eyes sparkled with not-so-secret delight. "Glad to be of service."

"Me too. I should sell myself to the study of anesthesiology."

"You'd make a mint." He kissed my neck. "I never sleep better than after I fuck you. Come here. This way."

Somehow, he lifted me and settled back into the chair with me on his lap. I wasn't really sure it would work because we're the same size, but he opened his legs and let my butt fall between. I laid my head on his shoulder, and it felt...really nice.

Much better than sitting and watching the traffic alone.

"I could learn to live like this."

He smiled and sighed. "Me too."

"It's not impossible." I wrapped my hand over the nape of his neck. "It's not. But you're...you. You're fast, and fearless, and up for any challenge. You're miles ahead of me. Give me a chance to catch up."

"I will." He tilted his head to kiss me. "I am. There's plenty of time."

"For you, maybe." I couldn't help thinking about our age difference.

"For us. Don't fret. Let's enjoy this time we have together. What will you wear for the awards banquet?"

"I brought a couple suits. You can help me choose."

"I only brought one." He pulled me back against his chest. "You'll have to live with it."

His stomach rumbled loudly.

"Oh, dinner." He was hungry. *Shoot.* "I didn't make reservations. Let me call down."

I rose to make the call. The clock showed ten after eight. "How does eight thirty sound?"

"Good. I'll take a quick shower and dress." He leered at me. "Want to join me?"

"If I do, we won't get to the restaurant in time. Or I'll be alone because you'll be asleep."

His cheeks reddened. "Good point. Be out in a minute."

The shower ran while I chose slacks and a shirt to wear underneath a tweed jacket with my earth tack on the lapel.

Epic came out in a towel and we switched places. He got ready while I took a quick shower. When I returned, he wore the earrings I'd bought him.

"You brought them?"

"I never go anywhere without them."

"I have the pin on my jacket." I showed him.

"Then I'll just have to orbit you tonight and maybe cause a rising" — he glanced at my crotch — "tide or two."

I rolled my eyes. "That's just awful."

"I'm afraid it's canon now."

When I was ready, we went to the elevator together. I pressed the Down button. "Why'd you press down? Isn't the restaurant up?"

"You can't get there from here. The restaurant tower has its own elevator."

He took my hand. "You have to go down to go up?"

"Yup."

"What if you want to go up?"

"You press Up." I pointed out the obvious.

"But you can't get to the restaurant from Up?"

"Not from this elevator. It doesn't go there."

He blinked his wide blue eyes. "And you wonder why I want to live in St. Nacho's?"

"No, I don't." I kissed his cheek. "I wonder why you do a lot of things, but St. Nacho's? I get that."

He gave me a slow, *I've got plans for you* smile — one intended to convey that we were going to do what he wanted. Work remotely. Move to St. Nacho's. Get a place and put down roots.

He let me know, with that smile, that he'd take care of me,

empty my cache of worries regularly with great sex, make me eat well and wear sunscreen and hats.

I'd probably have to mini-golf again. Better not be on my birthday.

When we got to the ground floor, we switched elevators and rode all the way to the steakhouse on the top.

"After you, sweetheart," he said when the doors opened.

CHAPTER TWENTY-SIX

On Saturday, it rained. We had breakfast in bed and watched Animal Planet for a while.

Epic went to the bathroom, and when he came back, he carried a small duffel from which he pulled a slender, flexible, gift-wrapped package.

"What's that?" I asked.

"It's a present for you." I carefully took off the tape and opened it.

Inside, a crop with feathers at the end waited like dueling pistols in the first act of a play.

"You're not going to hit me, are you?"

"Nope. Not ever, unless you want me to." He'd bound my wrists loosely together with the warning I'd better keep them where he wanted them.

"There's no place to tie your legs," he complained. "It's almost as if they are actively trying to prevent their guests from tying one another up."

"I can't imagine why."

"Open your legs," he commanded.

I spread my feet apart.

"Keep them just like that." He tickled my arm with the feathers.

"Oh God, I begin to see the appeal here."

"Speaking of which"—he took out an eye mask—"I need to do something about that."

From that moment forward, Epic drenched me in sensation. He started by tickling me in places that weren't very sensitive at all. My shins. The tops of my arms. My hands. My feet.

And then he moved to places that tingled, that made me laugh, that made me squirm and groan and eventually, beg him to stop because begging was fun.

I didn't safeword, even though what Epic was doing felt like a gentle form of torture. I loved his special edging technique, but because of the blindfold, I never knew what was coming. I could only feel. Was he going to tickle me, or suck me, or finger me to insanity?

The care with which he took me to the brink and then pulled me back again and again took timing and patience, and I thought, maybe, love. The tickles, kisses, and soft touches he used to drive me into ecstatic highs and maddening need took me to that special place where the only reality was Epic and sensation, and peace.

He'd concentrate the long crop with the feathered tip on places that were mildly sensitive or downright annoying. Then he'd go back to the top of my ass crack, my super ticklish ribs, the nape of my neck, my balls and my taint, and—gods—my hole. I could have come from his attention to my hole alone.

When the tickling stopped, he used massage oils that warmed my skin. He held ice in his mouth and gave cold kisses, licks, and shivery damp play bites to my nipples. He applied chilly suction to my cock and balls.

Over the course of a few hours, he raised goosebumps over my skin and ignited every nerve in my body. Yet he still didn't let me come.

"Yellow. Please." I finally mutinied by shoving off the mask. I cried out. "You little *monster*. Please. Please, let me come."

"You come when I say. Not one second before." He cupped my face and glared down at me. "Got that?"

Oh God, oh God, bossy Epic lit a fuse inside me.

"Yes. All right." I heaved a shuddering sigh and prepared for the whole cycle to start over. "Yellow. No mask. I want to see you, please."

"Fine." He accepted my terms.

"I want to watch your face while you torture me."

"Mm. You'd like that? You want to see me when I own your tight pink hole?"

"God yes." Fingers of bright sunlight stretched into long golden bars on the floor before he relented and gave me what I asked for.

"Oh God." My head fell back against the pillow. "Oh God. Let me come. Let me *come*."

That time, Epic didn't stop. He sucked and swallowed until I was empty and limp—every muscle in my body loose and pulsing gently.

Epic crawled up beside me to undo the binding on my hands. We exchanged languid, cum-flavored kisses. I rolled him beneath me and lay between his legs.

"What do you need?" I asked.

He glanced at the clock. "What time is it?"

"Four-ish. You want to fuck me? You can pass out after for an hour, and we'll still make the banquet."

"You know me so well." His cheeks darkened. "Is me dropping out like that a problem for you? I mean, I could probably stay awake, but I always feel so good. I let my eyes close and boom, it's like being a kid again and I nod off."

Was that a gap in Epic's self-confidence? "Of course not. If you need sleep, sleep. I think it's charming."

"Says the man who stays awake half the night worrying about work."

"You know me so well." I turned his words back on him as he rolled us both and reached for the lube.

"C'mere you." I came. Rather, I came again once he'd worked his way into my body and pounded me through the mattress.

God, he was beautiful. He fucked with every cell in his body. He fucked like it made him happy just to be fucking and he laughed about the silly things sex makes people do. He didn't have an ounce of shame over squelching noises, or dripping sweat, or his 'O' face, when I knew mine was pretty slack-jawed and unhandsome.

We fell onto our backs afterward, and in no time Epic was asleep. I cleaned up, cleaned him, watched him sleep for a bit like a lovesick hound dog, and prayed he'd never know I was having stupid, purple-prose thoughts about his youth, and beauty, and goodness.

An hour later, he woke. We kissed in the shower. Kissed while applying shaving cream, kissed to mingle our colognes, kissed on our way out the door to the banquet.

I straightened his tie in the elevator.

He mussed my hair with both hands.

At the door to the correct ballroom, I handed my invitation to an usher, who led us to a table at the front of the room. AIM Environmental Energy's theme for the night appeared to be "nature is awesome." We had to dodge live trees and planters with twinkling lights that simulated fireflies.

"This is nostalgic." The room had a definite outdoor-wedding vibe. There were even ivy-covered trellises leading to the stage.

"I like it." I unbuttoned my jacket and sat in the spot reserved for me.

Epic sat beside me in a spot marked *guest*. "This reminds me of a Rainforest Cafe."

Me too, especially because they were playing trickling rain sounds in the background.

"It's nice." The room felt cool and smelled of earth and ivy. "I like the lights. Firefly populations are declining worldwide, so it's nice to pretend."

Epic nudged me with his elbow. "Silver lining, meet big ugly cloud."

"I'm just saying."

"Let's enjoy it."

I turned to see how serious he was. "I enjoy anything with you."

With a shy smile, he slid his arm around the back of my chair.

I found wine on the table and poured us both a glass.

Epic lifted his toward me. "To you, sweetheart. This is your night. I'm so glad your work is being recognized."

"It's the work of StolenLives, really. I only gather the information—"

"Don't you dare finish that sentence." Epic knew exactly what I did at work now. He'd spent a month writing algorithms to streamline my data-mining process. "This award has your name on it."

"I know that. I do." But I couldn't help it if I wanted to deflect a little. I didn't crawl inside a cave everyday with my computer because I wanted to stand out.

He gently tapped my nose with his index finger. "No. False. Modesty. You're awesome."

"All right."

Servers emerged to bring food to the tables as an emcee gave opening remarks. We sat with strangers. Epic tried to get to know them while passing wine and butter and salad dressing. He schmoozed effortlessly, chock-full of charm and good manners.

The entree came—meatless but created to please even a

carnivore's palate — and then came dessert — a trifle of fresh berries and cream and sponge cake soaked in sherry.

After the dishes had been cleared away, the awards ceremony began.

Epic craned his neck as person after person was called up and acknowledged for things like green architecture, creating kilns for pyrolysis to create biochar, and the introduction of next gen sterile drinking fountains to rid the world of the need for plastic bottles.

I frankly felt a little out of place because I certainly wasn't doing anything like that. Toward the end, I got a little worried that I might be at the wrong banquet, or that AIM Environmental Energies group was playing a trick on me.

"And finally," the speaker said. "I'd like to introduce a very special member of the AIM board of directors. As you know, Charles and Violet Alsop began with the dream of an environmentally sound energy strategy fifty years ago when it became obvious to some people that fossil fuels were finite and likely to destroy the planet."

I turned to stare at Epic, who did not meet my gaze. I nudged him. He didn't respond.

"Epic. Look at me."

He relented. "What?"

"Did you have anything to do with this?" I hissed.

"With what?" He finally turned to look at me.

"The award. Did you have anything to do with me getting this award?"

His eyes widened. "How could I? We just met last month."

He was right. Of course he was right. But why didn't he say anything when I'd told him what the banquet was and named the company hosting it?

"But—"

"Shh." He nudged me.

"Without further ado, I'd like to bring Violet Alsop to the stage. Vi?"

The woman who passed through the ivy trellis walked regally. Tall and pale with dark hair, she had—I noticed when she got to the microphone—phenomenally blue eyes, just like Epic's.

"Good evening, wonderful friends and colleagues." Talk about alternative energy sources, Violet Alsop's smile could have powered the entire city. "Before we leave tonight, we have a very different kind of award to present. Unlike our 'Greenies,' which recognize the technological advances in sound energy and environmental work, this one goes to Stolen-Lives, an NGO dedicated to eradicating human trafficking. More specifically, the award goes to Ryan Winslow, who successfully discovered and documented a sex trafficking ring in our own community."

I glanced Epic's way to find his face had gone soft with adoration for his grandmother. This was the woman he idolized. The woman who had his back when his parents' disapproval brought him down. I loved her already.

"Mr. Winslow's hard work and subsequent coordination with law enforcement saved young North Dakotans' lives. Through his efforts, many more will avoid the despair and degradation they experienced.

"As you know, AIM Environmental Energy's mission is to create a better world for humans through the manufacture of green technologies and alternate fuel sources. StolenLives is dedicated to preserving the dignity of humanity by ending traffic in human suffering.

"We are proud to support Mr. Winslow's—and StolenLife's —efforts with this special award, along with a corporate donation toward the work at StolenLives. Mr. Winslow?"

With Epic's aid, I barely kept from stumbling over my feet as I rose. I buttoned my jacket and smoothed my tie on my walk to the podium. It took *forever* to get there, with every eye on me like that. Somehow, I got through the trellis and walked to the podium to stand next to Epic's grandmother without falling. I wondered why it took both hands to present me with a relatively small sculptural glass figure of a flame, but when she handed over the absurdly heavy thing, all became clear. My name and the year had been engraved on the base.

"It is my pleasure to present the first ever AIM Humanitarian award. For myself, my community, my state, and all the people we serve, I would like to say thank you, Ryan Winslow, for the hard work you do to uncover these crimes and bring justice to the victims."

I had prepared a few words. That was before I'd realized the woman warmly holding my hand was Epic's much-loved grandma. His mother had cast me in the villain's role. How did his grandmother see me?

"Mrs. Alsop." I nodded to her before turning to the tables in the darkness beyond the bright lights of the stage. "Friends. Thank you so much for the wonderful introduction. You make what I do sound pretty heroic. The truth is, I sit in a room with a computer looking for little connections. My job isn't any different than what any other data analyst does day in and day out, except I focus on certain pieces of information that come up time and time again in human trafficking cases.

"Like a dog trained to track a certain type of scent—a tool, if you will—I do one thing pretty well."

I could guess who snickered at the word "tool." *Down in front.*

"There are so many others who share this with me—legislators, law enforcement, other NGOs. Too many to name. We all want the same thing: to end the suffering of human beings who have fallen victim to the greed of others.

"That said, I'm delighted to receive recognition for the work we do at StolenLives and even more thrilled that our work resulted in arrests and convictions. I can't stop—I won't stop—until there's no longer a need for what I do. Thank you."

People in the vast black space beyond the stage lights

applauded. I was able to make out our table, and Epic, who stood and whistled.

I felt strangely dizzy, even though I hadn't had much to drink. I wasn't sure whether I'd make it down the stairs without taking a header, but Epic met me at the bottom where he caught my hand and led me to the side until his grand-mother closed out her speech and came down to greet us.

"C'mon, Grandma. Let's go find somewhere you can meet Ryan properly." He led us out of the banquet hall. We found an empty seating area in a quiet corner and took it over. Mrs. Alsop and I sat side by side on a couch with Epic opposite, sitting on a cocktail table.

"So, I'm guessing tonight was a bit of a surprise." Violet Alsop's eyes twinkled. "Epic told me all about you, but he didn't want you to know about the family connection until the ceremony. I'm sorry if it was a shock."

"I should have done some research and found out for myself," I admitted as I glanced from one to the other. "This is just weird. Epic, you're the image of your grandmother."

"I know. I'm going to be almost as gorgeous as she is someday."

"That's my silly boy talking," said his blushing grandma.

"And"—Epic raised his hands—"you can totally see how this is pure coincidence, right? I didn't even know you when the list of awardees went out."

"And now you're working together." Mrs. Alsop took his hand in hers. "I'm so proud of you, sweetheart."

I leaned forward. "Mrs. Alsop—"

"Call me Violet, please."

"Violet." I tasted the name. It was very much like Epic's—fitting and fun. "It's a real pleasure to meet you. Epic talks about you so often that I feel like I almost know you."

"Same," she said. "Epic has been very impressed by what you accomplish at StolenLives. My daughter Chloe pressed for a different career path for him, but I think ultimately,

Epic would never have found what he's looking for in finance. He's always been a crusader. He's so much like my Charlie."

"Tell me about him."

"Oh, you don't want to listen to me talk tonight. We'll have lots of chances to get acquainted. I need to get back to my adoring public, and you need to go off and do whatever it is young people do. I'm afraid I can only vaguely remember...but Charles and I used to—"

"Ew, Grandma."

"I'm flattered," I said, "but I'm hardly young people."

"Compared to me you are." She patted my hand. "Age is only a number. Ask Epic. He can manipulate those to do whatever he likes."

I laughed because he could do that with me too.

I got to my feet when she did. "You are as unconventional as he is, aren't you?"

"I enjoy being the local oddball, if that's what you mean. I'm the one Epic gets that from."

"I can't wait to learn more. Do you think you could join us for breakfast in the morning?"

"I'd be delighted. Epic, text me a time and place. I'll see you then." She gave a little wave and then sailed back into the ballroom—a flagship for beautiful women of any age, anywhere.

"Is Violet the reason your parents are Alsop-Gray and you only go by Alsop?"

"I didn't want to be hyphenated for the rest of my life." He put his hands on his knees. "Chloe and Steven didn't mind after a while. They both adore her, despite the fact that she undermines them with me."

"She loves you very much."

A smile lit his features. "She's going to love you too. I promise."

"I hope so."

"There's no doubt. She said you reminded her of 'her Charlie.' There could be no higher praise."

I swallowed a sudden tightness in my throat. "I love you, Epic."

He bit his lip. "I know. Same goes."

"I know." I didn't need him to say the three little words out loud yet. Or ever. He showed me through every word and every action how he felt about me—about us.

With the banquet out of the way and me finally away from the public eye, it was natural to breathe a sigh of relief.

Epic and I sat with our knees bumping, holding hands. My heart was full, and my mind empty. The pilot light within me—my obsession with work—hadn't gone out, but when Epic was around, he helped me make more efficient use of my "fuel."

Obviously because he was one of the A's in AIM Environmental Energy.

Gods. I should have learned more about AIM before we came. I should have looked the company up, but I'd been too focused on the job and too blown apart by Luis getting married. I hadn't bothered to look too deeply into something I thought was a bit of a waste of time.

Just goes to show how wrong you can be about things.

My dad once told me to hold a quarter in front of my eye and of course, I did. He asked me what I could see, and duh, I saw silver and not much else. Then he told me to move the quarter six inches away.

My job was just like that quarter. When I distanced myself even a little, I found I could see everything I'd been missing out on so clearly. Love, certainly. People who wanted to support me and StolenLives. Friendships I'd let slide, like Dan and Cam. Meals I'd missed. Things I did that harmed my body.

As long as I was with Epic, I knew I'd be able to keep the distance I needed from work to truly thrive. Maybe it was a bit risky, putting my whole life in the hands of someone who was barely out of school, but on the other hand, that person was Epic.

Who's on first?

Exactly.

"Let's go." He stood and held out his hand.

"All right." I let him lead.

EPILOGUE

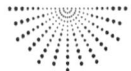

S ix Months Later

WE BOUGHT a vintage bungalow three blocks from the beach where we could hear the music from Nacho's Bar if we left the windows open. Ken the real estate wizard had flipped the property lavishly. Inside its blue-and-white master bedroom, I opened my eyes, wondering what exactly had teased me awake. Ah, yes—the aroma of coffee and banana-nut bread.

I reached out, but Epic was long gone. The sheets on his side of our bed had cooled. I checked the time. Already eight? *Yikes.* I had international calls to make, and I didn't want to miss my window.

I showered quickly and dressed. No shave today. I entered the kitchen in a hurry and found Epic sitting at the table reading on his tablet. As always, he looked relaxed but still put together. Button-down, jeans cuffed at the ankle, boat shoes with no socks.

"Why didn't you wake me?"

He glanced up. "Why should I? You've still got time for a nice breakfast."

The bowl of berries on the table looked luscious. He'd set a place for me with Greek yogurt and honey and a couple slices of banana bread. When I sat, he poured me coffee.

"Thank you."

He dropped a kiss on my forehead. "Any time."

The table sat in the sunniest spot in our kitchen. Well, it was sunny when the morning mist, typical in St. Nacho's, burned off. He'd left the slider open with the screen closed, letting in a breeze from the sea and the sound of birds chirping in our orange trees.

"Lila got confirmation that there's been a disruption in drug trafficking through El Paso. No word yet if that's because the Mexican government made headway on those manufacturing camps, but it's good news either way."

"A step in the right direction." Along with drugs, there were always mules who might or might not be willing participants. The cartels ran prostitution, gambling, and pornography rings. We celebrated every sign they were slowing down as a win.

I ate the rest of my breakfast and helped Epic do the dishes.

Epic and I spent most of our time working remotely from St. Nacho's. I still traveled for business, and we flew to Canada for face time with Lila and our colleagues when necessary.

Truthfully, working remotely had changed very little in my day-to-day work schedule. In fact, lacking commute time and creating a state-of-the-art home office meant I could spend even more hours at work than before. Epic put a firm stop to that. A moratorium. A *hell no*.

Over the weeks we'd spent together, I'd learned to let Epic tell me when it was time to start and stop. Like today, when he turned off the alarm so I could get a bit of extra sleep or in the evenings when sitting down to a nice dinner could be a late affair but was not optional.

Epic still made sure I wore sunscreen. He bought me hats.

When I doubted he was getting anything out of the deal, I only had to see his smile, taste his kisses, or surrender my body to the delights of our bed to know whatever we had was real, and good, and lasting.

Happy Epic made everyone around him happy. It was his gift.

"Come on. I'll drive you to work," he said as he opened the sliding screen door. "Get a move on."

He chivvied me out to our back yard where Waffles, our Corgi, lay basking in the sunshine. The little dog barked happily and ran around our feet in an attempt to herd me toward the guest apartment we'd turned into a state-of-the-art computer lab.

These days, time at work passed differently. For one thing, there was a refrigerator in the office kitchen filled with healthy snacks and drinks like LaCroix and kombucha. There was a massive, down and leather couch wide enough for two-person napping and...other things sometimes.

We'd hired Waffles as our PA. She mostly sat in my lap and snored softly or chased a laser pointer because the local vet, Dr. Davies, said Corgis are prone to unhealthy weight gain.

I couldn't remember the last time I felt tired, or hopeless, or lonely.

"Hey, don't hog the dog." Epic reached out with grabby hands.

"I'm not hogging." I curled around her protectively. "She wants to be here."

"Because she's got Stockholm syndrome from you hogging her. Let me take her for a while."

I handed Waffles over without waking her.

"Love you," he kissed me gently before going back to his desk.

"Love you more." I glanced out the window just in time to see the breeze knock a flutter of fragrant orange blossoms off our trees. Tiny white petals drifted past the window like snowflakes.

I let out a huge sigh. Our life was going to be...awesome. Epically awesome.

WHAT TO READ NEXT?

Want to spend a holiday in St. Nacho's? Try **Winter Solstice in St. Nacho's**, a taut and tender tale of compassion, redemption, and unlikely romance featuring a character you might remember from **A Much Younger Man**...

Luke is desperate to rescue the boy he once tutored. Can a winter solstice miracle bring them a second chance at love, or will Tug's dangerous addiction destroy their happiness forever?

"Everything is possible at the library."

Luke cheerfully provides his patrons with whatever they need, even if that means administering Naloxone when they overdose in the library bathroom.

Tug's a heroin addict. He's in the grip of a powerful addiction. He has no self-esteem. He sees no way out. When old crush Luke offers help, Tug's willing to see what he can get out of the deal. But there's a terrible cost to exploring his painful past and claiming his second chance.

Miracles happen for the men of St. Nacho's. Will Tug seize a new life and the chance to be with Luke? Or will he give in to the siren's song of a drug he can't resist?

Z.A. Maxfield pens a taut and tender second chance gay romance. If you believe a good man can find love even on the darkest, longest night, buy "Winter Solstice in St. Nacho's" for an HFN you will believe in today.

Feel like revisiting the original **St. Nacho's** stories? Before **The Men Of St. Nacho's** started finding their age gap lovers, there was Cooper and Shawn in **St. Nacho's**, Ken and Jordan in **Physical Therapy**, Yasha and JT in **Jacob's Ladder**, and Cam and Dan in **The Book of Daniel.**

Cooper's running from his past. Will a quiet young man offer him a future?

Cooper Wyatt has silenced his guilt for three years. A violin prodigy thrown out of Juilliard and implicated in a tragic car accident, the troubled musician struggles to find a new home. But when he arrives in a sleepy California seaside town and meets a deaf busboy who makes his heart sing, he hits the ultimate emotional crossroads.

Shawn Fielding doesn't let his hearing problems stop him from living life to the fullest. Though he may be shy, he dances and studies theater at the local college. And a conflicted instrumentalist's sexy grin aimed his way brings dire warnings from friends that not all love songs end happily.

Realizing he's falling for the handsome brown-eyed student, Cooper deliberately remains distant to avoid causing more pain. But Shawn believes the only way to heal the other man's soul is to help him speak the truth.

Will Cooper make peace with his issues and finally take his rightful place in Shawn's arms?

If you like stories about tough men and hard choices, I suggest you try **The Brothers Grime Series.** Life is full of dirty jobs. That doesn't mean you can't fall in love while doing them!

One man's tough job is a path to love.

The Brothers Grime is Jack Masterson's way of helping people in crisis after disability ends his career as a firefighter. Jack's people get to a scene long after the physical trauma ends. They don't solve crime or rescue the victims. They help people move on. The new job is all Jack wants or needs, until he gets the call about old flame Nick Foasberg's suicide.

Ryan Halloran's cousin Nick has been on a downhill slide for a long time. Despite that, Ryan does everything he knows to help. Ryan only understands part of what happened between Nick and Jack in high school, but after Nick's suicide, Ryan agrees both he and Jack need closure. They work together to clean the scene and despite the situation, heat flares between them.

Jack is keeping a painful secret and fighting his attraction to Nick's lookalike cousin, Ryan. Ryan calls himself a magnet for lost causes and worries Jack might be the next in a long line of losers.

Despite his misgivings, despite the past and the mistakes they've both made, Jack gives Ryan something to look forward to, and Ryan gives Jack a reason to stop looking back, in Grime and Punishment.

Do you want something totally different? How about a paranormal fantasy series with romance, adventure, and a little more...bite?

Begin **The Deep Series** today!

There's no leverage like seduction...until love takes a big bite out of Adin's plans.

As the Indiana Jones of historical erotica, there is no document Adin Tredeger can't unearth. Why he would risk the biggest coup of his career to join the mile-high club is beyond him. Nevertheless, the disarming, dark-eyed vampire Donte somehow enters Adin's locked airplane washroom and has him completely nude and coming apart, all without a whimper of protest.

From that moment, Adin and Donte engage in an international battle of wit and cunning. The prize is a priceless 500-year-old journal with illustrations so erotic the Marquis de Sade would blush.

Yet Donte's desire for the journal goes far beyond simple possession. He wrote it. And he's not above using every trick in his otherworldly arsenal—including seduction—to get his journal back.

Chemistry draws them together even as fortune tugs them apart. When a third party enters the chase, will Adin and Donte join forces to fight an enemy with a deadly goal—to erase Donte from history forever?

ACKNOWLEDGMENTS

I could not have begun this new series without a book bible for the St. Nacho's Series, which Susie Selva painstakingly created. Susie wears all the hats on the editorial side, and has done a fantastic job taking the noodles that come out of my brain and turning them into a book I can be proud of.

Without Susie, this book would not have been possible.

Also, another great big thank you to LE Franks, Morticia Knight, Belinda McBride, and Sue Brown for being my partners in Writerly Shenanigans. For all you do to help foster an environment of commerce, cooperation, enthusiasm, and community, I love and thank you!

ALSO BY Z.A. MAXFIELD

Novels

Crossing Borders

Drawn Together

Family Unit

ePistols At Dawn

Gasp!

The Pharaoh's Concubine

Rhapsody For Piano And Ghost

The Long Way Home

Home the Hard Way

The St. Nacho's Series

St. Nacho's

Physical Therapy

Jacob's Ladder

The Book Of Daniel

Winter Solstice In St. Nacho's

Men of St. Nacho's Series

A Much Younger Man

A Flighty Fake Boyfriend

The Brothers Grime

Grime and Punishment

Grime Doesn't Pay

Partners in Grime

The Deep Series

Deep Desire

Deep Deception

Deep Deliverance

The Bluewater Bay Novels

Hell on Wheels

All Wheel Drive

The My Cowboy Series

My Cowboy Heart

My Heartache Cowboy

My Cowboy Homecoming

My Cowboy Promises

My Cowboy Freedom

Honky Tonk Hellion

The Stirring Series

Stirring Up Trouble

All Stirred Up

Novellas

Lights! Camera! Cupid!

Blue Fire

Fugitive Color

Through the Years

Holiday Stories

I Heard Him Exclaim

Lost And Found

Secret Light

What Child Is This?

ABOUT THE AUTHOR

Z. A. Maxfield is a fifth generation native of Los Angeles, although she now lives in the Inland Empire.

She started writing in 2006 on a dare from her children and never looked back. Pathologically disorganized, and perennially optimistic, she writes as much as she can, reads as much as she dares, and enjoys her time with family and friends.

If anyone asks her how a wife and mother of four manages to find time for a writing career, she'll answer, "It's amazing what you can do if you give up housework."

Look for ZAM on Social Media!

COPYRIGHT

www.ingramcontent.com/pod-product-compliance
Lightning Source LLC
Chambersburg PA
CBHW030125180626
46812CB00002B/568